THE WAY THINGS WERE

I can't believe what I just found while I was digging through my old riding journals. The diary I kept the year we moved to Willow Creek! I hadn't seen it in ages, and I was kind of afraid I'd lost it somehow. I'm really glad I didn't.

The diary is sitting here next to me on my bed as I write this. I haven't so much as peeked at it yet. That's because part of me sort of doesn't want to open it up and reread about any of that year right now. It could be a little scary to remember everything I was thinking back then, how I was really feeling from day to day right in the middle of everything that was happening. . . .

Other books you will enjoy

CAMY BAKER'S HOW TO BE POPULAR IN THE SIXTH GRADE
by Camy Baker

CAMY BAKER'S LOVE YOU LIKE A SISTER
by Camy Baker

ANNE OF GREEN GABLES *by L. M. Montgomery*

HORSE CRAZY (The Saddle Club #1) *by Bonnie Bryant*

AMY, NUMBER SEVEN (Replica #1) *by Marilyn Kaye*

PURSUING AMY (Replica #2) *by Marilyn Kaye*

THE CASE OF THE MISSING MARBLES AND THE CASE OF THE RISING
MOON (The Adventures of Shirley Holmes) *by John Whitman*

THE SADDLE CLUB

CAROLE: THE INSIDE STORY

BONNIE BRYANT

A SKYLARK BOOK
NEW YORK • TORONTO • LONDON • SYDNEY • AUCKLAND

Special thanks to Laura Roper of Sir "B" Farms

RL 5, 009–012

CAROLE: THE INSIDE STORY

A Bantam Skylark Book / November 1999

ISBN 0-553-48678-0

Published simultaneously in the United States and Canada.

Bantam Books are published by Bantam Books, a division of Random House, Inc.
Its trademark, consisting of the words "Bantam Books" and the portrayal of a
rooster, is Registered in U.S. Patent and Trademark Office and in other countries.
Marca Registrada. Bantam Books, 1540 Broadway, New York, New York
10036.

PRINTED IN THE UNITED STATES OF AMERICA

OPM   0 9 8 7 6 5 4

*I would like to express my special thanks
to Catherine Hapka for her help
in the writing of this book.*

CAROLE HANSON'S RIDING JOURNAL:

I can't believe I'm starting a new journal already. I've been making so much progress with Starlight's training lately that I think I must have filled up my last riding journal in about two months! Speaking of Starlight, he was really well behaved in riding class today, which I plan to make notes about in just a second.

But first I want to jot down a few words about something that's bothering me (even though it really has nothing to do with Starlight and so maybe isn't the right kind of topic for a riding journal). I just got home from TD's a few minutes ago. Stevie and Lisa and I went there for sundaes as usual today, though for a change we talked more about people than horses, namely Max, who was acting so weird he barely managed to teach our class. He kept sneezing and forgetting what he was talking about—definitely *not* the usual brisk, efficient, super-organized Max Regnery!

Oops, I almost forgot what I was writing about. Anyway, as I was saying, I got home and found an e-mail from Cam waiting for me. (I printed it out and taped it here.)

FROM: CamNelson

TO: HorseGal

SUBJECT: Big news

MESSAGE:

Hi, Carole! How are you? Are you enjoying your summer vacation so far? I'm definitely enjoying mine, even though my school let out only six days ago. I've ridden Duffy every single day since then. Actually, I've been spending so much time at the stable that Mr. Barclay is starting to make jokes about charging boarding fees for me as well as for my horse!

But that's not really why I'm writing. I wanted to tell you that I've decided something really important. And I knew you'd appreciate it more than anyone else.

So here goes: I've decided that I want to be a three-day event rider when I grow up. See, I just read this really inspiring article in a magazine. It was a biography of Luanne Hall, a famous three-day eventer. She kept talking about how it was all her single-minded practice and devotion to her sport that made her so good. Plus she said that she already knew she wanted to specialize in combined training by the time she was seven years old!

So I guess that means I'm really behind already. Don't think I'm not a little nervous about that! Still, I'm really excited. Now all my work with Duffy will be aiming somewhere.

And I really feel like this is the right decision for me. I've always loved watching combined training events at horse trials and stuff. And I always thought it was really cool that riders and their horses have to be good at more than one thing—I mean, they need to be polished enough to compete in the dressage section, as well as being strong and bold enough to make it through the cross-country course and the stadium jumping. It will be a real challenge to train for something like that. I can't wait to get started!

Anyway, I wanted to tell you about this right away, since I knew you would understand what a big deal it is. I know you want to work with horses for a living someday, too, and I really hope you figure out a way to do it that feels as perfect for you as this does for me.

I'd better sign off now. I want to see if the U.S. Combined Training Association has a website.

I was thrilled at first, since I hadn't heard from Cam since before school let out for the summer. Sometimes I really wish we lived closer to each other—it would be nice to see him and talk to him in person more often, instead of mostly chatting over the computer. Still, Stevie claims it was fate that she met Phil at riding camp. She says it means they were meant to be together, so it doesn't matter that they live in different towns and go to different schools and can't see each other very often. So maybe it's the same thing for us, especially since Cam and I have so much in common and hardly any of the boys at Willow Creek Junior High are interested in horses. Of course, I don't really think of us as an official couple, like Stevie and Phil. At least not really.

Uh-oh, I was kind of getting away from the topic there again. The point is, Cam has already figured out what he wants to do with his life. And he's right—a lot of the great riders started preparing for their careers when they were younger than I am now. So where does that leave me? I mean, I already know I want to work with horses someday, somehow. But I have no idea what, exactly, I want to do. I've thought about becoming a riding instructor and stable owner like Max, an equine vet like Judy Barker, a competitive rider, a trainer, a breeder. . . . The possibilities are practically endless. My friends like to tease me by saying I'm scatterbrained about everything except horses. But after reading Cam's note, I feel like maybe horses are the thing I've been the *most* scatterbrained about, in a way, because some of the careers I'm interested in require an awful lot of special training and preparation. I've been losing a lot of valuable time puttering around, going on trail rides with my friends and goofing off, when I should have been trying to decide what to do. Maybe putting off thinking about the future has been a big mistake.

The problem is, even when I *do* think about it, I have no idea what I want to do. It's really bothering me. I know I should probably call Stevie and Lisa to talk about it instead of wasting all these pages in here. But for once, I'm not sure that's the greatest idea. I mean, I know my best friends would help me if they could—after all, helping each other whenever help is needed is the only rule we thought was important enough to include when we started The Saddle Club (except being horse-crazy, of course, which practically goes without saying for the three of us). Still, even if they *wanted* to be helpful, I'm not sure they *could* be. After all, Stevie can't be serious about anything for more than two seconds at a time (except maybe fighting with her brothers), so she might have trouble understanding why this is so important. Besides, she's kind of distracted right now with her own problems, since her mom announced last week that she's on strike—at home, that is, not at her law office—and that all four of the kids have to start helping out more at home. Stevie's first job was the laundry, and she managed to mess up and turn all her brothers' underwear pink (by accident, not on purpose).

That leaves Lisa. She would probably be totally organized and sensible about this whole topic, because that's just the way she is. (When he's in a silly mood, Dad sometimes calls my friends Loony Lake and Analytical Atwood, which actually describes Stevie and Lisa pretty well, though I'd never say so to them.) It could be kind of helpful to have that kind of perspective on this problem, I guess. But I can't help thinking it might not be the right way to look at it. Lisa would probably insist on starting off by making a list of pros and cons—you know, which horse-related careers pay the most, which require advanced schooling, which would mean

5

I'd have to travel away from home a lot, and so on. And it might be hard to explain why those things aren't as important to me as doing what I really want to do—whatever that is. Sometimes Lisa gets so caught up in what's logical that she forgets that logic can't always give you an answer.

I just read over what I wrote so far, and I really don't think this kind of stuff is what my old riding instructor had in mind when she insisted that all her students keep a careful, detailed journal of their progress as riders. When we moved to a different base, I stopped keeping a riding journal for a while, but then I realized I actually missed it, so I started again and I've kept it up off and on (mostly on) ever since. Writing things down really does help keep me focused on what I'm doing each day when I climb into the saddle, and how my riding could be improved. Dad would probably say it has something to do with discipline—that's a word I heard an awful lot on all those Marine Corps bases we lived on before we finally settled here in Willow Creek. And I guess I could use more discipline to help me make a decision about my life. So I guess it doesn't matter that I used up a few pages on stuff that doesn't *exactly* have to do with riding or training—at least not directly. After all, it does have a lot to do with what kind of riding or training (or instructing or breeding or veterinarianing or whatever) I'll be doing for the rest of my life.

But back to what I was saying before. No matter how Stevie and Lisa might try to help, they really wouldn't be able to make my decision for me anyway. After all, it's my life I'm talking about here, so I should probably just keep this to myself for a while and try to handle the decision on my own, in a mature way. If I really focus on possible careers, I'm sure I can come up with the right decision before too long.

In fact, I just got a good idea for a way to get started. I still have all of my old riding journals, dating from way back when I was seven. I think I'll go dig them out of their box in the back of my closet right now and see if anything I wrote in them gives me any clues about what I'm really meant to do with my life.

CAROLE HANSON'S RIDING JOURNAL:

I can't believe what I just found while I was digging through my old riding journals. The diary I kept the year we moved to Willow Creek! I hadn't seen it in ages, and I was kind of afraid I'd lost it somehow. I'm really glad I didn't.

The diary is sitting here next to me on my bed as I write this. I haven't so much as peeked at it yet. That's because part of me sort of doesn't want to open it up and reread about any of that year right now. It could be a little scary to remember everything I was thinking back then, how I was really feeling from day to day right in the middle of everything that was happening.

Still, another part of me wants to read it, and I think that part is getting stronger the longer I sit here and think about it. I guess my quest for a career can wait a few more minutes while I take a quick look. I'll just read a tiny bit, only the beginning part from right after we moved into our house. That much will be safe.

Dear Diary:

Now that most of our unpacking is finished (AT LAST!!!) I finally have time to write about our latest move. Our last move, as Dad keeps claiming. We'll see about that. I know he got a promotion (Mom and I keep calling him Colonel Hanson and saluting whenever we see him, which he thinks is a riot), and that means we might get to stay put for a while instead of moving around from base to base all the time. That's why he and Mom decided to buy a regular house in an actual town instead of living on a base like we usually do.

I'm still trying to get used to that. My room is almost as big as our entire apartment was on the last base. Well, maybe not quite that big. But it's a lot bigger than I'm used to, and I'm really not sure what to do with all this space. At least for once I won't have to agonize over which of my horse posters to hang up. Here there's plenty of wall space for all of them. I may even have to get some more to cover it all up!

I'd better hurry and get settled, though, since summer is almost over. Pretty soon I'll be busy getting used to a new school, a whole crowd of new people. The only difference this time is that most of the kids won't be from military families, so they may be kind of different from the people I'm used to hanging around with. Dad says Willow Creek is just far enough from Quantico that there might not be any other kids from the base at my new school! Actually, I guess that's not the only big difference. I'm going to have to get used to the idea that I may be at this new school for a long time instead of just a year or two.

8

Mom and Dad are both pretty excited about the idea of staying put for a while, I think. When I look through my bedroom window I can see Mom outside in our backyard— our backyard! What a concept!—planting the tulip and daffodil bulbs she bought this morning, even though the guy at the store said it's way too early. She's so excited about having a real garden at last instead of just a few pots of herbs and flowers on a windowsill. She can't wait to start planning a big vegetable garden like the one her family had when she was a kid and planting roses and flowering cherry trees and who knows what else to decorate the yard. Dad keeps moaning and complaining about having to spend his precious time off mowing the lawn, but Mom and I can both tell he's only kidding. He's really happy that Mom is so thrilled about living here.

I'm kind of excited, too, even though moving was even scarier this time than it usually is. I know I'll feel a lot better once I've had a chance to check out the local stable where I'll be taking lessons. At first when I heard Dad had been transferred back to Quantico, I thought I'd just go back to riding at the Quantico stables, which made leaving Prince Charming and all the other horses at our old base a little easier (and Mr. Wellstone, too, of course—he was a great teacher, especially when it came to dressage). After all, the last time Dad was stationed at Quantico, we lived on base and I got to know the people and horses there really well. I loved taking lessons from Margery Tarr, and there are some really great horses there, too, like Black Lightning and Major and of course adorable little Soda Pop.

But I guess the base is a little too far for Mom to drive me every day, especially if she gets a job in a real estate office here in town like she wants to. Luckily Margery understands why I won't be coming back, and she even promised not to hold it against me as long as I come to visit once in a while. Ha! Ha! Anyway, she recommended a stable right here in Willow Creek—she says it's the best one in the area. I forget what it's called, but I know it had kind of a pretty name. Something to do with trees or forests, I think. Pine Valley Stables? Maybe something like that, I don't know.

I just hope it really is as great as Margery says it is. I'm keeping my fingers crossed until my appointment to visit it tomorrow. . . .

FROM:	LAtwood
TO:	HorseGal
TO:	Steviethegreat
SUBJECT:	The future Mrs. Maximilian Regnery
MESSAGE:	

Hi, guys! Both of your phone lines are busy, which makes me think you may be talking to each other. I wish I were talking to you both, too, because I have big news. Our problem (well, actually Max's problem) is solved! Mom invited someone from work over to dinner tonight. Her name is Tiffani, and she's a model at that expensive store at the mall, Paris Chic. She's perfect! I mean literally *perfect*. She's tall, slim, and gorgeous, with the sleekest, straightest blond hair you can imagine, and these huge green eyes with long lashes. Plus she's really friendly and nice. I asked her how old she was, and even though Mom just about had a fit (she said it wasn't a polite question), Tiffani told me she's twenty-three. I know that's younger than Max, but it's not *too* young, you know? I mean, it wouldn't seem like a huge age difference once they'd been married a few years. Also, even though Tiffani isn't a regular rider right now, I found out she's been on horseback a few times before, and when I invited her to the Fourth of July picnic, she said she'd love to come. She even seemed kind of interested in learning more about horses. Isn't that great?

Because once Max gets an eyeful of Terrific Tiffani, we won't have to worry about him being lonely anymore. He'll know that she'll be the perfect wife!

CAROLE HANSON'S RIDING JOURNAL:

I just taped in an e-mail from Lisa, even though neither Stevie nor I got it until after Lisa had already told us her news about Tiffani in person. She was pretty excited because she's totally certain that this Tiffani woman is Max's ideal mate. I'm not so sure about that—it really doesn't sound like she's much of a rider at all, which makes it hard to believe she and Max could have anything important in common—but for once Lisa just won't listen to logic.

Today at Pine Hollow Lisa and I spent our schooling session working on serpentines (Stevie was late because her mom is still making her do extra housework), and Max stopped by the outdoor ring to watch us for a few minutes. At first I was a little nervous about that, since Starlight wasn't bending quite right and I knew that meant I wasn't communicating what I wanted properly. But I shouldn't have worried. Max was almost as distracted and confused as he was yesterday, and when Lisa asked him how he thought we were doing, all he said was "Hmmm. Yes, yes, that's very interesting." I think I started to write in here before about how weird Max was acting during class—like he was on another planet, as Lisa put it. But I might not have mentioned what my friends and I decided afterward during the Saddle Club meeting we had yesterday afternoon over ice cream at TD's. We started out trying to figure out why he was suddenly acting so odd and nervous, and we ended up deciding that he was just nervous because Deborah Hale, this newspaper reporter from Washington, D.C., has been hanging around Pine Hollow doing research for a story about horse racing. If she thinks all horsepeople are as out of it as Max has been this week, I can't imagine what kinds of horrible things she's going to end up writing in her article!

Anyway, something Lisa said while we were talking gave us our new idea. "Maybe Deborah Hale is Max's new girlfriend," she suggested. "That would explain his acting weird and forgetting stuff. He might be nervous around her."

Stevie and I thought about that for a moment, then I shook my head. "I can't believe that Max would be interested in someone like her. She doesn't even ride." That much was clear just from watching Deborah in action that day. She hardly knew one end of a horse from the other.

Still, thinking about Max's love life—or to be accurate, his total lack of any love life that we know about—made us realize that poor Max isn't getting any younger. He's almost thirty already! If he's going to have any hope of passing Pine Hollow down to his heirs someday, he needs to find a wife soon. And we figure The Saddle Club is the perfect group to help him find the perfect woman!

That's when Stevie had an even more brilliant idea. "I'm one step ahead of you guys," she told us. "I was thinking about a certain annual event at Pine Hollow that would be the perfect opportunity to introduce Max to hundreds of eligible women."

"I give up," Lisa said after a moment. "All I can think of is the picnic."

"Same," I agreed, remembering that Pine Hollow's annual Fourth of July picnic is coming up next weekend.

"Right!" Stevie cried. "The Fourth of July picnic!"

"But it's not the type of thing that draws single women," I reminded her. "Usually it's just the riders and some of the parents."

"Don't you see?" Stevie waved her hands around so much that she almost tipped her water glass into her blueberry-and-pineapple sundae. "That's where we come in. It'll be up to The Saddle Club to bring in every prospective wife we can think of. Then Max can choose one—with our advice and consent, of course."

That gave me something to think about. I'd never even

considered the possibility that Max might end up marrying someone we didn't like. It was a scary thought. After all, we'll end up stuck with whoever he marries for as long as we ride at Pine Hollow, so it would be a whole lot better if he just found someone nice in the first place.

As usual, it didn't take Stevie long to swing into action. She started by making a list (on her napkin) of qualities we should look for in a potential mate for Max. I remember the whole list because it pretty much sums up what I was thinking, too: Mrs. Max must be (1) horsey (or at least very interested in learning about horses), (2) friendly, especially toward Max's students, (3) interested in helping Max out around the barn, (4) in good health, (5) smart, (6) beautiful.

But that wasn't all. Before we left TD's, Stevie almost managed to convince our waitress to come to the Fourth of July picnic. It turned out she has to work that day, but it's probably just as well. The waitress fits most of the categories, but she's a little weak in number two, at least when it comes to Stevie. I have the funniest feeling she'd be perfectly happy if Stevie never came in and ordered another one of her crazy mixed-up disgusting sundaes ever again!

It was yesterday evening that Lisa came up with Tiffani. Then this morning Stevie convinced her science teacher from last year, Ms. Cartwright, to come to the picnic and bring her two single sisters along with her. Actually, the only reason Stevie was talking to Ms. Cartwright in the first place was because she never turned in her final project, but that's Stevie for you. She can almost always turn a negative situation into a positive one if she puts her mind to it.

14

It was getting to be my turn to come up with some candidates, and luckily I had the perfect opportunity, since today was Bring Your Daughter to Work Day at Quantico. While Dad was busy taking care of work, *I* was busy tracking down every nice single woman on the base, including my old riding instructor, Margery Tarr. She's definitely my top choice. Margery is twenty-six, she's as horsey as can be, she's super-nice, smart, and beautiful. No offense to Stevie's and Lisa's women (not to mention my dad's administrative assistant and the others I invited to the picnic), but I'm sure Max will love Margery so much that he won't even notice the others are there.

In any case, writing about running into Margery reminds me of my old diary. I only read a little bit the other day, like I planned, but now I can't seem to stop thinking about it. I know I really should make some notes here about the problems Starlight and I were having with those serpentines (that's why I picked up my journal to begin with, after all), but maybe that can wait a little while.

Dear Diary:

I thought it would be a lot harder than usual fitting in at this school, since it's so different from what I'm used to. But the kids here are mostly really nice—it turns out they're not that different from the kids at any of the base schools. Well, not very different anyway. It still feels kind of strange to be the only military brat in most of my classes, or having to explain the difference between a sergeant and a colonel and a general, or having people think that Dad drives a tank to work and has top-secret meetings with the President. It's only been a couple of weeks, though. I'm sure I'll eventually get used to that stuff, too.

School may only be okay so far, but Pine Hollow is downright great. It's even more wonderful than it seemed at first—I could tell right away I was going to love it. I guess that's really no surprise, though, since I've loved every stable I've ever seen. But Pine Hollow is really pretty special, I think, even compared to other stables.

I started off riding a really sweet old dapple gray named Pepper. Once Max (that's the owner's name, Max Regnery—he inherited the stable when his father died a few years ago, and he runs it now with some help from his mother. Everyone calls her Mrs. Reg for short.) saw that I know what I'm doing, he suggested that I try riding a few of the more challenging horses. My favorite so far is Delilah, who's a gorgeous palomino with great gaits and a really sweet, gentle temperament—though I also like this lively bay gelding named Diablo and also Comanche, who is a deep chestnut gelding with a ton of spirit and a mind of his own. Another girl in my riding class usually rides Comanche, though. Her name is Stephanie Lake, but everyone calls her Stevie. She's good friends with a girl named Dinah Slattery, who usually rides an Arabian named Barq. They're sort of nice, though in my opinion they could both stand to be a little more serious about riding. They spend way too much time playing pranks on this snobby rich girl in our riding class named Veronica diAngelo. None of them (Stevie, Dinah, Veronica) goes to my school. They're all students at this pri-

16

vate school across town called Fenton Hall. There are a few kids in my riding class who go to my school. There's this really quiet, nice girl named Lauren Michaels, and a less quiet (but still nice) girl named Polly Giacomin who is a pretty decent rider. Most of the other kids are from Fenton Hall, but some of them seem nice, like this really pretty girl named Meg Roberts and this other girl whose first name is Anna, and I think her last name is McCormick or McMahon or something with a Mc in front. I'm hoping to get to know some of them better, especially Polly and Meg and Lauren. I think maybe I could be real friends with them.

And like I said, I already know I'm going to be great friends with Delilah and Diablo and all the other horses. They're wonderful. Of course, that's not stopping me from still trying to convince Mom and Dad to buy me my own horse soon, like maybe for my birthday this year (that's coming up in just a couple of months, after all) or Christmas, or maybe even both. I wouldn't need any other presents if I had my own horse. I think Mom is mostly on board with the idea, especially after I spent two hours talking to her about it last Sunday afternoon while helping her pull weeds out of this overgrown flower bed at the side of the house where she wants to make a rose garden. Plus she already sort of promised I could have my own horse someday soon, after I found that lost pony while we were living in that rented house this past summer. Dad seems a little more skeptical about the whole idea, but I think he may be coming around. We'll see. I'm keeping my fingers crossed, because having a horse of my very own at last would make our new home perfect!

CAROLE HANSON'S RIDING JOURNAL:

Okay, I opened this journal to make some notes about mounted games, but I'll get to that in a second. First I just have to write down something that happened at Pine Hollow earlier today, because it was so strange. It had to do with Max, of course. These days *everything* strange seems to have to do with Max.

My friends and I had made plans to go for a trail ride together. Stevie was late because she'd been stuck at home negotiating with her younger brother, Michael, to do her chores for her. That meant Lisa and I had already tacked up our horses by the time she finally arrived, but we left them tied outside and went in to help her with Topside.

As we were leading Stevie's horse back out a few minutes later, we heard Max instructing someone on how to tack up. "That's weird," Stevie commented. "Doesn't he have a lesson in about two minutes?"

Lisa nodded. "Yeah, and usually he'd get another student to help, or ask Red."

She was right about that. Mostly Max counts on all of us students to help each other out—he thinks that makes us better riders. But Red O'Malley always pitches in, too. That's why he's such a good head stable hand.

We came around the corner and saw Delilah cross-tied in the aisle. Max had a bridle slung over one shoulder and a saddle in his hands. That reporter, Deborah Hale, was with him.

"Now, do you remember how to put the saddle on?" Max asked her, gently and patiently.

Deborah stared at Delilah's back. "Umm," she said nervously, "you, um, put it in the middle of the back?"

I cringed on her behalf, figuring she was in for one of Max's famously stern lectures. When he teaches someone something once, he expects them to remember it. And we all knew that he'd taught Deborah this particular lesson before.

But Max just bit his lip and nodded. "Right," he told Deborah. "That's right. That is definitely right. *Eventually* the saddle should be just about in the middle. But the important thing to remember is that you put the saddle forward on the withers and then slide it back toward the croup—and not vice versa—so that the hair underneath lies flat. Okay?"

Deborah nodded. I thought she looked kind of unhappy. "Okay," she said.

Stevie, Lisa, and I looked at each other in amazement. Whatever had been getting to Max earlier in the week was obviously still distracting him. I mean, he was about to be late for a lesson, and as far as I know, Max Regnery the Third has *never* been late for a lesson in his whole life.

"Why don't we offer to help out?" I whispered to my friends.

"I'll take Topside and wait outside," Lisa offered. "You guys tack up Delilah, since you're a little faster."

I handed Topside's reins to Lisa, and she led the bay gelding away. Then I turned to the adults. "Hi, Max. Hi, Deborah."

They looked up in surprise. I guess they'd been so engrossed in what they were doing that they hadn't noticed we were standing there watching them.

Deborah seemed kind of relieved at our interruption. "Hi, girls," she greeted us warmly. "How are you?"

"Fine," Stevie said. She glanced at Max. "Listen, I know you've got that adult class starting right now, so why don't we tack up Delilah for Deborah?"

Max just stood there for a few seconds, as if he didn't even understand what Stevie was talking about. He stared from Deborah to Stevie and me and then back again. "You really want to tack up Delilah?" he asked us at last.

"That's right," I said cautiously. It might have been my imagination, but I thought Max looked a teeny bit annoyed with us for some reason.

"Well, all right," Max said. "But make sure you check over the tack carefully." Then he took off for his lesson.

The whole thing was pretty weird. But enough about that. I've really got to think of some good mounted games to play at the Fourth of July picnic. That's sort of because of the idea I had to make sure our plan to fix Max up would really work. My friends and I were talking about the picnic on our trail ride after we helped Deborah with her tack, and we were a little worried that even with all those single women coming, Max might be so busy with the students and horses that he wouldn't even notice how smart and beautiful and friendly they are.

"Wait a minute, I've got an idea," I said. "Maybe we could do some kind of introduction to the horses at Pine Hollow. We'll just say that our friends want to try riding and learning more about horses."

20

"Do you think he'd do it?" Stevie asked, meaning Max.

"Absolutely," I said. "Look how nice and patient he was with Deborah. I was thinking—I'll bet he's like that with all the single women."

"You think so?" Lisa asked, looking a little dubious.

"Sure," I replied. "Why else was he being so nice? I've never watched an adult lesson, but I'm sure he's easier on them than on the younger riders."

"Actually, he gets after them, too," Stevie said. She explained that she had once given a jumping demonstration to a beginning adult class, and that Max had been barking commands nonstop.

Still, we all agreed that my plan just might work. "If he's as nice to the women at the picnic as he is to Deborah, they're all going to think he's wonderful," I pointed out. "And he's bound to find at least one of them irresistible."

Stevie nodded. "Okay," she said. "So who's going to be the one to tell Max that more than a dozen strangers—who also happen to be young, attractive, single women—are coming to the picnic?"

None of us was looking forward to that. But it turned out to be surprisingly easy. First of all, we ran into Mrs. Reg when we got back to the stable. She started talking about how many new adult riders had started taking lessons lately, and how that was great for Pine Hollow because it meant a lot of their friends might also decide to start taking lessons. So that should help make all the extra people we invited seem a little more normal.

Plus, when we told Max our idea about introducing the horses and everything, he just nodded. "Great," he said.

"Sounds like an excellent idea. And in return, I have a favor to ask of you three. I was thinking we could have a mounted games demonstration at the picnic."

He explained that he'd been trying to get more students interested in signing up for Pony Club games. He thought that if we showed people how much fun the games are, more of them would want to give it a try.

So that's why I need to think of some ideas. We already came up with a few possibilities, like a costume race and the traditional baton relay race. And of course Stevie voted for her personal favorite, the super soaker target shoot.

Mounted Games: Ideas

1. Shadow Tag: This one's always fun and really fast-paced, which should make it fun for the audience.

2. Musical Tires: We played this a lot at one of my old stables. Just like musical chairs, except riders trot around a line of tires on the ground, and when the music stops, riders have to dismount and run to stand in one of the tires.

3. ???

I'm sure I'll think of more ideas soon. Now that I think about it, mounted games have always been some of my absolute favorite things to do on horseback. Maybe that should be a clue in my quest for the perfect career. After all, if I end up being a riding instructor like Max, I would get to supervise that sort of thing all the time. Plus it must be really fun teaching kids (and adults, too) to love horses and riding. I think I could be really good at that. I already like talking to people about horses, and I even enjoyed helping Deborah with her tack earlier. Of course, Max is so busy running Pine Hollow and teaching all us students that he doesn't have much time for anything else, like competing in shows himself or training young horses (or dating eligible women, obviously—ha ha!). Seriously, though, I guess I'll have to think about whether that kind of stuff is important to me, or if it's more important to share what I know with new riders.

This isn't going to be easy. *Aargh!* How do people ever decide what to do with their lives?

FROM: Steviethegreat

TO: HorseGal

TO: LAtwood

SUBJECT: Pony Club games

MESSAGE:

Okay, I've been thinking about ideas for games to play at the picnic, and since this is going to be such an important day, I decided we ought to have at least a couple of really special games instead of just the usual old egg-and-spoon or shadow tag or costume race stuff. Even the super soaker thing doesn't seem quite exciting enough this time, though it might be okay to start things off with. Anyway, here's what I've come up with so far.

(1) Watermelon Stomp: Since we'll probably have watermelon at the picnic anyway, we would just have to get a few dozen extras. We'd make all the riders line up in a circle at the edge of the ring, then scatter the watermelons around in

the middle. You'd get points for every watermelon your horse stepped on and smashed. I think Max would really appreciate how challenging this one would be—after all, a rider would have to have really good control of her horse to convince it to step *on* the melon instead of *over* it. So it would really show off our riding skills.

(2) Zebra Race: In this one, we could set up buckets of black and white paint (nontoxic of course, Carole, so don't have a heart attack) at one side of the ring. The riders would start at the other end, riding bareback. They would have to ride across, dismount, and paint stripes on their horses to make them look like zebras. Then they would have to lead them back across the ring to the finish line. We would have to work out some kind of scoring system that would give some points for finishing faster than the others and some for artistic merit. Maybe the audience could vote on which zebra stripes looked the most convincing or something.

That's all I've got for now, but I'm still thinking. Naturally, we could still also play some of the old classics like musical tires or whatever. But I think my games would definitely liven things up, don't you?

FROM:	LAtwood
TO:	Steviethegreat
TO:	HorseGal
SUBJECT:	Pony Club games (2)
MESSAGE:	

Hi, Stevie. I just got your interesting list of games for the picnic. They both sound really creative and everything, but I think they might not be quite right for *this* demonstration. After all, part of what we want to do here is convince some of the women (at least the ones who aren't already riders) how much fun riding is. And it might be better to do that with some slightly simpler games. I mean, if these women get all dressed up in their pretty summer picnic clothes, they probably aren't going to be too thrilled if the horses start stomping on watermelons and squirting juice and seeds all over the place. (Not to mention the whole safety issue, and what Max would say about the state of the ring afterward.) Ditto for the paint idea. That could get kind of messy, too, and we don't want to be stuck hosing off our horses when we could be introducing Max to his future wife, do we?

Anyway, I've come up with a list of games that will be fun and easy to understand. Here they are:

1. Baton or Flag Relay Race: A classic, so we should probably do it, especially since it's really easy to understand what's going on.

2. Costume Race: Active and funny and also easy to follow.

3. Super Soaker Target Shoot: As you always say, Stevie, this one's usually a big crowd pleaser. And if a few people in the audience get sprinkled by a few stray drops, it's no big deal. (Unlike being sprinkled with watermelon juice or black paint, ha ha.)

What do you think? Maybe we can talk about it on the phone later and figure out a final list to give to Max.

On another topic, I've been thinking about all the women we've invited to the picnic. I know we were talking about it on the trail ride the other day, but have either of you stopped to think about just how Max is going to react when he sees them all? I mean, thirteen single women is a lot. Think about it. We have my two: Tiffani the model and my dad's secretary, Nicole. Stevie, you invited five, right? Your teacher and her two sisters, your old baby-sitter, and the waitress from TD's. (I still can't believe you convinced her to take the day off and come after all!) And Carole, you came up with *six* single women from the base, plus those two married women and their husbands who overheard you talking about the picnic.

So basically, we're talking about *a lot* of (mostly) single women. All I can say is, Max had better fall in love with one of them. Because if he doesn't and he figures out what we're up to, he's going to kill us!

FROM: Steviethegreat

TO: LAtwood

TO: HorseGal

SUBJECT: The more the merrier

MESSAGE:

Don't worry about having too many women at the picnic. The more Max has to choose from, the more likely it is that he'll find one he likes. Right?

CAROLE HANSON'S RIDING JOURNAL:

I'm not sure Stevie is right about "the more the merrier" stuff she wrote in that e-mail. Sometimes I think that having too many choices makes things harder, not easier. After all, there are about a million interesting careers I could have that would involve horses, and so many of them sound like stuff I could really end up loving. It won't be easy to figure out which one is the most important to me when they all could end up being so much fun.

For instance, I just pulled out my information packet from Moose Hill Riding Camp, because I remembered we'll be getting ready to go there just a couple of weeks from now. As I was looking through all the stuff they sent, I was getting really excited. I mean, what could be more perfect than spending an entire week out in those beautiful woods, riding every single day, having cookouts, sitting around the campfire, and seeing old friends and making new ones? Actually, just about the only thing that could be better than that would be to spend an entire summer at Moose Hill! That makes me wonder if I shouldn't think more seriously about working someplace like that when I grow up, or maybe even managing and running it, like Barry does at Moose Hill. I'm sure his job is a lot of hard work (any job that involves horses is), but it must also be sort of like going on vacation for a living. That could be a cool way to do the kind of stuff I was thinking about before—teaching people to appreciate horses and riding, watching kids learn how to be better horsepeople, and all that sort of thing. Plus, since most camps are only open for the summer, it would mean I would have time for competitive riding or training or whatever during the rest of the year. Sounds pretty good . . . Maybe I can talk to Barry and the counselors while I'm at Moose Hill. I'm sure they could give me a better idea of what their jobs are really like and whether I would like doing the same kind of thing someday.

Anyway, I'd better sign off now. I was going to sketch out a training schedule for Starlight tonight—I really want to start working more on his flexibility, and he could use some refresher lessons on gait changes. But I'm running out of time, since I promised to check in the attic for extra old clothes for the costume race at the picnic tomorrow. Stevie wants to make sure everything is absolutely perfect so that Max will be able to fall in love without worrying about anything else. *Sigh.* A matchmaker's work is never done!

Bar None Ranch
17 Sidewinder Drive

May 12

Howdy, Carole!

What's new back East? I haven't heard from you in a while, so I thought I'd drop a note and let you know what's going on out here at the ranch. Mostly it's a lot of nothing. The latest crop of dudes just left last night, and the next group doesn't arrive until tomorrow, so it's a rare day off for all of us here. That doesn't mean we're all lounging around eating bonbons in front of the TV, of course. Dad is out with Walter and one of the other hands repairing fences, and Mom is out at the grocery store stocking up for another week's cooking.

I thought you might like to know that Christine and I had an out-of-town-member Saddle Club meeting, just the two of us. We went out at dawn a couple of days ago on a bareback ride across the desert to watch the sunrise, just like we did that time when you guys were here. It was great, of course, though not nearly as much fun as when we're all together. Maybe if I work on my parents and you work on yours, we can convince them that you and Stevie and Lisa should come out here for another visit. What do you think? School's letting out soon....

Oops, I just heard a car pull in, which means Mom is back from the store. I'd better go help her put stuff away. Write back sometime and let me know how you're doing, and give my best to Stevie, Lisa, Max, Red, Phil, Cam, Starlight, Topside, and oh, just about everyone else at Pine Hollow.

> Saddle Club Forever!!!!
> Your friend,
> Kate

Dear Kate,

Sorry it took me, like, two months to write back to your last letter. It kind of got lost for a little while. Actually, I just found it stuck in with the information packet from Moose Hill (that's the riding camp where Stevie, Lisa, and I go every summer, in case you forgot), which arrived in the mail the same day back in May.

Anyway, it sounds like you and everyone out at the Bar None are doing pretty well—or at least you were back in May! You'll have to write back and let me know how things are going out there these days. I'm sure you're busy with hordes of dudes who are thrilled with all the wonderful people and horses at the Bar None (not to mention your mother's fantastic cooking!). In the meantime, I have some good news and some bad news to report.

I'll start with the good news. I'm sure Stevie would say I shouldn't give it away right at the start, so I'll give you the background first. Have we ever told you about Pine Hollow's Fourth of July picnic? We hold it every year, and it's always lots of fun. All the riders and their parents and friends are invited, and Max fires up the barbecue and serves hamburgers and hot dogs and stuff while everyone talks about horses.

This year Stevie and Lisa and I already knew it was going to be even more special than usual. See, we decided it was past time for Max to settle down with some nice, horsey woman. He's seemed kind of lonely lately, and besides, we wanted to make sure he would have some heirs to take over Pine Hollow someday, just like he took it over from his father, and his father took it over from *his* father before that.

But you know Max—he hardly ever thinks about anything except horses, horses, horses. Normally there's nothing at all wrong with that, but in this case we were afraid it might keep him from finding the wife of his dreams. So we decided to step in and make it a Saddle Club project.

We figured the picnic would be the perfect place for Max to meet lots of new people, so we invited all the young, attractive single women we know. They all showed up, along with the usual crowd, and everything seemed to be going pretty well. The weather was hot and sunny, the sodas were cold, and everyone was enjoying themselves. Max and Mrs. Reg seemed a little confused about all the extra people we'd brought, but they didn't ask too many questions, so we didn't offer too much information.

At one point we were talking to Max (and introducing him to some more of the women) when he mentioned that he wanted to make an important announcement. Not right then, though—he scurried off toward the tack room to "take care of things," and we were a little afraid that we'd scared him off. You know, by overwhelming him with so many beautiful, intelligent women.

We were getting hungry at that point (if you think baby-sitting little kids is tiring just try baby-sitting thirteen adult women sometime!), so we went to get in line for burgers while we were discussing Max's behavior. Mrs. Reg and Deborah Hale—oh, I almost forgot to tell you, Deborah's this newspaper reporter who's been hanging around Pine Hollow doing research—anyway, the two of them were cooking. We were a little surprised to see Deborah there, since we figured Max would be too busy during the picnic to help her with her research. *Especially* since he had his hands full with tons of single women as well as the usual horses and students and stuff!

In any case, she didn't seem to be having much fun. She kept squinting and wiping her eyes from all the smoke blowing into her face, and it didn't help her mood at all when she noticed that some of the hamburger meat was green. It turned out it was just Stevie's brother Chad's way of getting back at her for turning his underwear pink (don't ask!). He had dyed the meat green with food coloring before she brought it over to Pine Hollow. (We volunteered to bring some of the food for

31

the picnic since we were inviting so many extra guests.) The green meat thing was actually sort of funny once we figured it out, but I guess Deborah wasn't amused. Mrs. Reg smoothed things over, though, and we suggested that Max give his demonstration for the beginning riders. He was muttering something about his big announcement, but we figured that could wait a few more minutes.

The demonstration went really well, we thought. All the women seemed interested in what Max was teaching them, and he took his time with each one of them, which we thought was a good sign. I was especially excited when he recognized my old riding teacher from Quantico, Margery Tarr, and it turned out they knew each other already. (Margery didn't need to learn anything at the beginners' demonstration, of course, but she was interested in seeing Max's teaching methods, since she's an instructor herself.) They seemed to like each other so much that for a few minutes I was sure she would end up being the one. But then Max says, "Hey, Margery, are you still seeing that same guy?"

"I sure am," Margery replied. "And he still refuses to learn to ride. I guess blah blah blah."

Okay, she didn't really say "blah blah blah" at the end. Probably not, anyway. I didn't hear a word because I was so disappointed.

Still, at least Max had twelve other women to choose from, and I figured they were all madly in love with him by then, so I wasn't too worried. I *was* kind of surprised to hear that Margery was in love with someone who didn't even ride, though. I mean, she's just about as horsey as a person can be. Sometimes adults are hard to figure out, you know?

I didn't have much time to think about that, though. There was a shout from the direction of the barbecue pit, and when we turned to see what was happening, we saw flames.

"Oh no!" Deborah yelled.

Mrs. Reg had been standing near us, watching Max's lesson, but she acted fast. There was a bucket of partly melted ice nearby. She grabbed it, ran toward the barbecue, and sloshed it over the fire.

"Nothing to worry about!" she called. "A hamburger just caught fire for a second." Then she turned to Deborah. "Are you okay?" she asked her more quietly.

Deborah nodded, but I thought she still looked pretty upset. I'm not sure, but I think there were even tears in her eyes.

"Is she all right?" Max asked, looking worried.

Stevie was closest to him, so she answered. "Yeah, it looks like the smoke really got to her, though." She looked at Deborah. "You should splash your eyes with cold water!" she yelled to her helpfully.

Deborah didn't answer. She just turned and ran into the stable. We had no idea what was wrong with her. And we didn't have much time to worry about it, since all those women were still waiting for Max to go on with his demonstration.

Anyway, she reappeared a little while later, after the riding demonstration was over. Stevie had helped Mrs. Reg finish the cooking, and by then everyone had moved on to dessert. Max was talking to a whole group of women about the history of Pine Hollow. After a little while, though, he got up and went to get some more dessert.

We followed him, pretending we were still hungry, too. "Are you having a good time?" Stevie asked him innocently.

"I'm having a marvelous time," Max said. "Your friends are really great fun. It was a good idea to invite them. And now I think I'll sit with my mother. I want to talk with her for a moment."

33

"Oh, no!" I blurted out, thinking about our plan. Not wanting Max to catch on, I quickly added, "I mean, please sit with us. It's the big picnic, and it only comes once a year."

Max hesitated, but then he gave in. "All right, if it really means so much to you. I suppose I can speak with Mother later. But I do have an announcement to make," he added firmly.

"An announcement?" Stevie asked. "Oh, I get it." She waved her hands to silence the crowd. "Everyone, Max has an announcement to make. And that is that the mounted games demonstration will start in five minutes. So get your seats now!" She turned back to Max. "Good thinking. We've got to keep this show on the road, or the fireworks will be starting before we know it."

That's another Pine Hollow tradition—watching the Willow Creek town fireworks from that little hill behind the stable. It's a great spot to see them from.

"Actually," Max said, "that wasn't the announcement I had in mind. But it's all right. I'll make it later."

After that we all got to work setting up for the games. The costume race and the relay races went very well. Everyone seemed to enjoy watching them, and I *know* my friends and I had fun doing them.

Then it was time for the grand finale—Stevie's favorite, the super soaker target shoot. Before we got started, though, we noticed one problem. One of the targets we'd set up was tipping over because the easel holding it had broken.

Lisa and I just kind of stood there and stared, not sure what to do. But Stevie thought fast. She told us that she noticed Deborah standing on the outskirts of the crowd, looking kind of out of it, and she figured this would be a perfect way to get her involved in things and maybe help her have some fun at the picnic. So she asked her if she would mind standing in for the broken easel—holding up the target.

Deborah agreed. I guess she was happy to have something to do. In no time at all, everything was ready to go.

Just as Stevie had predicted, the crowd loved the game. People roared when the riders missed wildly, and they cheered on their favorite riders. I'm pretty sure most of them—even the adults—were wishing they could take a turn with the water guns themselves.

Stevie was very pleased with the reactions, of course. "Everyone seems to be having a blast," she said at one point, looking around with satisfaction.

Betsy Cavanaugh was standing nearby and overheard our conversation. She pointed to Deborah. "Everyone but that poor woman holding up the target, you mean."

We all looked over at Deborah. Most of the water that missed the targets (and that was a *lot* of water) was hitting her, and she didn't look too happy about it. "Gee," Stevie said, looking worried. "I thought she might enjoy getting splashed. I guess I was wrong."

Stevie was ready to stop the game right then and there, since Deborah obviously wasn't having any fun. But we decided five more minutes wouldn't make much difference, so we continued, figuring we could apologize to Deborah later.

But after the race ended, we were all so excited that we sort of forgot about her for a little while. We were too busy talking about the games, squirting each other with the leftover water, and so forth. Lisa had noticed Deborah hightailing it to the Regnerys' house, so we figured she was inside changing into some dry clothes.

But then we heard a door slam, and we saw Deborah coming

35

out of the house carrying a suitcase. A taxicab had just pulled into Pine Hollow's driveway, and Deborah headed straight for it without so much as a glance at any of us.

We were all kind of surprised at that, but Max was downright dumbfounded. He stared after the cab with a totally weird look on his face.

"Uh, Max?" Stevie said. "Max?"

He hardly seemed to notice her at first, but then he shook his head. "Not now," he practically whispered. Then he ran toward the house.

Lisa shook her head as we all stared after him. "I have just one question," she said. "*What* is going on?"

None of us knew the answer to that. We held a quick Saddle Club meeting to discuss it, trying to figure things out. All we could agree on for sure was that Max seemed pretty upset about something, so we decided to do what we could to help. We got the picnic back into full swing by inviting everyone to help with some easy stable chores, since we figured Max could use some help after the busy day. Most of the guests seemed happy to help with stuff like tossing fresh hay down from the loft and moving fence posts around for the jumping demonstration some of the younger kids were supposed to give. We weren't sure we could convince them that mucking out stalls was a fun picnic activity, though, so we decided to tackle that one ourselves.

While we were hard at work in the stall closest to the office hallway, we overheard Max and his mother talking inside in urgent, hushed tones.

"Why be stubborn at a time like this?" Mrs. Reg demanded.

"It's *not* stubbornness, Mother," Max protested. "I just know there's nothing I can do."

"Nothing? That's not true. You could go after her," Mrs. Reg said.

"Forget it. It's no use. She's never going to speak to me again."

My friends and I stared at each other, trying to figure out what they were talking about. They mumbled a little bit after that, so we couldn't understand them. But then Max burst out with his bombshell.

"It's off!" he exclaimed. "Everything concerning Deborah Hale is off! I'm just thankful I was spared the embarrassment of asking her to marry me in public and then having her run off."

I don't know how my friends felt when they heard that, but I felt as if my entire body had just gone numb. I couldn't believe what I'd just heard, or what it meant. We had ruined the lives of two people. On top of that, we could forget about seeing an heir for Pine Hollow anytime soon.

Stevie was the first one of us to speak. "I have a pit in my stomach the size of a black hole," she announced.

That pretty much summed it up. We had just realized that all of Max's weird behavior, all of his patience with Deborah and his absentmindedness lately, was because he was falling in love with her!

We ticked off all the problems we had created for the man we were trying to help. "We brought thirteen single women to the picnic where Max was planning to propose to another woman," Stevie said.

I winced, remembering something that Max had mentioned to us earlier. "Not only that," I pointed out, "but he'd told her that the people at the picnic were his best friends."

"So we made him look like a playboy," Lisa said.

"And we made her cook green hamburgers," Stevie added.

Lisa nodded. "And we let her get soaked by squirt guns."

We went on like that for a little longer before realizing we had

37

to do something. Max's current problem was one hundred per-cent our fault, and we couldn't just sit around wringing our hands if there was any chance we could fix it.

The trouble was figuring out how to find Deborah and getting her back to Pine Hollow. To make a long story short, we tracked her down by calling the taxi company. The dispatcher told us Deborah had taken the cab to the bus station, so we knew that was where we had to go—and fast.

Stevie hung up the phone. "So what's the fastest route to the bus station?" she asked Lisa and me.

"I think you go straight downtown past the mall," Lisa said. "But who are we going to ask to drive us? We can't exactly explain things to Mrs. Reg or Max. And all the parents are busy with their children, getting ready for the fireworks."

Leave it to Lisa to look at things the sensible way! We knew she was right. It was just starting to get dark, but it wouldn't be long before it was time to start gathering on the hillside for the fireworks.

Luckily I had a brilliant idea, if I do say so myself. "Actually," I told my friends, "straight downtown is not *the* fastest route. It's only the fastest route by car, if you get my drift."

They got it right away. In a matter of seconds we were racing for the tack room. We didn't bother with saddles—just grabbed bridles and hard hats and took off. Soon we were mounted bare-back on Starlight, Barq, and Topside and setting off across the fields at a brisk trot, which quickly became a canter.

When we reached town, we decided to take a shortcut through the park, where workers were setting up for the fire-works display. As we passed the bandstand, some of them turned to wave at us, looking a little surprised to see three horses wan-dering through the park.

"What's the big finale going to say?" Stevie called to them good-naturedly.

" 'America the Beautiful,' what else?" one of the workers answered with a grin.

We didn't stick around to chat any longer. We hurried on toward the bus station. When we got there, we were afraid we were too late. A bus was just pulling away, and Stevie actually chased it for a while on Topside. Max would have killed her if he'd been there—it was a pretty crazy and dangerous stunt, even for Stevie—but the bus actually stopped. However, as it turned out, Deborah wasn't on it. She was waiting back at the station for a different one. So we went over to her and Stevie and I managed to totally confuse her with a lot of long, rambling explanations about green hamburgers and eligible women, mixed in with a few apologies.

Finally Lisa stepped in, speaking in her most mature and responsible voice. (You know the one, Kate!) "Deborah," she began, "none of us is proud of what we've done this week—even though we did it without knowing what we did. We turned your stay at Pine Hollow into a nightmare. We thought we were helping Max by inviting a lot of women we know for him to meet, and you by trying to include you in Pine Hollow's craziness. We didn't realize that we were just getting in the way. But now that we know that Max was *already* in love, we want to do everything we can to make things right again."

At first Deborah just nodded along and smiled politely at Lisa's words. But suddenly she did a double take and grabbed Lisa by the arm. "What did you say? Max was already in love? How could he? I mean, with whom?"

It took about a second for us to realize that Deborah still didn't know what we were trying to tell her. "With *you!*" all three of us cried in unison.

It took some doing to convince Deborah that we knew what we were talking about and that it was really true. We also explained about how Max's "big announcement" was going to be the moment when he asked her to marry him.

Deborah seemed a little stunned by it all. Her face was sort of blank for a minute, and a few tears squeezed out of her eyes. But it turned out she was crying for joy, because she said that marrying Max would be a dream come true.

"Now, if he'll only get around to asking me!" Deborah said.

"What do you mean, asking you? You're a modern woman, aren't you?" Stevie said.

Lisa and I shook our heads frantically. We were afraid that Stevie was going to step in with one of her big plans and mess everything up again. But she didn't pay attention.

"When you want to get the scoop on a big story, do you wait for it to come to you?" she asked Deborah.

"Of course not," Deborah replied promptly. "If I didn't go after it, I'd never get the story. But what exactly are you getting at?"

Little did she know. Stevie had just concocted another of her plans, and it was a doozy. See, she had remembered the finale at the fireworks display, when they spell out a message. And with a little help from Deborah, she managed to arrange things with the park workers to replace the words *America the Beautiful* with the words *Marry Me Max*. Isn't that romantic? The best part is, Max never so much as glanced at any of the other eligible women who were gathered on that hillside watching the display. He had eyes only for Deborah. And he said yes. Well, actually he didn't really say it. He was too overwhelmed. But he answered with a kiss, and everybody cheered louder at that than at any of the fireworks. It was an absolutely wonderful end to a very interesting day!

So that's the big news—Max is getting married! He and Deborah haven't set a date yet, but we're already looking forward to the wedding.

By the way, in case you're wondering why I'm so thrilled that Max is marrying a woman who doesn't know a farrier from a fetlock, it's mostly because they love each other. But also, on the ride back to Pine Hollow—Deborah rode Starlight with me—she asked me all kinds of questions about horses and riding and seemed really interested in the answers. So I think she'll learn fast. The way I see it, she really doesn't have much choice! Ha ha! Seriously, though, it's still kind of weird to think that Max ended up with a woman who wasn't even on our list. I guess finding the right person isn't always as straightforward as you might think, huh?

So that's the good news. Pretty great, huh? But now you're probably wondering about the bad news. Remember how I started this letter by saying I'd found your letter in my Moose Hill packet? Well, the bad news is about Moose Hill. Stevie and Lisa and I were just starting to get really excited about going back there this year when we found out that the whole thing is off. The camp is having some kind of wiring problem that means they have to close down for at least a month! Can you believe it? So we're stuck here cleaning tack, mucking out stalls, and suffering through one of those famous Virginia summer heat waves when we should be getting ready to pack up and head for the cool green hills of camp. Not that we wouldn't be cleaning tack and mucking out stalls there, too, of course, but Max is a lot tougher than the staff at Moose Hill. And it's not like we don't all still love Pine Hollow. But you know what I mean, right?

Anyway, I'd better finish this. It's getting late, and my hand is about to fall off from all this writing. Besides, thinking about how much fun we're going to be missing at camp makes me want to go stick my head under a pillow and moan. *Aargh!* Do we have rotten luck or what?

Your slightly depressed friend,
Carole

CAROLE HANSON'S RIDING JOURNAL:

Writing to Kate today reminded me that I'm supposed to be figuring out what to do about my career. It's been weeks since Cam wrote to me about becoming a combined training star, and so far I'm no closer to deciding what I want to do. After all, Kate is only a few years older than me, and she's already hung up her stirrups after an incredible career as a champion show rider. Of course, that turned out to be the wrong career for her in some ways—even though she's a fantastic rider and has won a million blue ribbons, it didn't make her happy because she got so caught up with wanting to win all the time that riding wasn't fun for her anymore. I'm sure Dad would say I should learn from other people's mistakes and think really hard about whether I might feel the same way if I became a competitive rider.

And I have thought about that—ever since I met Kate, actually. It's hard to know what would happen, but I'm pretty sure I wouldn't have the same sort of problems as Kate had. For one thing, she started competing in some pretty major shows when she was really young, which is probably harder than doing it when you're a little bit older. Besides, I think it just depends on each person's personality. Kate ran into trouble because she was so super-competitive that she couldn't think about anything else, not even enjoying herself, so she was miserable. I think Stevie might have a little bit of that same kind of personality. When she's competing at something (especially when she's competing against Phil or her brothers), she gets so caught up in winning that she sometimes forgets she's supposed to be having fun. On the other hand, Lisa isn't that interested in beating other people. But she has such high standards for herself (which is why she always gets straight As, keeps her room spotless, and is super-organized about everything) that she might make herself miserable by putting a lot of pressure on herself, which comes down to sort of the same thing.

I guess I'm kind of different from any of them in that way. I love riding in shows, and I love winning—but always in that order. The most important thing to me is making sure my horse and I are working well and safely together, and that's what I love about all riding. I don't think any amount of pressure or desire to do well in a show could make me forget that.

So maybe that means I could really enjoy a career as a competitive rider if I wanted to. Of course, if I decided to go that way, my decision making wouldn't be over by a long shot. I would still have to figure out what kind of event to specialize in—jumping (Hunter or Jumper divisions), dressage, three-day eventing like Cam, or even something like endurance riding or carriage driving.

Thinking about Kate also makes me think about Western riding, since that's the kind she mostly does on her parents' dude ranch. I've really enjoyed learning about that kind of riding during visits to the Bar None. It's different from what we do at Pine Hollow, but it's still a lot of fun, and it would be cool to learn more about it—maybe even try barrel racing again like we did that one time. If I start training right away as a competitive English rider, will that mean I won't have enough time to do that kind of thing? I mean, I know I would never want to switch to Western riding full-time and be a professional barrel racer or anything.

Probably not, anyway.

No, definitely not. This decision is complicated enough. I shouldn't make it any more difficult than it needs to be. I like Western riding as an occasional thing, but in my heart I know English riding is my true love. I know that as surely as I know Starlight is my true horse and Stevie and Lisa are my true friends. I only wish I were that clear and certain about what my true career calling is. . . .

This decision is turning out to be even harder than I thought. There are so many possibilities to consider, and it's hard to figure out what any of them would really be like if I were doing it full-time. And now it looks as if I won't have a chance to check out the life of a riding-camp counselor first-hand, at least not this year. *Sigh!*

Dear Diary:

Happy birthday to me! It's hard to believe it's already my birthday, which means Thanksgiving is almost here—I al-

ready feel like we've lived in Willow Creek a lot longer than three months.

But back to my birthday. We didn't do anything too exciting, just a nice dinner at home (Mom made all my favorite foods and Dad got takeout ice cream from Tastee Delight, this new place that just opened at the little shopping center at the edge of town). After dinner I opened my presents. Mom and Dad got me a subscription to my favorite horse magazine, a new model horse (the Appaloosa, the one I've been wanting—I can't believe Mom remembered!), and a really nice pair of breeches. Aunt Elaine sent a neat video about show jumping. Aunt Joanna and Uncle Willie gave me a gift certificate so that I could pick out some more model horses for my collection. And my relatives in Minnesota all chipped in for a really nice watch with a gold jumping horse on the face. The only thing that would have been better than all that great stuff is a real horse of my own. I was still kind of hoping I'd come downstairs this morning and find Mom and Dad waiting to drive me off to some stable or other to pick one out—but oh well. There's always Christmas, right? Otherwise, though, it's been a practically perfect day.

Oh, I almost forgot. Somehow the people at Pine Hollow found out it was my birthday, too. I think Lauren probably told Max. She's so sweet! She got me a mug shaped like a horse's head and a cute birthday card with a picture of a gorgeous dapple gray Arabian mare on it. Mrs. Reg baked a cake (with a picture of a horse on it in icing that looked exactly like Delilah!) and everyone sang. Stevie Lake and Dinah Slattery kind of goofed off during the song—they

45

changed the words to "Happy birthday to you, Your horse lost a shoe, The blacksmith's in prison, Cuz he stole a kazoo." Don't ask me where they came up with those words, since they don't even make any sense. But that's pretty typical for them—they can't be serious about anything.

Anyway, it was really one of the best birthdays I can remember. Actually, these days my whole life seems almost too good to be true. I think I'm finally starting to believe that my family and I are here in Willow Creek forever—or at least for the foreseeable future, which is pretty much the same thing as far as I'm concerned.

One of the things that's helping make it real is that we're planning a vacation. Mom and Dad are really gung ho about going away somewhere this year as a family. Not just a weekend at the beach or whatever, but a real vacation, somewhere far away, for a whole week. We've never really done anything like that before, since we always seem to be either getting settled in someplace new or packing up to move again.

But it sounds like we're definitely going somewhere during my winter break next month. The only question left is where we should go. Believe me, we've already had plenty of arguments about that! Ha ha! Mom is pulling for some secluded mountain lake she read about—I think it's in, like, West Virginia or someplace like that. She wants to rent a cabin up there and relax for a week. Dad and I agree that that sounds pretty boring (not to mention cold, since it will be the middle of winter), but that's about all we agree on. He wants to go to some golfing resort in Florida near the beach. He's been trying to convince Mom and me that we

46

would love lounging around on the sand while he's off on the links. Neither one of us is convinced, of course. I can't believe they're not more excited about my idea. It's to go out West to this Arizona dude ranch I read about. I've always wanted to do something like that—I've only been Western riding a few times, and I think it would be fun to learn more about it, maybe see some calf roping and barrel racing and stuff, and take trail rides through the desert. And like I told Dad, the brochure says there's a public golf course just outside the nearest big town, which is only seventy miles away.

I'm not holding my breath, though. I have a feeling we're going to end up on the beach this year after all. But that's okay, I guess. I'm sure I can find someplace to go riding, and maybe we'll even get to see Aunt Joanna and Uncle Willie. That way I could at least go riding with Sheila, since she has her own pony (unlike me, boo hoo!). Besides, I have to remember that we can take vacations every year, now that we're living in one place. So if we don't make it to that dude ranch this year, it just means I have a whole year to convince Mom and Dad that we should go there next year! (And the year after that, and the year after that, and again the year after that . . .)

Okay, I didn't think *anything* could make me feel better about not getting to go to Moose Hill this year. But then along came Kate. . . . I still can hardly believe we're going out to the Bar None again! I have never been so glad that Kate's father was a pilot in the Marines, or that he retired, or that he has that part-time job flying that businessman's private plane, or that the businessman has to come to Washington a lot, or that we live so close to Washington. . . . Oh, you know what I mean. Sometimes I think we're the luckiest girls in the world! I can't wait to see Kate again, and Colonel and Mrs. Devine, and Christine and John and of course wonderful Stewball. Riding Stewball again just might even make me forget how unfair it is that practically everyone else in the entire world has their own horse except for me. But I almost feel like Stewball is mine— he's like my horse away from home! Ha ha!

Anyway, I don't know if you two will even see this message before we leave tomorrow, since it's, like, three A.M. right now. But I was just too excited to sleep!

Git along, little dogies!!!!!!!!!!!!!!

CAROLE HANSON'S RIDING JOURNAL:

It's amazing how even the nighttime sounds are different here at the Bar None than they are at home. I'm lying on my bunk in our usual cabin right now, writing this. The others are asleep already, and I'll probably join them soon—it's been a long and exciting day. But I'm still a little too keyed up to sleep quite yet.

By the way, I've discovered yet another horse-related career: horseback acting! I don't think that's the career for me, though. It's not quite as easy as it looks, as Stevie discovered.

It all started when Kate announced, almost as soon as we arrived yesterday afternoon, that she had volunteered all of us (herself and Christine included) to play robbery victims in the Wild West show in Two Mile Creek. It's a reenactment of a Wild West bank robbery and shoot-'em-up that's held every day on the main street of town. It's really fun to watch, and we were all thrilled at the idea of being a part of it.

But that wasn't the only big news Kate had for us. We were sitting down to dinner last night when she turned to me, Stevie, and Lisa. "I almost forgot to tell you about the auction," she told us. "It's just about the biggest news around here right now. I was about to tell you before, but then we got distracted talking about other things, and I forgot."

"An auction?" I asked, not really understanding what she meant at first. Actually, I was picturing this auction I went to with Dad once where they were selling a whole bunch of musty old rifles and Civil War uniforms and other military memorabilia. The only interesting things they had at that auction were a few pieces of antique tack. "What kind?"

"The best kind—a horse auction," Kate said. She explained that ever since Walter and John Brightstar had started working at the Bar None, the Devines had more well-trained horses than they knew what to do with. "It's going to take place at the end of the week," Kate went on. "My mom seems determined to make it into a big event. She's going to sell a lot of baked goods and canned preserves, and she'll have sandwiches and things for sale, too."

"It sounds perfect," I declared.

"Good," Kate said, her eyes sparkling. "Because I promised Mom and Dad that you guys would help out. I hope you don't mind."

"Mind?" Stevie raised an eyebrow. "The only thing we'd mind is if you *didn't* let us help!"

We talked about the auction and the Wild West show all through dinner. By the time we finished it was still light out, so we went out to the big corral near the barn to say hello to the horses. I was happy to see Berry again, and Lisa was glad to see Chocolate. But nobody was as thrilled as Stevie was to see Stewball. I swear, sometimes I think that girl and that horse were separated at birth! They have more in common (namely their fun-loving, mischievous, slightly ornery personalities) than most people do with their actual blood relatives! Ha ha!

Naturally, I couldn't wait to see Moonglow, the mare Kate got at the wild horse roundup, and Moonglow's foal, Felix. Kate had told me a lot about the two of them in letters and phone calls, but I hadn't seen them yet in person, since she got them right after our last visit to the Bar None.

"Where are they?" I asked her eagerly. "I'm dying to see them."

"They're in the barn," Kate said.

"Why are you keeping them in the barn?" I asked, glancing at the herd of horses in the corral in front of us. "Isn't Felix old enough to stay out with the herd yet?"

"Oh, he's old enough, all right," Kate said with a laugh. "I can't remember if I explained why I named him Felix."

"It is an unusual name for a horse," I said.

"But a good name for a cat, right?" Kate said. "And you know what they say about cats and curiosity. Well, Felix is about the most curious foal I ever met. Last week he decided to see how a cactus would taste."

"Oh no!" I exclaimed. "Is he okay?"

"Oh, sure. The cactus was tiny and definitely took the worst of it," Kate assured me. "We're just keeping Felix and his mama inside for a week or two until we're sure he's completely healed." She chuckled. "He may be nosy, but he's not stupid. I don't think he'll make that mistake again. Come on, I'll introduce you to them."

We headed into the barn, leaving the others out by the corral. Moonglow and Felix were just as wonderful as I was expecting. Moonglow is a gorgeous pale gray mare, and even though she was a wild horse not too long ago, she's already really sweet and friendly, though a little shy with new people. And Felix is positively adorable! His little

51

bottlebrush tail never stopped moving, and he ran right over and sort of bleated at Kate and me as soon as we approached the stall. It was so cute! I'm sure Kate will have a lot of fun training them both, especially with Walter's and John's expert help. It almost made me wish I had a foal to train—at least until I remembered how much work I still have to do with Starlight!

Anyway, we went to bed pretty soon after that since we were tired from the trip out. This morning we woke up bright and early for one of Phyllis Devine's five-star ranch breakfasts, then got ready to head into town to rehearse for the bank robbery show. Christine had ridden over from her house before breakfast, so all five of us rode to Two Mile Creek together. While we were in the corral getting our horses, John Brightstar saw us and asked where we were going. When he heard the answer, he burst out laughing, then teased us mercilessly about being in the "Wild West Dude Show," as he called it.

We really didn't pay that much attention to him, though. He's always joking around, and besides, we were all too excited about being in the show to care much what anyone said. But I did notice that Lisa started blushing as soon as John began teasing us, and I had a pretty good idea why. The last time we visited Kate, Lisa and John became pretty good friends. More than friends, I guess—they actually kissed once or twice. Stevie and I were completely clueless about it at the time, though. It wasn't until we were home again and Lisa sort of admitted the whole thing that we had any idea. So this time I'm planning to keep an eye on the two of them. I don't want to be nosy or anything, but I also don't want to be oblivious again.

When we arrived in town, Kate introduced us to Chuck Pierce, the director of the show. He also stars in it as Outlaw Buck McClanahan, the "head varmint," as Kate says. Chuck instructed us to tie our horses (he called them critters) to a hitching post in front of the sheriff's office. Kate explained that Chuck liked to have some horses around during the show to give the place an authentic Wild West look. Then we headed over to the high-school gym for the rehearsal.

"First things first," Chuck said when we got there. "We have to get you gals properly gussied up."

"Awesome," Stevie said. "Do we get spurs and hats like yours?"

"Not quite," Chuck said with a smile. He pointed out a tall red-haired woman on the other side of the gym. "Go over and see Cassie, there. She'll get you outfitted."

We did as he said, and in a matter of minutes we were dressed in our costumes for the show. I think Stevie was a little disappointed to find out that those costumes looked more like something out of *Little House on the Prairie* than *Gunfight at the OK Corral*—in other words, long calico dresses and crisp white bonnets.

"Remember," I told her, "we're supposed to be the helpless victims, not the cowboys."

Stevie still couldn't help grumbling a little, especially when she saw Cassie emerging a moment later dressed just like Chuck, with her long red hair pinned up and tucked under a black cowboy hat.

Next Cassie explained more about the show and our parts. "We're a vicious band of desperadoes," she explained with a smile. "So remember to look scared. You girls are going to be walking along innocently in front of the bank when we come out of it with our guns blazing. When we see you, each of us will grab one of you as a hostage and start dragging you toward our horses. You should all be screaming and crying out the whole time, but not so loud that the audience can't hear the rest of the dialogue."

"Then what happens?" I asked. When we'd seen the Wild West show before, there hadn't been any hostages.

"While you're being carried toward the horses, one of you faints." She pointed to me. "Think you can do that?"

I placed one hand over my forehead and pretended to swoon, crumpling dramatically to the floor. My friends applauded my performance.

"All right, you win the part," Cassie said with a grin. She assigned parts to the rest of the "victims." Lisa was supposed to wriggle free of her bad guy and run for cover. Christine got to wrestle the gun away from the robber holding her and march him into the jail. And Kate and Stevie would just be carried over to the horses, where the robbers would drop them. They were supposed to run for cover offstage when the shoot-out with the posse began.

I could tell that Stevie was a bit disappointed once again. I'm sure she was hoping for a more active role. Still, I knew that we would all have lots of fun, no matter what parts we were playing.

We practiced our section of the show a few times with Cassie and Chuck and the other robbers. Then Chuck said we had time to change out of our costumes and go grab some lunch before we had to get ready for our debut performance.

First we went to check on our horses, who were fine, and then we wandered aimlessly around town. "I couldn't eat a thing," Stevie declared once or twice, and I knew what she meant. I was too excited to even think about lunch.

"I'm not hungry, either," Lisa said. "But I definitely am thirsty. I've never had to do so much screaming in my life."

"Me neither." Suddenly Stevie stopped in front of a store. "Let's go in here a minute."

"The candy store?" Christine said. "I thought you weren't hungry."

"I'm not," Stevie replied, and she disappeared into the store. The rest of us shrugged and followed.

Like a lot of downtown Two Mile Creek, the candy store was decorated like an old-fashioned Western shop. Glass jars, filled with every kind of candy I could imagine, lined the walls. Stevie was already at the counter placing her order.

"Rock candy!" Lisa said as the shopkeeper handed Stevie a bulging paper bag. "I should have known."

"It's one of her favorite treats in the world," I explained to Kate and Christine.

"It's one of mine, too," Christine said as Stevie rejoined us. "I hope you're planning to share, Stevie."

55

We left the shop and strolled down the sidewalk. "Don't worry, I'll share," Stevie said. "But this candy is mostly for medicinal purposes. I've got a little bit of a sore throat from all that screaming, and I wouldn't want to lose my voice." She gave a weak-sounding cough.

I raised my eyebrow suspiciously. "You don't sound very sick to me," I told her. "But as long as you stick to that promise to share, I won't say a word."

Sensible Lisa suggested we should probably try to eat something other than rock candy before the show, so we headed over to a hamburger place for lunch before going back to the gym. We got dressed in our costumes again, then crowded around the full-length mirror in the locker room to make last-minute adjustments.

"Stevie, what are you doing?" Kate asked at one point.

I glanced over and saw that Stevie had a guilty look on her face. She also had her dress hitched up above her waist and was shoving the bag of rock candy deep into one of the pockets of her jeans, which she had left on beneath the long skirt.

She started babbling about her so-called sore throat again, so we teased her until she passed the candy bag around again. When we went back out into the main part of the gym, still sucking on our candy, one of the other performers asked where we'd gotten it.

Stevie fished the bag out of her pocket again. "Help yourself," she said. Stevie is nothing if not generous. Even after all the "bad guys" had helped themselves, she still had plenty of candy left, and she stuck it back in her pocket.

"This is great," said a performer named Sam as he sucked

on one piece of candy and stuck a second piece into the pocket of his costume. "Rock candy is my favorite."

"Mine too," Stevie told him. "I guess that must be why we're paired up together, huh?" Sam was the one who was supposed to kidnap Stevie during the show.

Pretty soon it was showtime. I think my friends and I were a little nervous, but we were looking forward to the show, too. The five of us huddled in the doorway of a jewelry store near the bank. At exactly three o'clock, we stepped out and started strolling down the street, trying to look as natural as we could in our old-fashioned costumes. I glanced over and saw that the bad guys' horses were lined up at the hitching post in front of the bank.

As we neared the bank, the sounds of gunshots came from within, and a curious crowd began to gather nearby. A moment later the bank's doors burst open and the five desperadoes backed out, holding large sacks of money and firing their six-shooters into the bank. My friends and I did as Chuck had taught us, throwing up our hands and shrieking in terror. Chuck—or, rather, Outlaw Buck McClanahan—whirled around.

"Looky here, boys!" he called loudly to his comrades. "I think we found us some hostages!" He grabbed Kate by the shoulder, and then I sort of lost track of the others as Cassie grabbed me by the arm and started to drag me toward the horses. Just as we'd practiced, I went only a few steps, wriggling and screaming, before giving one final cry and pretending to faint dead away.

My eyes were closed, but I could still hear the others

shrieking and yelling and carrying on. After a moment or two, when I figured nobody was looking at me anymore, I cracked one eye open a little. I didn't want to miss the whole show!

I was just in time to see Lisa's dramatic escape. She wriggled her way out of her captor's grasp and dashed down the sidewalk, almost tripping over my limp arm on the way. She ran past the jail and made her escape into the sheriff's office just beyond, shrieking all the while.

At almost the same time, Christine was wrestling the gun away from the outlaw who had grabbed her. When she got it away from him and pointed it at his head, the crowd cheered excitedly. Christine really hammed it up, making the robber put his hands behind his head and then jabbing the gun at his back as she prodded him toward the jail. The onlookers cheered again as the two of them disappeared inside.

But I was only half watching at that point. I'd caught a glimpse of something going on farther down the street, where our horses were tied. Berry, Chocolate, Spot, and Arrow were just standing there where we'd left them, looking fairly relaxed and unimpressed with all the shouting and gunfire. But Stewball was another story. He had his head up and his ears were pricked toward us.

I was a little worried about him. I hoped the strange noises weren't spooking him. But I was kind of surprised, too. Stewball was a hardworking, sensible cutting horse who normally didn't spook easily.

As I watched, he seemed to get even more agitated. He stamped his feet and snorted loudly, still staring toward us.

Or, rather, toward *Stevie*. She was still struggling with Sam, her "captor," and letting out piercing screams.

I guess it was all too much for Stewball. Suddenly he whinnied and reared, snapping the lead rope holding him to the hitching post. He reared again and then, realizing he was free, he galloped straight toward Stevie and Sam! He stopped in front of them and reared once more, neighing and squealing and pawing the air with his front hooves.

The rest happened pretty fast. I guess Stevie and Sam were both startled, and I think the rest of the actors were, too. For a second I was tempted to get up and hurry over to help calm Stewball before someone got hurt, especially since just about everyone else was standing and staring at the horse in surprise.

But Stevie acted fast. As she told us later, she figured that if Stewball was so determined to become a part of the performance, she was going to let him, even though it meant deviating a bit from the script.

She wriggled out of Sam's grip. The minute she was free, Stewball stopped snorting and stood perfectly still. Sam, meanwhile, turned to run in the opposite direction. Stevie quickly tightened the girth on Stewball's saddle, hitched up her skirt, and leaped aboard. Without any direction from her (or so she claims, anyway), Stewball took off after Sam. The crowd went wild. Everyone continued to cheer and holler as Stevie and Stewball chased Sam down the street. Sam searched desperately for someplace to hide, but every time he veered toward the sidewalk, Stewball was there before him, herding him as well as he would any stubborn calf.

Finally Sam reached the other horses. He ran over to Spot and tried to mount him, not realizing that Kate had loosened the girth. The big Western saddle slipped sideways under Sam's weight and dumped him back on the ground. Spot looked around as if wondering what on earth was going on, which the crowd absolutely loved.

Even from my limited view, I could tell that Stevie was having a ball. As Sam cowered behind Spot, she ripped off her bonnet and waved it above her head as if it were a cowboy hat. "Get 'im, Stewball!" she cried.

Finally Sam made a break for the little stand of trees just beyond the hitching post. He shinned up one of the trees and perched on one of the lower branches. That didn't faze Stewball one bit. He raced up to the tree and started rearing against the trunk as if trying to follow Sam up there.

Luckily Stevie managed to stay in the saddle. I could tell she was trying to get her horse under control, but she wasn't having much luck. Stewball definitely has a mind of his own!

I guess it's a good thing Stevie's mind is just as wacky as that horse's, because she finally figured out what to do. She told Sam to give Stewball the extra piece of rock candy he still had in his pocket. And what do you know? As soon as he did, Stewball calmed down right away!

The crowd had been laughing hysterically through the last part of Stewball's performance, and when he crunched on the candy they burst into wild applause. Stewball turned to see what all the noise was about, bobbing his head slightly as he did. I guess it looked like he was taking a bow, because everyone laughed and clapped even harder.

So that was The Saddle Club's first and only appearance as victims in the Wild West show. After it was all over, Chuck politely (sort of) and firmly (very) asked us *not* to repeat our performance.

Still, we were feeling pretty pleased with ourselves as we headed back to the gym to turn in our costumes. "Stewball was pretty great, wasn't he?" Stevie said. "I always suspected he was the smartest horse I'd ever met, and now I know it for a fact. What other horse would have come galloping to my rescue that way?"

For the rest of our time in town that day, people kept coming up to Stevie and congratulating her and Stewball. She loved every minute of it, of course. "He really is the most wonderful horse in the world," she told one group of people. "I'd be happy if I never rode another horse in my life besides Stewball."

That made me raise an eyebrow in surprise. It sort of sounded like she meant it. Of course, anyone would think Stewball was pretty wonderful after what happened today, so I'm sure she was just excited.

Whew! I just realized I've been writing for a long time. It's getting late, and my eyelids are starting to feel like they have lead weights attached to them. Besides, I really shouldn't be filling up this journal with silly stuff like the Wild West show. I mean, I only brought it along in the first place in case talking to Kate gave me any ideas about my career, or in case I wanted to make some notes about Western riding or anything like that.

So maybe I *should* write a few words about the differences

61

between English and Western riding. I mean, it's always an interesting learning experience to switch to Western after not doing it for a while. It makes me think about riding more consciously because I have to remember to do stuff like neck-reining. Here are a few of the other big differences that come to mind right away:

English: gaits are walk, trot, canter
Western: gaits are walk, jog, lope
English: shorter stirrup length
Western: longer stirrups—always feels weird at first!
English: smaller saddle
Western: big, deep-seated saddle with horn in front
English: bits are usually . . .

CAROLE HANSON'S RIDING JOURNAL:

HEH HEH HEH! THIS JOURNAL HAS NOW BEEN HI-JACKED!!!! *HEH HEH HEH HEH HEH!!!!!!!!*

I, Stevie Lake the Magnificent, am here to rescue this journal from terminal boredom. Also from terminal drool, since I just woke up and saw that Carole was using it for a pillow. I guess she was so bored by all the dull stuff she was writing about English vs. Western riding that she fell asleep right in the middle of writing it.

I mean, give me a break. Drool aside, most girls' diaries would be full of juicy stuff about boys, or at least complaints about idiotic brothers or something normal like that. But when I glanced at the open page of this, it was all loping versus cantering! That's Carole for you. But I'm going to do her a favor, for her own good. I'm going to show her what a *real* diary is supposed to be like!

Dear Diary, This is Carole Hanson writing. I'm at the Bar None Ranch with my wonderful, almost supernaturally incredible friends. Yesterday we went out riding on the range. I was feeling kind of blue because I missed my hunky boyfriend, Cam, so much. I couldn't stop dreaming about grabbing him in a big hug and smooching him and stuff.

So imagine my surprise when I saw a lone rider cantering—oops, I mean *loping*—across the desert toward me and my friends.

"Who is that handsome fellow?" my friend Lisa asked, shading her eyes with her hand.

I felt my heart begin to flutter wildly, for I recognized my one true love, the man of my dreams. "Oh, be still my heart!" I intoned. "It's Cam! But what is he doing here?"

Cam brought his horse to a stop just in time to answer my question. "Carole, my darling!" he exclaimed, leaping out of the saddle and rushing to my horse's side. "I missed you so much, light of my life! I couldn't take another breath without seeing you again. So I rode all the way across the country from Virginia to be with you."

"Oh, Cam!" I said lovingly. I dismounted and put my arms around him.

But before our quivering lips could meet, there was an evil shout from the horizon. Three riders wearing hideous monster masks galloped toward us in a cloud of dust. "Oh no!" my friend Kate cried. "Who are those masked men?"

63

"Heh heh heh!" the tallest of the hideous threesome yelled. He had an obnoxious, whiny voice and a soccer T-shirt. "Stand and deliver, ladies! We are here to rob you!"

"You can't do that!" Cam said gallantly. "I won't let you!"

"Oh yeah?" snarled the middle-sized varmint, a weasellylooking fellow. He grabbed a rope from his saddle and lassoed Cam before he could make a move. "What are you going to do about it, lover boy?"

"Stop it! Stop it!" I cried, horrified at the thought that my poochy baby Cam might get hurt by the three bad guys, especially since I had just recognized them as my long-lost evil brothers Chap, Alfred, and Miguel. And the most frightening realization of all?

They weren't wearing masks!

Those were their real faces!!!!!

I knew I had to help Cam if I could. After all, he was just trying to protect me. I did the only thing I could do. I turned to my wonderfully talented friend Stevie. "Help him, Stevie!" I yelled in a panic. "Use your skills as a black belt kung fu master to save us all from these horrible beasts!"

"Your wish is my command," Stevie agreed, leaping out of the saddle. "I am always ready to fight for the cause of good against evil. And my trusty steed, Stewball, can help. He's a black belt master, too."

"Really?" said the smallest of the three bandits, sticking his thumb in his mouth and sucking it like a baby. "I didn't know horses could do martial arts."

"He's a very special horse," Stevie said as she proceeded to . . .

Well, I guess Stevie thinks she's pretty amusing. I woke up this morning to find her scribbling away in here, cackling at her own wit the whole time. Give me a break. It's a good thing I woke up when I did and yanked this journal away from her, before she went crazy and filled up the whole thing with her silly story! I'll definitely have to remember that I can *never* let Cam see this journal!

Anyway, this morning we went on a ride through the desert. It was really nice to just get out there and ride, especially since we were so busy with the Wild West show yesterday. At breakfast and during the ride, Stevie was acting all mysterious, kind of quiet and smiley, but she wouldn't tell us why. She said she did have something on her mind, but she wanted to wait until the time was right.

We were back at the barn after the ride, and John Brightstar was helping us untack the horses, when Stevie finally came out with it. I guess Lisa and John were chatting about the horse auction, and Stevie overheard them as she was leading Stewball toward the corral gate.

"Hey, John," she called loudly. "I thought I'd better tell you that one of the horses you'll be cutting out for the auction is good old Stewball, here."

Kate and I couldn't help hearing that. "What are you saying about Stewball?" Kate asked Stevie. "I don't think my parents are planning to sell him."

"Oh, yes they are," Stevie replied. She looked around at

all of us and grinned. "I wanted to wait to tell you all the big news when Stewball could be with me to hear it." She slapped the horse fondly on the neck. "*I'm* buying Stewball. Kate, your dad agreed to it. He's arranging to have him shipped to Virginia right after the auction."

"You're kidding!" Lisa exclaimed, which was pretty much what we were all thinking, I guess.

"I talked to my dad last night," Stevie said. "Stewball's coming home to Pine Hollow."

"That's wonderful!" Lisa exclaimed. "Isn't that wonderful, Carole? Stewball's going to live at Pine Hollow!"

It was all such a shock that I wasn't sure what to say. "It *is* wonderful," I agreed cautiously. "You're sure your parents really agreed to this, Stevie?"

But John had a different question for Stevie. "What's a dude like you going to do with a cutting horse like Stewball out East?" he asked bluntly.

For a second Stevie looked taken aback. Then she put her hands on her hips and glared at John. "For your information, John Brightstar, Stewball is a very smart horse. He very well may be the smartest horse you or I have ever met. In fact, he's a whole lot smarter than some wranglers I could mention. That means he's more than capable of learning anything anyone tries to teach him. I'm sure he'll make a great English riding horse."

John shrugged and turned to fiddle with Chocolate's stirrups. "That's probably true," he said calmly. "I just wonder whether he'll like it."

"Of course he will," Stevie replied. "He'll love it. And I

66

know he'll especially love being with me, just like I'll love being with him."

John still didn't quite seem convinced, but Lisa and I were happy to see Stevie so happy. She's been wanting her own horse for a long time—just before we came out here, she was getting all grumpy because Polly Giacomin got her own horse, and she hasn't been riding as long as Stevie has.

Anyway, we spent a lot of the rest of today talking about Stewball—or, to be more exact, listening to Stevie talk about Stewball. When she's really excited about something, it can be hard to shut her up. So we mostly didn't even try.

I spent a little time thinking about the steps Stevie would need to follow to retrain Stewball to be an English horse, since I figured she would need some help. It seemed like a pretty interesting challenge, and I was sure it would keep Stevie really busy for a while, maybe even busier than training Starlight keeps me. Sometimes it's harder to teach a horse how to change something he already knows how to do (like switching from neck-reining to English-style aids) than it is to just teach him a brand-new skill.

Anyway, Lisa disappeared after dinner, and Stevie was off talking to Frank Devine about the arrangements for shipping Stewball or something, so I was in our bunkhouse alone (rereading that silly story Stevie wrote in here, actually), when Kate came in, looking serious.

"I've been wanting to talk to you and Lisa alone," she said.

I rolled over on my stomach and looked at her. "Well, since Lisa's not here, you'll have to settle for just me," I said. "Talk."

Kate took a deep breath. "I don't think Stevie should buy Stewball."

"What?" That made me sit up straight. "Why not?"

"I just don't think they're a good match," Kate replied.

"Not a good match!" I practically sputtered. "What are you talking about? They're the perfect match. That's why she always rides him when we come out here, remember? Anyway, your father obviously thinks otherwise, since he's the one who agreed to sell him to Stevie. Don't you think he knows what he's doing?"

At that moment Lisa walked in. "What's going on?" she asked, obviously noticing that I was kind of upset.

"Kate doesn't think Stevie and Stewball are a good match!" I exclaimed. "She doesn't think Stevie should buy him. Can you believe it? I mean, I know Stevie has been driving us a little crazy by talking about Stewball all the time, but that's only natural. They're perfect for each other. Don't you think?"

Lisa sat down on the bunk beside me. "I'm not sure," she replied quietly.

My jaw dropped. "What do you mean, you're not sure? What is everyone around here thinking?"

Kate explained. "When I said Stevie and Stewball weren't a good match, I wasn't talking about their personalities," she said. "But the fact is, Stevie's interests and talents are in English riding. And Stewball just isn't an English riding horse."

I wasn't totally convinced by that. I mean, normally I respect Kate's opinions when it comes to horses. But I was sure Stewball could be retrained, and I said so.

Kate nodded. "There isn't anything Stewball couldn't learn and do pretty well," she agreed. "The problem is that he'll be a pretty good English horse instead of an outstanding Western horse. That just seems like a waste to me."

"I don't know," I said. "I still think the most important thing is for Stevie to have a horse that makes her happy."

Kate paced the small room for a minute. Then she turned to look at Lisa and me. "I didn't want to go into this, because you know how I feel about competition," she began.

I was all ears. Kate doesn't talk much about her past on the horse show circuit, so naturally I was curious about what she was going to say. I couldn't imagine what her feelings about competition could possibly have to do with Stevie and Stewball.

"Stevie is a fine English rider, and she's getting better all the time," Kate said. "She's probably capable of going on to win plenty of ribbons. It's possible she could even make a career for herself if she wants to, especially in dressage. But that's not going to happen on Stewball. He'll never be good enough to help Stevie compete at a high level in dressage. He's a terrific horse, but he just won't be championship material. He'll hold her back every time. And that's not fair to either of them."

That really made me think. I was starting to see that Kate might have a point.

I've been thinking about it ever since. Kate and Lisa and I agreed that we have to try to convince Stevie to think twice about what she's doing. (By the way, it turns out that John Brightstar had just been telling Lisa the same sorts of things that Kate was saying.)

So I'm sitting here again after everyone else is sound asleep, still thinking. Maybe I should come up with a list of pros and cons. That's probably what someone logical like Lisa would do. It's worth a try.

PROS: Why Stevie should buy Stewball
and
CONS: Why Stevie shouldn't buy Stewball

PRO: Their personalities are a perfect match.

CON: Stewball's personality also makes him a perfect Western cutting horse (even though Stevie's personality somehow works just as well for an English rider, which doesn't really make sense on a list like this, I guess).

PRO: Stevie is ready to have a horse of her own, and her parents agreed to buy Stewball for her over the phone, which is practically a miracle, and Frank Devine thinks it's okay, too.

CON: Stevie can talk anyone into just about anything, and maybe in this case that includes herself. If you know what I mean. Maybe she's not thinking clearly because she's so crazy about Stewball.

PRO: Stevie really, really loves Stewball. And isn't that the most important thing?

CON: Maybe it isn't the most important thing. Maybe if she *really* loves him, she should love him just the way he is instead of trying to change him, even if it means they can't be together all the time.

Oh, forget it! This doesn't seem to be working out too well. I think lists of pros and cons are supposed to be a lot less complicated than that one. Besides, I'm not sure a list like that is going to convince Stevie to change her mind (if anything can). It might work for Lisa, since she usually makes important decisions based mostly on logic, because that's how she is. Stevie, on the other hand, usually goes with impulse or emotion—she's really not the logical type.

It kind of reminds me of my parents. Talk about opposites attracting—Dad has always been pretty logical and sensible, like Lisa, while Mom was always more impulsive and emotional, like Stevie. And what about me? I'm not really sure. Maybe a little of both.

Talking about all this decision-making stuff just keeps reminding me of the big decision I'm trying to make about my career. I think maybe that decision has to combine both types of decision making. I have to be logical about it, so I'll know what I'm getting into, but I also have to make sure that whatever I come up with is something that feels right to me emotionally as well.

I just hope I inherited enough from both my parents to be able to do it!

CAROLE HANSON'S RIDING JOURNAL:

Well, so much for our big plans to talk Stevie out of buying Stewball. Thanks to us, she's more convinced than ever that he's the horse for her! We tried to show her what the problem was by setting up a sort of fake English horse show in the desert. We figured maybe that would help Stevie see how wrong it would be to make him try to change.

Unfortunately, we forgot to let Stewball in on the plan. He actually did pretty well, at least compared to the other horses, which just reinforced Stevie's belief that he can do anything she asks him to do. So now she's happier than ever with her decision, and the auction is tomorrow. Yikes! I'm not sure what else we can do except try to be supportive. And I'll still help Stevie with retraining Stewball, of course. After all, what are friends for? Even if I'm sure now that she's doing the wrong thing . . .

Okay, I've got to stop thinking about that. Let's see, what else happened these past couple of days? For one thing, I helped Kate's mother, Phyllis, make cookies and lemonade today for the auction. Even though it didn't have anything to do with horses, I still had a really nice time. It sort of reminded me, a little bit, of how Mom and I used to help Dad make his special-recipe cookies when I was little. I miss those days a lot, but it was nice to think about them while I was helping Phyllis.

Oh well, it's getting late. I'd better put this away and get some sleep. I'll need plenty of rest if I'm going to be ready for tomorrow.

Hello, Saddle Club!

You only left the Bar None a week ago, but I miss you like crazy already! Christine and my parents miss you, too, of course.

Oh yeah, and so does John—one of you in particular, wink wink! Ha ha! Stop blushing, Lisa—it's true!

Anyway, how are you adjusting to life back on the East Coast? Stevie, are you holding up all right without Stewball? For what it's worth, I meant what I told you before—I think you made the right decision. And I even overheard my father telling my mother that he thinks it was very mature of you to think about what's best for Stewball.

So now that the auction is over and you guys are gone, things are pretty quiet around here. There are plenty of dudes around, of course, but it's just not the same. I'm already looking forward to your next visit!

Love,

Kate

Dear Kate,

Hello! It's the Willow Creek chapter of The Saddle Club here. We decided to get together and write back to you. We're typing this on Lisa's computer, so we'll have to identify ourselves as we write. This is Lisa writing right now, by the way.

(Carole) Hi, Kate! How are Moonglow and Felix doing? I'm so glad I finally got to see them in person. Or should it be "in horse"? Well, you know what I mean.

(Stevie) How's my good buddy Stewball? Give him a big hug for me, okay? Speaking of Stewball, I'm still hoping to find his English-riding twin sometime soon. I figure that I'm in pretty good shape, really. Since I convinced my parents to get me a horse *once*, it should be even easier next time, when the *really* right horse for me comes along. But for now I guess I'm pretty happy going back to riding good old Topside. And I'm glad I figured out in time that Stewball belongs there at the Bar None. No matter how much I miss him, I'm glad he's in a place where he's so happy. He could never be that happy living most of his life in a barn. It's like I told your father, Kate—I want Stewball to spend the rest of his life doing what he does best, which is cutting and herding. And he should be rewarded for his hard work by being able to do what he loves best, which is playing with the rest of his herd out on the range. After seeing all the horses and their new owners at the auction, seeing how perfect they all were for each other, I finally realized that Stewball and I might be perfect together when I'm visiting the Bar None, but not full-time.

(Lisa) Wow, was that really Stevie Lake writing that? Who knew she could be so serious?

(Stevie) Ha ha, very funny, Lisa. You'd better watch it or I'll start asking you more questions about exactly how you and a certain cute young wrangler said good-bye before we left the ranch.

(Carole) Don't remind me about that! I was going to keep an eye on those two this time, and I totally forgot about it because there were so many other things going on. So once again, I have to totally rely on Lisa to tell me what happened.

(Stevie) I know. And she never quite seems to tell us *all* the juicy details, does she?

(Lisa) You see what I have to put up with, Kate? Maybe

I should move to the Bar None permanently just to get away from my nosy friends!

(Carole) Come on, Lisa, you know we're just kidding! Besides, romance is in the air these days, right? Kate, remember how we told you about Max and Deborah's engagement? Well, they're as lovey-dovey as ever. It's kind of scary sometimes. I mean, Deborah actually has Max thinking about *china patterns*, of all things! Still, Deborah is really nice, and it's pretty cute to see how happy they are together.

(Stevie) Yeah, it was so positively adorable to see how Max wasn't even paying attention when Judy Barker was giving that talk about performing leg checks today at our Horse Wise meeting. He kept glancing at his watch and then looking at the door, like he couldn't wait to escape and go be with his beloved. Gee, I guess that means he didn't find our nine millionth lesson on locating the flexor tendon as thrilling as I did. By the way, Kate, in case you couldn't guess, that last part was supposed to come across as sarcastic.

(Carole) Don't worry, Kate, I'm sure Stevie knows that leg checks really aren't anything to joke about. It's very important for any rider to understand just how important and fragile a horse's legs are. After all, those legs have to take an incredible amount of strain and pressure every day just carrying around the weight of the horse's body. I mean, at certain times when a horse is galloping, his entire weight rests on just one leg, which is pretty amazing when you think about it. And besides, there are so many things that can go wrong, it would be irresponsible not to be extra careful about it. For instance, a check could reveal problems with the tendons, wounds, splints, and so on. Plus you have the whole subject of foot troubles, which is another serious—

(Stevie) MAYDAY! MAYDAY! Horse-crazy lecture in progress! Evacuate! EVACUATE!!!!!

(Carole) Very funny, Stevie. And you don't have to laugh QUITE so hard, Lisa.

(Lisa) Yes, I do. Poor Kate. She thought she escaped from your twelve-hour horse lectures when you left. But you've found a way to share the joy with her long distance.

(Stevie) No kidding. But I guess by now Kate knows as well as we do that Carole Hanson eats, sleeps, breathes, thinks, and even *writes* nothing but horses, horses, horses.

(Lisa) Well, that and horses, of course.

(Stevie) Right. And don't forget horses. And then of course there's her great interest in, let's see, what was it again? Oh yeah—horses.

(Carole) Okay, Kate, I think we'll have to sign off for now. I have a couple of friends to strangle. Bye!

(Lisa) Bye, Kate! Write again soon!

(Stevie) Bye, K—AAAAH! SHE'S CHOKING ME!!!! CALL NINE-ONE-ONE, QUICK! BEFORE IT'S TOO LA— gurgle, gasp, *thud*. . . .

Love,

The Saddle Club (Virginia chapter)

CAROLE HANSON'S RIDING JOURNAL:

I've been thinking a lot over the past few weeks about how some things just aren't meant to be, no matter how much somebody wants them. I guess Stevie's decision about Stewball last month got me started on that topic. After all, she really, really, really wanted Stewball to be her horse forever. For a while all she could think about was how much she cared about him, and that made her think that nothing should stop her from being with him all the time. And she and Stewball are so obviously crazy about each other that, for a while, the rest of us (well, Lisa and me, anyway) thought that made perfect sense. When all along there was just this one thing—namely, the fact that Stewball's true home would always be out West while Stevie's is back here in the East. That meant it couldn't work out, no matter how much Stevie wanted it to.

I guess I'm still thinking about this because of my old diary I found back in June. Looking at the first few entries reminded me about how my family always dreamed of having a home of our very own where we'd live, just the three of us, for years and years. Maybe that's sort of the same thing, you know? If it weren't for that one thing . . .

Well, this is getting too depressing and serious. Besides, it's *definitely* not the kind of thing I'm supposed to be writing in here. I've been lazy all summer about this journal, actually. Now that school has started again, I'll have to get back to writing the stuff I'm supposed to be writing in here, like training notes and notes about my career (since that *does* have to do with riding).

Training notes first. This time the notes aren't going to be about Starlight, though—at least not directly. Today (Thursday), Starlight and I held another training session with Lisa and Prancer, and it went really well. We concentrated on obedience and precision, putting the horses through some basic dressage exercises to see how much Prancer has learned. Then we tested her some more by having her follow Starlight around the ring. First we had them both walk. Then I asked Starlight to trot, but Lisa didn't let Prancer break into a trot to keep up, like the horse wanted to. Instead she kept her at a walk so that Prancer would know she always had to respond to what her rider wanted her to do. That's an important lesson for any horse, of course. But Prancer is even more competitive than most horses because of her early training, so we want to be certain that she learns the lesson well. We went on with the same exercise for a while, shifting gaits back and forth. She did really well, and so did Lisa.

Sometimes when I'm watching her these days, it's hard for me to believe that Prancer started out her life as a racehorse. I mean, it's impossible to forget that she's a Thoroughbred, of course—just looking at her long, graceful legs and sloped shoulders is enough to tell you that. But even though she still needs more training, she's adjusting really well so far to her new career as a pleasure horse.

Speaking of careers, the whole time I was watching Lisa and Prancer today, I was thinking about how interesting it would be to concentrate on training full-time. It must be really interesting to spend all your time thinking about how to help horses get better at whatever they're supposed to be doing, whether you're a trainer who specializes in one sport, like jumping or racing, or whether you mostly just work with general riding horses. Then there are the people who train their own competition horses, like our friend Dorothy DeSoto used to do before she retired from competition— that's one way I could combine two interests, riding and training. Or there are people who train horses for very specific purposes, like to be police horses or for therapeutic riding or the circus or whatever.

It's amazing to think how many different careers there are out there! I mean, there are about a million kinds of trainers alone. And beyond that, there are a *billion* other careers working with horses.

I guess maybe I should consider myself lucky that at least I've narrowed things down that far. Because if I had to choose out of every possible career in the world (military officer like Dad, lawyer like Stevie's parents, accountant/businessperson like Lisa's dad, newspaper reporter like Deborah, doctor, dentist, teacher, travel agent, musician, telephone repairperson, waitress, politician, farmer, truck driver, chef, plumber, artist, engineer, carpenter, actor, salesperson, tree surgeon . . .) I would probably go crazy. Although I just remembered one other career I could definitely cross off my list—bug specialist! Those creepy-crawlies we saw when Dad and I went to the Insect Zoo at the Smithsonian last weekend with Marie Dana and her mom were really gross. I'm not usually squeamish about that sort of thing, but somehow, seeing so many insects and spiders in the same place kind of freaked me out. It's just a good thing I didn't say so to Marie—she would have teased me even more than she already does.

That reminds me. I should probably stop writing soon and go get the guest room ready for when Marie gets here next Tuesday. She'll be staying with us for a couple of weeks while her mother's in Europe on business, and I'm looking forward to having a temporary sister. I've always wondered what it would be like not to be an only child.

More importantly, I really want Marie to feel comfortable while she's staying with us, especially since she'll be having her birthday while she's here. And that probably won't be easy in any case, since it will be her first birthday since her father was killed in a car accident.

It's probably going to be a really difficult time for her, but I want to make it a little easier if I can. Actually, I just had an idea for something that might help me get some perspective on what Marie's going through. Maybe I should get out my old diary and read a little more. I mean, I kind of stopped reading it a while back after I finished those first few entries, the easy parts. But if it will help me help Marie, I guess I could try to read a little farther. The guest room can wait. . . .

Dear Diary:

Well, we put it off until the middle of December, but my crazy family finally decided on a vacation spot! After all our weeks of arguing (or "debating," as Mom likes to call it) we decided to rent a condo at this resort in the mountains. It's not that place in West Virginia that Mom wanted—there was nothing to do there except stare at the water and twiddle your thumbs (at least that's the way Dad described it the other day, which made Mom laugh so hard she almost choked on the cookie she was eating). But some friend of Dad's at the base told him about this resort, which is in Vermont. Dad's friend has been there a bunch of times and said it has a lake and nice scenery (for Mom), a stable and tons of riding trails through the woods and mountains (for me), and a swimming pool and lots of other sports facilities (for Dad). There's no golf course, but Dad said that's what compromise is all about. Besides, I think he's kind of excited about learning to ski. None of us has ever done it before, and we're going to sign up for family lessons as soon as we get there. That should be fun, though of course I'm looking forward to the riding trails even more than the ski trails, ha ha!

Anyway, it really does sound like a great place. Mom and Dad have been joking that we're making up for all those years without vacations by packing every possible vacation activity (except golf, Dad keeps adding) into this one trip. Actually, it's kind of funny—I think they're even a little nervous about that. Mom made doctor's appointments for us all to have checkups before we go to make sure we're ready for all that active outdoor stuff. And Dad is already talking about how he wants to get ahead on his paperwork at the office before we leave. He claims it's so he can relax and not worry about work while we're on vacation, but Mom said she thinks he's secretly afraid he's going to break a leg or two learning to ski and doesn't want to fall behind at work while he's recuperating! Ha!

I'm definitely not going to waste time worrying about anything like that. And I'm sure that once we get there my parents will relax and have fun. Maybe while we're at the resort, I can even get Mom and Dad into the saddle for a nice trail ride! Now that would be what I'd call family fun!

Dear Diary:

This is a week when

I mean, I can't

What can I say about this? It's too crazy to write down. Crazy. That's what it is. Crazy. I really don't even want to try to talk about it, because

Okay, I have to start again.

This has got to be a mistake. It's got to. There's no way it could be real. I mean, we're supposed to be leaving on our big vacation in just a couple of weeks. That's what's supposed to happen, right? It's supposed to be this way: We plan our vacation. We go on our vacation. We have a great time and live happily ever after.

Here's how it's not supposed to be: We plan our vacation. We go to the doctor to get checkups before the vacation. The doctor finds something suspicious in one of Mom's tests. The doctor tests her again. Then he sends her to a specialist. The specialist says

I can't write it. I can't write it down. Mom and Dad are

downstairs; I'm not sure what they're doing. Probably talking about what the doctor said. I mean, it's only four-thirty in the afternoon and Dad came home from work as soon as Mom called him.

It can't be true. There has to be a mistake. Aren't they always showing stuff on the news about how doctors make mistakes all the time? They're only human, right? It can happen.

Anyway, Mom is going to a different specialist tomorrow for a second opinion. She made the appointment right after the first one called.

So here's what's probably happening. Mom goes to a crazy specialist who doesn't know what she's talking about. Crazy specialist gives her some crazy news that can't possibly be true. Realizing this, Mom wisely makes appointment with a different specialist. She goes to see the new specialist, and the new specialist immediately tells her she's the healthiest person he's ever seen in his life. Everything is fine, we all go off on vacation together like we planned and have a wonderful time, and no one ever mentions the word cancer again.

Oops. I didn't mean to write that word down. But it doesn't matter. Because it can't possibly be true.

And just to prove that everything's totally normal and there's nothing to worry about, I think I'll do something totally normal now, like go over to Pine Hollow. Maybe that will help me stop thinking about this for a while, at least until they tell me it's all a horrible mistake.

FROM:	HorseGal
TO:	Steviethegreat
TO:	LAtwood
SUBJECT:	My new sister
MESSAGE:	

Hi, guys! I hope you're both still thinking of lots of fun things to do while Marie is here. Like I told you at TD's earlier today, she's coming after school tomorrow, and I want to make sure she doesn't have time to miss her mother too much. Or her father, either, of course.

Anyway, so far I think what we have on the schedule is trail rides, possibly a picnic in the woods, and of course the big birthday sleepover in the loft at Pine Hollow.

Still, like I told you today, I also want to give her a little time to settle in before we do any of that stuff. She likes riding well enough, as you know from meeting her before, but she's not quite as horse-crazy as the three of us. So I want to make sure we do stuff that she wants to do, even if it doesn't always involve horses. I hope you understand.

By the way, in case you're wondering, Dad and I still haven't come up with any brilliant ideas for Marie's birthday gift. But we're going to keep thinking. I'm sure it will be easier to come up with something good when she's actually here.

I can't believe she's coming tomorrow. I can't wait!

P.S.—Stevie, in case you can't tell, I'm still definitely not interested in trading my new "sister" for your three monster brothers. So don't even bother to ask again! Ha!

FROM: Steviethegreat

TO: HorseGal

CC: LAtwood

SUBJECT: Take my brothers, please!

MESSAGE:

Just kidding about my brothers! (Not really . . .)

Anyway, I think it's a good idea to keep Marie distracted while she's staying with you. You definitely don't want her getting all bitter and sad again, like she was when we first met her. I mean, I know that was pretty soon after the accident and everything. But we should make sure she's having so much fun during these two weeks that she doesn't have time to start feeling depressed. Sounds like a job for The Saddle Club to me!

By the way, I still can't believe how weird Max and Deborah were acting the other day. Remember? When Max was helping Deborah jump down from the fence as if she'd break her leg if she tried it by herself, and how he was blabbing about china patterns as if it wasn't the most boring topic in the world? I know Deborah was sort of laughing at us for being worried, but I can't help it. It's like they're both becoming different people just because they're engaged now or something. I hope they get over it soon, because frankly I can't stand too many more conversations about china patterns!

FROM: LAtwood

TO: HorseGal

CC: Steviethegreat

SUBJECT: Marie

MESSAGE:

I agree with Stevie, mostly. I think you should try to keep Marie distracted from too many sad thoughts. But if she does start to miss her parents (especially her father) while she's staying with you, I think you need to be ready to listen and understand. I know you'll be great at that, Carole.

Anyway, let me know how the first day with your new "sister" goes, okay? Good luck!

And by the way, Stevie, in response to what you said in your e-mail, I think you can stop worrying. Max and Deborah aren't going to turn into totally different people just because they're together. I mean, some of the ways they're changing are actually *good* changes, like Deborah's becoming interested in horses, right?

Besides, I'm pretty sure the china pattern thing is temporary. They'll probably never mention the topic again once the engagement is over, the china is in the cupboard, and they're happily married. You might just as well start worrying that Carole is going to stop spending time at Pine Hollow forever just because she might not go there for a few days while Marie is settling in! Ha ha!

CAROLE HANSON'S RIDING JOURNAL:

My math teacher is out sick today, so I have a study hall. I can't concentrate on my English homework, which is what I should be doing, so I figured I'd write a few words in here instead.

Unfortunately I don't have any training news to report, since I haven't seen Starlight since the day before yesterday. I miss him already!

But what I really want to write about is something that happened a couple of periods ago, before lunch. It really wasn't anything that major, it just made me think about things differently. But first, maybe I should explain a few other things that have been happening lately.

It started pretty much as soon as Marie's mother dropped her off at my house yesterday. Dad and I invited the two of them in and then took them upstairs to show Marie to her room. "You'll be staying in here, Marie," I told her politely as I opened the guest room door and ushered her in.

"Nice," Marie said when she took a look around.

I was happy that she liked it. I'd put a lot of effort into making it cozy and inviting. I'd tucked the flowered bedspread over some extra-fluffy pillows and brought in my favorite hooked rug from my own room to add some brightness to the wood floor. Some roses from the garden trellis were in a vase on the dresser. And to add the perfect finishing touch, Snowball was curled up on the bed fast asleep. (I didn't have anything to do with that part—the contrary cat probably just realized the bedspread was freshly laundered and wanted to shed black fur all over it! Ha!)

Anyway, Dad and Mrs. Dana said a few nice things about the room, too. Then Marie spoke up again. "I'm a little surprised," she said, stepping farther into the room with a puzzled look.

"What do you mean, hon?" Mrs. Dana asked.

Marie shrugged. "Well, knowing that Carole did the decorating, I would expect to see some more horsey stuff. You know—some hay, maybe a saddle or two. Or at least a few dozen horse posters."

Dad and Mrs. Dana laughed, but I couldn't help feeling kind of embarrassed. I could only imagine what Marie would say when she got a good look at my room across the hall—after all, practically every inch of wall space is covered with posters and pictures of horses. Normally I wouldn't be the least bit embarrassed about that, of course, but sometimes Marie can be so sarcastic. . . .

But that was just the beginning, really. Dad suggested we all go down and have a snack before Mrs. Dana had to leave to catch her plane. When we got to the kitchen, he whipped a plate of chocolate chip cookies out of the oven.

"I've been keeping these warm for you," he told Marie. "I baked them this afternoon from my own secret recipe." He winked at me.

"Yum!" I exclaimed. "You haven't made your secret-recipe cookies for ages, Dad!" I stopped to think. "In fact, I can't remember the last time you made them."

"Well, this is a special occasion," Dad said.

I didn't think too much about that at the time. But later . . .

Anyway, after Mrs. Dana left, Marie and I went upstairs to unpack her suitcases. As we put her clothes away in the dresser (Snowball woke up when we came in and kept trying to help by taking her socks out when our backs were turned and batting them under the bed), Marie suddenly realized that she'd forgotten to pack her portable CD player. She's really into music, and she seemed pretty upset about it. "How am I going to make it through two weeks without any music? I can't fall asleep without it!"

"No problem," I reassured her. "You can use my clock radio while you're here. I have an alarm clock I can use."

"Really?" Marie asked gratefully. "Thanks a lot, Carole. Hey, it doesn't just play the farm report or anything, does it?"

"Ha ha," I said, rolling my eyes. I was just starting to remember how Marie liked to make jokes about absolutely everything!

Still, I was enjoying having her around for most of the rest of that first day. Then it was time to start our homework.

"You can have my desk to yourself tonight," I told Marie. "I have to write a two-page essay for English class, so I'll be downstairs using the computer."

I was still on the first paragraph of my essay when Marie came into the room.

"Uh, hi, Carole," she said. "When you said you had a paper to write, that reminded me that I'm supposed to write one, too. It's for extra credit in my social studies class. Do you think I could use the computer when you're finished?"

I bit my lip. I knew I should offer to let Marie do her work first, since she was a guest. On the other hand, Marie's paper was only for extra credit, while mine was an assignment, so I wasn't sure what to say.

Dad must have come into the room just in time to hear what Marie said. "Carole, why don't you let Marie do her assignment first? She's our guest, you know." He had this sort of disapproving tone in his voice, like he was surprised he even had to tell me such a thing.

I felt pretty guilty then. "I was just going to say the same thing." I saved my document and then let her use the computer while I went to help Dad with the dishes.

He said he wanted to talk to me about something. "It's about Marie," he said seriously. "I just wanted to make sure you know how important it is that we give her extra-special care. It hasn't been that long since she lost her father, and it's sure to be tough on her to have her mother so far away for such a long time."

"I understand," I said. "I'm being nice to Marie. And I've got a lot of special things planned for her, especially on her birthday."

"That's good, honey," Dad said. "But it's important to remember to be nice and consider Marie's feelings in little ways as well as big ones. For instance, I noticed you took the last of the rice at dinner without asking Marie if she wanted more."

I frowned. "I guess so, but she already had lots on her plate."

"Even so, you should have asked," Dad said.

I didn't think that was really fair. But I promised Dad I'd be more careful, and that was that.

Until today. There were five minutes left in my English class this morning when a student I didn't recognize came into the room and handed a piece of paper to my teacher.

Ms. Blackburn read the note. "Carole, could you come up here, please?"

Surprised, I went up to the desk. "What is it?"

"Your father is on the phone for you," Ms. Blackburn said. "You're excused to go to the principal's office to take the call."

My heart started pounding and my head started spinning. Why would Dad be calling me at school? As I walked down the hall toward the principal's office, I tried to tell myself that this wasn't like the last time he'd called me to the office phone. It couldn't possibly be anything like that at all.

I tried to put the memory of that terrible day out of my mind. Still, I couldn't help being nervous as I picked up the phone. "Hello?" I squeaked.

"Carole? Is that you?" Dad sounded as cheerful as ever.

"It's me, Dad," I said. "What's wrong?"

"Listen, honey," he said. "I thought I'd better remind you about the juice. I know you were pretty sleepy this morning, and I was afraid you'd forget."

"The juice?" I repeated blankly. I didn't have the foggiest

idea what he was talking about. I *was* pretty sleepy this morning. Marie kept the radio on until almost midnight last night. It was just loud enough to keep me awake, but I didn't want to ask her to turn it down. After all, she was a guest.

"That's what I was afraid of," Dad said. "Remember, I told you and Marie that we only had one insulated cooler bag, so I put both your juice boxes in with your lunch. You'll need to give Marie her juice box before lunch. I know you two have different lunch periods, so I thought I'd better remind you."

"Thanks, Dad," I said mechanically, finally remembering the conversation he was talking about. Still, I couldn't quite believe that was the whole reason he had dragged me out of class. "Are you sure that's all?"

"That's it, sweetie," he said. "Now don't forget, okay?"

I left the office feeling a little confused. But when my head started to clear, my confusion turned to relief, then annoyance. By now I'm on to anger.

Having Marie stay with us was supposed to be fun. And I guess in some ways it sort of is. But it's also causing a lot more problems than I expected. Dad's ragging on me for eating too much rice and scaring me half to death with emergency phone calls about juice. I had to stay up extra late working on my English paper after Marie finally finished hogging the computer for her extra-credit report, and then when I finally could go to bed I couldn't sleep because her music was so loud. Plus when I went to give her that stupid juice box before her lunch period, it made me late for my next class and my teacher chewed me out in front of everyone!

It's hard to believe Marie is already upsetting our life so

92

much when she hasn't even been staying with us for twenty-four hours yet. How am I supposed to survive two whole weeks with my new "sister"????

(later)
I'm starting to think that everyone around me has been taken over by aliens. Why has having Marie around made everything seem so totally different?

Things have only gotten weirder since I wrote all that stuff earlier today. I spent the rest of the school day stewing about what happened with the phone call and the rest of it. So by the time Marie and I got to Pine Hollow this afternoon, I wasn't exactly in the greatest mood.

And my friends? They didn't even notice! Stevie was all excited and proud of herself because she managed to talk Max into letting us use the hayloft for Marie's big birthday sleepover. And Lisa just grinned away as if that was the greatest news ever in the history of the world. It didn't help that Stevie reported that Max said he'd been looking for something special to do for Marie himself. I mean, I know we all said we wanted Marie to have a nice time and everything, but you'd think she was Queen of Sheba the way everyone is carrying on over her!

Anyway, after they all finished making a fuss, we finally left on the trail ride we'd planned. But not before Marie cracked a few jokes about how messy the tack room was, which didn't exactly make me feel sisterly.

I was trying my best to be a good hostess, so as we started across the fields to the woods, when Marie mentioned that she was a little rusty because she hadn't been riding much lately, I offered to give her a few pointers. "From back here I'll be able to see what you're doing wrong," I said helpfully, since I was riding behind her. "For instance, right now your heels should be down more, and your arms look a little stiff."

Marie adjusted her position. "Better?"

"A little," I said. "But now you're leaning back too much, and your legs are too far forward. You look like you're sitting in a chair."

"Oops." Marie adjusted again.

"Okay, that's better," I said, glad that she was improving, at least a little. "Now let's work on the way you're holding the reins. Don't curl your wrists, and keep your thumbs pointing up and your elbows in. . . ." I kept on advising her like that as we rode down the trail, trying to be as helpful as possible.

A few minutes later we heard the sound of hoofbeats on the trail ahead. It was Simon Atherton. As usual, he looked as if he might fall out of the saddle at any moment. His elbows were sticking out at a crazy angle, his toes were practically pointing straight up, and—well, like I said, *as usual*. Anyway, it turned out he was riding alone because Veronica diAngelo had ditched him. Big surprise there. He's had a huge crush on her for ages and she just hates it. I don't know if that's got more to do with the fact that Simon's kind of nerdy or that his family doesn't belong to the Willow Creek Country Club and drive a car that's more expensive than my house.

Ugh. I keep getting off the subject here. I can't even seem to *think* straight since Marie has been here! The point is, for some reason Marie suddenly decided to ride back to Pine Hollow with Simon rather than continuing the trail ride with us. Don't ask me what *that* was all about. She said something about wanting to be there when Dad came to pick us up, so maybe that was it.

My friends and I rode on. "It's unusual for your father to pick you up on a weekday, isn't it?" Stevie asked me.

She wasn't the only one who'd noticed *that*, believe me. "Yeah, well, a lot of unusual things have been going on around here lately," I said, feeling kind of grumpy.

Stevie and Lisa changed the subject after that. But by the time we headed back toward the stable, I was starting to feel kind of bad about how Marie had left. I was really trying to be helpful when I corrected all those things about the way she was riding, but I realized it might have come across as, well, maybe a little mean. More like criticism than helpful advice. For some reason, though, I just hadn't been able to stop myself.

I mean, even if Marie has been sort of annoying since she's come to stay, even if Dad has been acting strange because of her visit, it wasn't very polite of me to act that way. I decided I was just overtired from not sleeping much, and maybe a little shaky because of that phone call at school. I vowed to try to do better.

So when we got back to the stable, I insisted that Marie just hang out and relax while my friends and I did all the work taking care of the horses. Instead of appreciating how nice I was being, Stevie and Lisa actually started criticizing me! They seemed to think I was depriving Marie, making her feel left out because I hadn't begged her to muck out Starlight's stall with me! They didn't even seem to notice how hard I was trying to be nice. I couldn't believe it—it was as if they were turning into different people, too, right along with Dad and Marie.

"Give me a break," I snapped at them. "Marie doesn't have to hang around with us every single second, you know."

I guess that wasn't a very nice thing to say. But again, I couldn't seem to stop the sharp words from popping out of my mouth.

So I guess I have to include *myself* with all the people who have been taken over by aliens, huh?

Dear Diary:

I'm glad the holidays are finally over. I never thought that Christmas and New Year's Eve could be so totally miserable.

The thing that made it the worst is the way Mom and Dad have been acting. They're trying so hard to act like everything is normal that it's totally abnormal. Dad has been cracking so many corny jokes lately that I'm ready to tear my hair out. And that's not all. He even dressed up as Santa Claus on Christmas Eve! Can you believe it? He hasn't done that since I was about five years old. And he seemed totally shocked when I didn't jump up and down and squeal at his silly ho ho hos like I used to back then. Give me a break!

And then there's Mom. She's not acting quite as weird as Dad, but in a way that makes it even worse. How can she act so normal when everything has changed? Sometimes I just want to scream at her, to shake her and shout out, "Come on, Mom, you have cancer! Don't you even realize that?"

If I didn't have Pine Hollow to go to every day, I'm not sure what I would do. Of course, things aren't totally normal there, either. I finally told Lauren about my mom's diagnosis. I thought she should know, since she's my best friend in Willow Creek. Or at least I thought she was. Now I'm not so sure—I think she's been avoiding me, though I could be imagining things, I guess. But I know she must have told other people, because now everyone seems to know. Max and Mrs. Reg have both spoken to me about it, saying if I ever need to talk to anyone, etc. etc. etc. It's nice of them, I know, but I really don't feel like chatting about that particular topic too much.

The worst part about it all is that a lot of the other kids (at school as well as Pine Hollow) look at me with this weird expression—sort of sympathetic, sort of sad, sort of nervous, sort of curious. It's like they think that just because my mom has this horrible disease, suddenly I'm a whole different person or something. How weird is that? About the only people who haven't treated me much differently are Veronica diAngelo (she's as snobby as ever) and Stevie Lake and Dinah Slattery. The day after I told Lauren about my mom, the two of them came up to me as I was leading Delilah out of the stable before our riding class.

"Hi, Carole," Dinah says, right out. "We heard about your mother being sick. We're sorry."

"Yeah," Stevie added. "That really stinks."

I couldn't help smiling a little at that. It was just about the

97

truest thing anyone had said since that first doctor's visit. "Thanks," I said.

That was the entire conversation. I continued on my way with Delilah, and Stevie and Dinah went back to where they'd left their horses. And after that, the two of them went back to acting just the same way they always do, joking around and goofing off and getting yelled at for talking too much in class. And not giving me that weirdo sympathetic-sad-curious look at all. For some reason that makes me feel a little less like a being from another planet during riding class.

Anyway, no matter how many strange looks the others give me, there's no way I'd stop going to Pine Hollow. It's the only place that feels comfortable and safe most of the time these days. Other than what he said that one time, Max still treats me just the same as always—in other words, he still yells at me to keep my heels down and my hands steady. And of course the horses haven't changed their opinions at all. Delilah still lets her head droop whenever she thinks I'll let her get away with it, Barq still pins his ears back when Delilah and I come a little too close, and Pepper still pokes his head out and snorts at me every time I pass his stall.

I really don't know what I would do without them.

CAROLE HANSON'S RIDING JOURNAL:

I'm sitting in Starlight's stall right now, and I just opened this to write down that the farrier came by and fitted Starlight with new calked plane shoes this afternoon. But I also happened to see what I wrote about Marie in that last entry. It's amazing how much your thoughts and feelings can change in just a week or two. I figure maybe I should write down what happened during the rest of her visit, so that I'll remember it someday years in the future, when I'm looking back over these notes for tips I can use for my career as a _____. (Fill in the blank: trainer? riding instructor? vet? competitive rider? breeder? camp counselor? cowboy? I still have no idea.)

Actually, it all seems kind of embarrassing now. But like Max always says, we sometimes learn best from our own mistakes. I wasn't too embarrassed to write down the time a few months ago when Starlight stumbled a little when I wasn't paying enough attention to the terrain, and I fell off and landed in a gigantic mud puddle. So I guess I shouldn't be too embarrassed to write about this, either. Maybe if I do, I'll remember never to act like such a jerk again.

It started on Thursday evening, the first week of her visit, when I came downstairs looking for a snack and some help with my homework. I discovered that Marie and Dad had eaten all the good cookies in the house and that they were already working on Marie's homework together. That kind of set me off. Especially when Dad looked up and said, "Oh, hello, sweetheart. Is your homework all done?"

"No," I replied through clenched teeth. "I haven't even started it yet. I came down to get some cookies, but I see that *somebody* has already eaten them all. I guess that *somebody* never stopped to think that I might like a snack, too. But then, that *somebody* never stops to think at all from what I can tell. She just cracks some stupid joke and does whatever she feels like doing."

Marie's face was turning redder and redder through my whole speech. At the end she burst into tears and ran out of the room. I could hear her footsteps thumping up the stairs, and then the sound of a door slamming.

Dad stood up, his face thunderous, like it only gets when he's *really, really* mad. "Just what was that all about, young lady?" he demanded. But before I could answer, he said, "No, I don't want to hear. Whatever your problem is, there's no excuse for taking it out on Marie the way you just did. She has done nothing but be a charming guest since she arrived. You, on the other hand, have been grouchier and ruder than I've ever seen you. I'm surprised Marie has been able to put up with you this long."

I folded my arms across my chest, willing myself not to cry. "Fine. Take her side. As usual."

Dad had already opened his mouth to go on with his yelling, but when he heard what I'd just said, he looked surprised. "Her side? Carole, I'm not taking anybody's side here. I'm just pointing out—"

"You're just pointing out everything that's wrong with me and everything that's wonderful about her," I interrupted. "I bet you wish Marie were your daughter and that I was the one going home after a couple of weeks."

Dad just stared at me for a moment, though I didn't quite dare to meet his eyes. "Is that really what you think?" he asked at last.

I shrugged. "Well, what else would I think, after the way you've been gushing over her and ignoring me?"

"Carole, are you telling me you're jealous of the way I've been treating Marie?" he asked. "Because you know as well as I do that she has been through some tough times lately. And if anyone could understand what she's going through, I thought it would be you. Now, it's obvious that you're upset, and you know I don't like to see that. But this time I think you're just going to have to think things through on your own—calmly and rationally. When you do, I think you'll see how ridiculous you're being and how poorly you've been treating Marie."

Part of my mind knew that what he was saying made sense. But a much louder and angrier part couldn't help thinking that he just didn't understand what I was feeling. Otherwise he would be comforting me, not scolding me.

So basically, that conversation didn't end very well. I managed to stay pretty much out of Dad's and Marie's way the next day, Friday. But by Saturday morning I was feeling more miserable than ever. I wasn't sure I could survive the sleepover we'd planned for Marie's birthday celebration. I also realized that Dad and I had never settled on the perfect gift for Marie, but at that point I wasn't about to remind him. I think I actually sort of hoped that he would forget all about it.

I decided to head over to Pine Hollow as soon as I got up. I really needed someone to talk to, and Starlight has always been the best listener there is. Plus I figured he was just about

101

the only one guaranteed not to start lecturing me about being nicer to Marie!

Dad and Marie were both still asleep, so I scribbled a note and took off. I spent the next hour or so grooming Starlight to within an inch of his life, complaining to him about Marie the whole time.

I had no idea at the time, but it turned out that Starlight wasn't the only one who heard those complaints. Stevie and Lisa were in the hayloft right above his stall the whole time. They'd gone up there to check whether the loft was ready for our sleepover, and they didn't really mean to eavesdrop, of course. But by the time they realized I was down there and heard what I was saying to Starlight, I guess they were sort of afraid to interrupt. So they just kept quiet and listened.

Then they started to plot. Or maybe I should say they just *continued* their plotting, since it turned out they were already worried about how Marie and I weren't getting along that well. But more on that later.

I was feeling a little better by the time our Horse Wise meeting started later that morning. It was an unmounted meeting that week, and Max decided to have a sort of pop quiz Know-Down. I'm always pretty good at answering the questions, and that day was no exception. Except that I might have interrupted once or twice when it really wasn't my turn, mostly to tell Marie that her answers were wrong.

That's probably at least part of the reason that Marie disappeared as soon as our class was over. Stevie, Lisa, and I looked around for her, but she was nowhere to be seen at Pine Hollow.

Wondering if she'd forgotten about our sleepover plans, I called home. "Hi, Dad," I said when he picked up. I felt a little shy—I'd never stayed angry with him for so long before. "I just wanted to make sure Marie is there with you."

"Marie?" he said, sounding confused. "But she's at Pine Hollow with you."

Well, that made me start to feel kind of worried. If Marie wasn't at home and she wasn't at Pine Hollow, then where was she? I did my best to reassure Dad, telling him she was probably around the stable somewhere. But I was already pretty sure that wasn't true.

I went to see if Stevie and Lisa had any ideas about where Marie might be, but both of them seemed to have disappeared, too. I wasn't worried about them, though. All my worries were for Marie.

I sat down to think. Where would she go? I tried to put myself in her place to figure it out.

At first I still had no idea *where* she was, but I think that's when I started to realize *why* she might want to disappear. I had spent so much time that day trying to avoid Marie that I hadn't stopped to think that Marie might also be trying to avoid *me*. After all, I'd been pretty mean to her for the past few days. Why would she want to spend her birthday with someone who couldn't speak to her without snarling?

Finally I figured out where she might have gone. I headed for the tack room and then Starlight's stall. After slipping a bridle on him, I led him out of his stall and mounted bareback. A few minutes later we were riding across the fields and through the woods toward the Danas' house, which is just a couple of miles from the stable. When we got there, the house looked deserted and still. I dismounted and tried the doors, but they were locked tight.

I was starting to think that Marie wasn't there after all when I heard a noise from the little garden shed in the side yard. It was Marie, and she was crying. I called to her, feeling terrible.

"Who is it?" she called back suspiciously. When I opened the door of the shed and poked my head in, she frowned through her tears. "What do *you* want?" she demanded. "Did you track me down so you could yell at me and humiliate me some more?"

I knew I deserved that. I had been mean and spiteful toward Marie all week. Somehow all my good intentions for her visit had turned sour, which meant that I'd done more harm than good when Marie was feeling her loneliest.

"Marie," I told her hesitantly, "I think I owe you a big apology. I mean a *really* big apology."

Marie looked wary. "I'm listening."

I poured out everything I was thinking, like how I hadn't been seeing her point of view at all, and I was jealous of all the attention she was getting, and that kind of thing. It was all true, too. I couldn't believe I hadn't seen it until then. I still can't.

"The funny thing is," I told her, "I've always wanted a sister or a brother. But now that I've actually had the chance to have one, I've realized that I'm just not very good at it."

"Well," Marie said thoughtfully, "I guess I wasn't really going out of my way to look at things from your point of view, either. I was pretty busy worrying about how I'd be able to deal with my mom's being gone and all, so I didn't stop to think about how you'd have to deal with having me in your house."

I thought that was pretty nice of her to say. We sort of smiled at each other a little then and promised we'd both try to do better from then on. We even shook on the deal. Oh, and I finally remembered to wish her a happy birthday.

By the time we got back to Pine Hollow, Dad had called there three times looking for us. We called him right back to let him know we were both safe and sound, and while Marie was talking to him, he told her he wanted to take the three of us out for a big birthday dinner before our sleepover.

I smiled when Marie put her hand over the receiver to tell me that. "He's probably plotting ways to get us to be nice to each other," I said. "Maybe he thought a restaurant meal would put us in a friendlier mood." I took the phone from her. "Hi, Dad," I said. "I wanted to tell you, Marie and I don't need to go out to dinner together."

"Carole!" he began, sounding angry. "I had hoped you'd—"

"No, no, it's not that," I interrupted him with a laugh. "What I meant was that Marie and I are friends again. I apologized for being such a rotten hostess all week." I caught Marie's eye. "And such a rotten friend. So you don't need to try to make us like each other anymore. We took care of that ourselves."

Dad chuckled. "Boy, am I glad to hear that," he said. "But still, that's all the more reason for me to take you girls out.

What better way to celebrate friendship than with a nice dinner? Besides, it's still Marie's birthday. Don't you want to give her our present?" It turned out that he had gone ahead and gotten her a present on his own. It's a nice case for her to carry her music CDs around in, and it even has a picture of a horse embossed on top, so it really did seem like it was from me, too.

Dinner was nice, and Marie and I were both in a great mood when Dad dropped us off for the sleepover. We went into the stable and climbed the ladder to the loft, where we could hear Stevie and Lisa talking.

"Hi, guys," I greeted them cheerfully. "Sorry we're late."

I noticed that Stevie had that sort of guilty look on her face that she always gets when someone *almost* catches her getting into trouble. But she just jumped to her feet. "No problem," she said. "Let's get this sleepover on the road!"

Marie and I put our stuff down. Then I remembered something sort of odd I'd noticed on the way in. Since my friends had been at the stable longer than Marie and I had, I figured they might know something about it. "So why's that fence netting hanging on the wall down there?" I asked them.

Stevie gulped. "Uh, what netting would that be?"

I gave her a strange look. She was definitely acting guilty about something. "Don't tell me you didn't see it."

Stevie shrugged. "I didn't see a thing. Did you, Lisa?"

Lisa just rolled her eyes and didn't answer.

"I have a feeling these two have something to hide," Marie said.

I nodded. "I think you're right. Should we try to bribe

them into telling us with the leftover birthday cake we brought with us?"

"Nah," Marie said. "Let's just toss them over the side and eat it all ourselves."

Stevie and Lisa gasped simultaneously. That made me more suspicious than ever.

"Aha!" Marie said. "That got a reaction. It must be a clue!"

"But what could it mean?" I said. "Were they planning to ambush us and steal our cake, maybe toss us off the loft during the night?" When I glanced at Stevie I noticed that the guilty look was stronger than ever. "Hey, what *were* you guys planning, anyway?"

Lisa glared at Stevie. "Well, it certainly wasn't my idea."

Stevie gave us a weak grin. "I'm just glad to see you two are getting along," she said.

We finally had to threaten her with tickling to get her to tell us the truth about what she'd been up to. It seems that Stevie had come up with one of her crazy plans to get Marie and me to be friends. It involved that fence netting, which she planned to string up as a safety net beneath the loft. Then she was going to somehow push Marie off the edge of the loft so that I would have to leap to her aid and save her life, thereby making us lifelong pals. (By the way, I definitely got the impression that Lisa wasn't totally on board with this idea. If I know the two of them, she was probably trying to talk Stevie out of it the whole time, and Stevie was just plowing on ahead and ignoring all her sane, sensible advice.)

It was a pretty crazy plan, even by Stevian standards. But

107

it just goes to show how crazy I was acting to make my friends go to such extremes.

Anyway, the rest of the sleepover was a lot of fun. And the second week of Marie's visit was a *lot* better than the first. I realize now that I was trying a little too hard to think of her as a sister, when I should have seen that just being her friend through a difficult time is important enough. I also realize (partly from reading a little bit more of my old diary the other day) that I should have already known better than to take out my own feelings of jealousy or helplessness or anger or whatever on other people, especially when those people are the very ones who could use my understanding the most.

Wow, I'm sounding an awful lot like some kind of psychologist here, aren't I? Maybe that's what I should be when I grow up, but it doesn't involve horses. . . . Unless . . . Unless there's such a thing as a *horse* psychologist.

CAROLE HANSON'S RIDING JOURNAL:

Yikes, I can't believe I haven't made any notes in here in weeks. It's partly Snowball's fault—I left this journal on the floor of my room, and she batted it under the bed (even though it's almost as big as she is!), so it took me a while to find it.

But I have good news to report, so I guess it was worth the wait. Pine Hollow is entering a team in the regional dressage rally in two weeks! Isn't that amazing? I mean, we enter the combined training rally every year, of course. But Max has never sent a team to the more specialized rallies, since he

108

believes it's more important for students to ride as much as we can rather than competing as much as we can. But he thinks this rally will be a good learning opportunity, so we're in!

I can't wait! I think the only one more excited than me is Stevie. Dressage is really her sport, and I'm sure she'll do great. I hope we all will. I'm still considering pursuing competitive riding as my career, and if I decide to go into combined training like Cam, dressage will be a big part of that, even though I'm not as into it as Stevie is. So this rally really could tell me a lot about what it might be like.

The rally isn't the only big surprise we had today, either, though the other one doesn't have much to do with horses. Well, actually it does, but only because it means Lisa is going to be so busy that she won't have as much time as usual for riding. Of course, that's not about riding so much as it's about *not* riding, so maybe I should say—

Uh-oh, I'm even starting to confuse myself here. So let me start again. The second piece of big news is that Lisa has been cast as the lead in the Willow Creek Community Theater's production of *Annie*. She's going to be an actress!

It's a little weird, actually. Ever since we started The Saddle Club, my best friends and I tell each other just about everything. But Lisa didn't breathe a word to Stevie or me about her decision to try out for the play until after she found out she'd won the lead. Not that I'm mad about that or anything, of course—just a little surprised. But maybe it seems more surprising because I didn't realize Lisa was so interested in acting. I never would have guessed she would do something like this, which seems kind of strange. I mean, she's one of my best friends, right?

Anyway, she says she's definitely not going to give up riding while she's rehearsing for the play, but it sounds like she'll have to cut back the time she spends at the stable. A *lot*. She actually made up a whole schedule, noting when she has to be at rehearsals and costume fittings and stuff, allowing time for Horse Wise and riding lessons, and working in time for meals, sleep, and homework. Of course, some of the times seem a little tight—like the way she's only allowed herself eight minutes to eat dinner. And she hasn't scheduled in any time for things that seem pretty important to me, like Saddle Club meetings or going to TD's for ice cream after lessons.

Besides, that was before we found out about the dressage rally. Now she has to work extra practice time into her schedule as well. And it's not as if she'll be entering on a well-trained show horse, like Topside, or even a fairly seasoned one like Barq. Max decided he wants her to ride Prancer in the rally, since Lisa has been making so much progress with her lately. He told her that if she put in two solid weeks of practice between now and the rally, he was sure she could do really well. But what I want to know is, how's she supposed to do that when she's spending all her time at rehearsals?

It's only been a few hours, really, since we found out about the play, and Stevie and I are already worried about how she's going to fit everything in. We talked about it a little after we finished practicing the dressage tests Mrs. Reg gave us after today's lesson. Lisa had already rushed off to a rehearsal, so the two of us took turns reading the tests to each other.

Actually, I ought to make a few notes about the practice here. After all, that's what this journal is supposed to be for! So I should mention that Starlight did okay on our first time through the test, but it took him a few beats to get into some of the gait changes. I've got to prepare him earlier, as I told Stevie.

"Yup," she said in reply. "Maybe a couple of strides before the A-mark, you can give the aid. He looks good, though."

"Thanks, but we're nowhere near as good as you two," I told her sincerely. "Dressage is just never going to be Starlight's favorite event."

Stevie remarked then that Topside would probably be happy doing twenty-meter circles and serpentines all day, which I had to agree with.

"The team is really lucky to have you two," I told her. "After all, the lowest score wins in dressage, and I'm sure you two are Max's biggest hope for low marks at the rally."

We went back to practicing then, staying at it until the horses started to get fussy and tired. It was getting on toward dusk by then anyway, so we decided to put the horses away and go to TD's for some ice cream to reward ourselves for our good practice session.

As we were heading into the barn, we saw Lisa running up the driveway toward us. It turned out her rehearsal had ended ten minutes earlier than scheduled, so she had rushed back to Pine Hollow, expecting to join us for some dressage practice.

111

We explained that we had just finished and really couldn't practice anymore. The horses were tired, it was getting dark outside, and the indoor ring was in use for an adult lesson.

"And anyway," I pointed out, "they'll be feeding Prancer in a half hour. Even if you could get tacked up in five minutes, she wouldn't be any fun to ride now because she'd be so cranky for her dinner."

"I'm feeling kind of cranky myself," Stevie joked.

Lisa didn't seem amused. "I guess that extra ten minutes is just going to go to waste then," she said sulkily.

"Ten minutes, huh?" Stevie said. "Well, if you've got an extra ten minutes, how about we spend them together at TD's?"

Lisa didn't bite. "I don't think I can go," she said. "I'm going to have to look at my time schedule again, and I need my computer for that. See you at class Tuesday." With that she took off, leaving the two of us to finish grooming our horses.

It was weird to be at TD's without Lisa. We didn't even sit in our usual booth. Instead we took a table for two. After we placed our orders, we sat back to talk about Lisa's big news and about how hurried she seemed already with her new schedule.

Suddenly Stevie leaned forward. "Carole, are you worried, too?" she asked.

"You mean about today?" I asked, thinking about the way Lisa had rushed back to Pine Hollow and then rushed away again just as fast.

"About today, tomorrow, the next three weeks—and after," Stevie said grimly. "For all we know, Lisa might find out she likes acting better than riding and—"

112

"And decide to quit Horse Wise, Pine Hollow, and The Saddle Club altogether so that she can devote her life to the stage," I finished for her. I'd been thinking more or less the same thing all afternoon.

"She can't keep up this schedule forever, that's for sure," Stevie said.

I had to agree with that. After talking about it a little more, we decided there was only one thing to do. We had to make it a Saddle Club project. Actually, I guess you could say that the project is *saving* The Saddle Club, because it really wouldn't be The Saddle Club at all without Lisa.

As usual, Stevie was the one who came up with a plan to get started. "Lisa is on the brink of making a huge mistake: abandoning the two most important things in her life—riding and us, her best friends," she said. "Unless someone helps her now, she could regret this for years. She needs help—and fast. We'll provide it. We'll be there for her at all times. Starting with Tuesday, no matter how tired we are, we'll stay after class, practice with her, coach her, give her advice. . . ." And so on. She had a lot more to say, though I don't remember all of it. The point was, we're going to do our best to be there for Lisa however she needs us so that she can make it through the next couple of weeks without feeling like she had to quit riding.

I just hope this doesn't turn out to be like the time over the summer when we tried to change Stevie's mind about buying Stewball. After all, those plans totally backfired—if she hadn't realized on her own that she was making a mistake, Stewball might be munching hay in his stall at Pine

Hollow right now. Of course, that's not the only time that a Saddle Club project has backfired. . . .

Never mind, though. This time will be different. It *has* to be. Lisa is counting on us, even if she doesn't know how much.

FROM: HorseGal
TO: Steviethegreat
SUBJECT: Our new Saddle Club project
MESSAGE:

Are the phones at your house ever *not* busy? I thought it was girls that are supposed to talk so much on the phone. But your brothers must spend all their free time calling their friends, because I've been trying to get through for almost an hour!

Anyway, I've been thinking more about Project Lisa (or maybe I should say Project Annie—no, on second thought, I think it should *definitely* be Project Lisa). I can't remember if we talked about this at TD's earlier, but maybe we could help out (more than usual, I mean) with Lisa's stable chores. She didn't really include any time on that schedule of hers for stuff like mucking out or cleaning tack, or even grooming Prancer after lessons. So we could pitch in and take care of most of that if she needs us to.

But I also realized that the physical stuff is really only the start of what we'll be doing. The more important part of our plan is just to support her and make her see that we're totally committed to getting through this situation and being there for her, and she should be confident that we can work together to make it happen. I was also thinking about that stuff with Stewball last summer, and also about the way we tried to set up Max with all those single women, and I think this is sort of like those situations in at least one way. It will be best if this is a realization that Lisa can come to sort of on her own, though of course we should do all we can to put her in a position to do that. Luckily our plan is perfect in that sense, don't you think?

Anyway, call me if you get this message tonight—if you can manage to chase your gossipy brothers away from the phone!

FROM: Steviethegreat
TO: HorseGal
SUBJECT: Oops
MESSAGE:

I just noticed your e-mail about Lisa when I went to the computer to send you an e-mail about the horrible dream I just had. I had to tell you about it right away (the dream, that is, not the e-mail), and I figured your dad might not be thrilled if I called, since it's three o'clock in the morning. I mean, the Colonel is pretty cool about most things, but . . .

Anyway, back to your e-mail for a second—I guess you

sent it on Saturday night, right after we came up with our project, so maybe it's a little out of date since it's already Tuesday. But I still think you're right about pitching in with stable chores. Of course, after the way Lisa ducked out halfway through today's lesson (not to mention the way she kept talking about that Hollie girl who's in the play with her as if she were the fourth member of The Saddle Club! Humph!), I think it's going to take a lot more than cleaning tack to get us all through this. By the way, I'm not exactly sure what you were driving at with all that other stuff about realizations and commitment and everything, but if what you're saying is that we have to keep doing everything we can to smooth her way for the next couple of weeks, then I'm with you.

At least she still sounded pretty much like the old Lisa when we talked to her on the phone earlier tonight (or maybe I should say *last* night, since it's technically Wednesday morning—oh, never mind). I mean, she really sounded like she wants to be in the rally as much as she wants to play Annie. Almost, anyway. But that doesn't mean we can relax. Now that I think about it, it was kind of, you know, un-Lisa-like for her to ask us to tell Max she was working with Prancer as much as she can. For one thing, "as much as she can" doesn't seem like much. For another, it's just not like her to ask people to cover for her. (That's *my* specialty, ha ha!)

Anyway, I guess the bottom line is that we have to do even more to help Lisa remember how great riding is. In fact, I'm starting to think we need to do more than that. We have to convince her that she definitely likes riding better than acting, just so there's no question of which one she'll choose in the end. After all, it's like we were saying on the phone after Lisa hung up—we're both afraid that being great at two things (riding and acting) is going to force her to choose. And if she doesn't do well at the rally because she hasn't had enough time to practice, she may think she's not as good at riding as she is at acting. And then . . . Uh-oh!

Speaking of not being good enough at riding, in between all this helping and convincing and Saddle Club projecting, I hope I have time to figure out how to stop riding like "a sack of potatoes," as Max put it in class this afternoon. (Double humph!) Still, I guess I really can't hold it against him. Topside is so wonderful that he could make any rider look bad by comparison. I just have to try harder to be worthy of him.

Oh, that reminds me of the whole reason I started writing this—my dream! Actually, it was more like two dreams in one. I'm getting kind of sleepy, so I'll just give you the short version. First I dreamed that Topside and I were getting ready to ride into the ring at the dressage rally. But instead of being at the Sunny Valley fairgrounds right here in Virginia, the rally was taking place in the middle of the track at Churchill Downs—you know, the racetrack where they have the Kentucky Derby. (Whoa, I know I must be getting tired—I can't believe I just informed Carole Hanson, the girl who knows everything about every riding sport, where the Kentucky Derby takes place! Ha!) Anyway, that was strange enough. But then when I went to mount Topside, I couldn't remember how to do it. I started to panic and ended up climbing into the saddle *backward!* But Topside was so professional and unflappable that he just walked right out into the ring and saluted the judges all by himself (he actually *saluted*, too—he lifted his hoof right up and touched it to his forelock and sort of bowed). It was all pretty much downhill from there. Sitting backward like that, I had a perfect view of Max watching from the audience, and he kept shaking his fist at me and yelling, "Sack of potatoes! Sack of potatoes!" over and over again. Then when we finally finished the test, instead of clapping, the audience threw potatoes at us. Not just whole ones, either. I got hit in the face with a big wad of mashed potatoes. Oh, and did I mention the horrible moment when I looked up and realized the judges for the event were my three brothers? I'm surprised my hair didn't turn white from shock as I slept.

The next part of the dream was even stranger. I was back at Pine Hollow after the dressage rally, cleaning Topside's tack. For some reason it took so long that I was still there scrubbing away at the stroke of midnight. (Maybe it took a while to wash off all those potatoes. . . .) The big, spooky grandfather clock in the hall outside Mrs. Reg's office chimed off the first few chimes. (I know, I know, there's no clock there. But this is a dream, remember?)

Suddenly an apparition appeared in front of me. It was the ghostly form of good old Pepper. "Greetings, Stevie," Pepper said in a dramatic voice. "I am the Horse of Pine Hollow Past."

I was so surprised that Pepper was talking (not to mention

the fact that he was there at all, since he died last fall) that I almost dropped my saddle soap. "What do you wish of me, Pepper?" I asked in a quavery voice.

"I wish to show you the past," Pepper replied.

So then I jumped on his back and he galloped off into the clouds. When we came down again I saw myself riding Comanche in the outdoor ring. Only it wasn't me the way I am now. It was me the way I was a few years ago, when I hardly knew you because you'd just moved here, and neither of us knew Lisa at all. Dinah was riding beside me on Barq, and we were laughing and having a good time.

So far so good. Pepper took me back to the tack room, and I went to work on that saddle again. But before I knew it, another ghostly form appeared. This time I recognized Cobalt. "Greetings, Stevie," Cobalt said, arching his neck dramatically. "I am the Horse of Pine Hollow Present."

"Okay, let me guess," I said, hardly even surprised this time to see him alive again. "You want to show me the present. Well, isn't it right here in front of me?"

I guess Cobalt didn't think much of my smart mouth, because he just grabbed my sleeve in his big teeth and dragged me off into the clouds again. A few seconds later we were looking down at the three of us (you, me, and Lisa, that is) in the hayloft at Pine Hollow having a sleepover, sort of like we did a little while ago when Marie was staying with you, only Marie wasn't there. It was just The Saddle Club, and I could tell we were having a great time. We were having a hay fight, and Lisa and I were trying to stuff as much hay as we possibly could down the back of your pajamas while you wriggled and laughed and tried to get away. It looked like so much fun that I wished I could go right down there and join in (even though I was technically already there). But Cobalt just grabbed me again and pulled me back to the tack room.

I was smiling as I kept cleaning my tack, thinking about all the good times we've had since we became friends and started The Saddle Club. Then I looked up and saw Farthing standing in front of me. (That's this crotchety old pony Max used to have who died a few months before you moved to Willow Creek.)

Farthing turns out to be the Horse of Pine Hollow Future, naturally. "Come, Stevie," he told me in a solemn voice. "I must show you your future."

I went along with him, expecting to see something nice, like me and Lisa being bridesmaids at your wedding to Cam (ha ha!), or the three of us taking a trail ride with our children, or something like that. Instead, we floated down over the Fenton Hall cafeteria. "Why are we here?" I asked Farthing, totally confused.

"This is the site of the gala Hollywood film premiere of Lisa Atwood's latest picture," Farthing said.

"Really?" I probably should have been surprised that they'd hold something like that in the Fenton Hall cafeteria, but at the time I was a lot more surprised that Lisa was a famous movie actress. I couldn't help feeling kind of proud of her, though. "Lisa is the star of the movie?"

"She's the star of *every* movie," Farthing informed me. "Every director in Hollywood refuses to make any film unless she agrees to star in it. But that's okay, because audiences have stopped going to any film that doesn't feature Lisa At-wood."

"Wow." As Farthing swooped us down for a better look, I saw that there was a long red carpet stretched across the cafeteria, and cameras were flashing everywhere as the press crowded around to catch their first glimpse of Lisa. I guessed that she was in the long, black limo that was just pulling up to the door. Everyone started yelling and cheering and calling her name and waving stuff for her to autograph.

Before the car door opened, though, I caught a glimpse of a couple of familiar faces in the waiting crowd. It was us—you and me. We were clutching a couple of envelopes and looking just as excited as everyone else.

"I can't wait to see her," the future me said.

"Me either," the future you replied. "I'm sure she'll love seeing these pictures of Prancer that we brought for her."

I was just thinking how nice that was of us (bringing the pictures, I mean) when the car door finally opened and Lisa stepped out. At first I didn't realize it was Lisa. She looked a lot more sophisticated than usual—she had all kinds of makeup on, her hair was piled up on top of her head with little tendrils falling down at the sides, and she was wearing this sparkly long red dress with matching red high heels that had to be four inches tall. Oh, yeah, and I think she had a red feather boa, too, but I'm not totally sure about that.

Anyway, we started yelling and screaming her name, jumping up and down and waving our envelopes. Meanwhile, all these huge linebacker-type guys in dark sunglasses got out of the car, too, and sort of surrounded Lisa. I guess

121

they were supposed to be her bodyguards. The whole group of them started down the red carpet, and Lisa still didn't seem to hear us.

She moved closer, pausing every few steps to pose for the cameras or to sign an autograph for her swooning fans. We screamed her name even louder, and the future you opened your envelope and pulled out a handful of photos. "Lisa! Over here!" you yelled. "It's us! We brought you some pictures of Prancer so you can see how well she's doing these days!"

"She's great!" the future me added at the top of my lungs. "But she misses you since you moved to Hollywood. We all miss you!"

Lisa was finally right in front of us, but she still didn't seem to hear what we were saying. She did see the photos you were waving at her, though. She paused and grabbed one of them. "Thanks for your support," she said in this sort of bored, haughty tone. "It means a lot to me to have fabulous fans like you." Then she took the pen that one of her bodyguards was holding out and scribbled her signature on the photo—right across a scene of Prancer in the outdoor ring!

It was horrible. "But why doesn't she recognize us?" I asked Farthing. "We're her best friends."

Farthing shook his head, making his mane flop around. "Not anymore," he intoned. "Acting is her only friend now."

By the way, I guess I probably should have mentioned that I fell asleep tonight reading A Christmas Carol—we have a quiz on it tomorrow in English class. So I guess that might have inspired the second part of the dream a little. But it was still pretty freaky, don't you think?

Whew! It's getting late (early?), so I should go. I'll see you tomorrow at the stable for dressage practice and Lisa duty. Wish me luck on that quiz. I'll need it!

P.S. Maybe I should send Lisa this list to remind her why she loves riding? What do you think?

Why Riding Is Better than Acting:

1. You don't get to spend time with horses when you're an actor (usually, anyway, unless you're acting in a cowboy movie or *National Velvet* or something).

2. Riding is much better exercise than acting (probably? Although now that I think about it, Lisa has to do a lot of dancing in this particular play. But that's not always the case, right?).

3. You don't have to wear lots of stage makeup and gunk in your hair when you're riding.

4. Riding gets you more fresh air.

5. It just is!!!!!!!!!!!!

CAROLE HANSON'S RIDING JOURNAL:

It's hard to believe that the dressage rally is tomorrow. I can't wait! Lisa's dress rehearsal for *Annie* is tomorrow, too. She invited Stevie and me to come watch—I can't wait for that, either. I've never been to a dress rehearsal before. Lisa says it will be just like watching the real play, at least as long as nothing goes wrong. The actors will all be in full costume and makeup, with all the lights and music and everything, just like in an actual performance.

It's been such a busy couple of weeks! I've hardly had time

to write anything about all the practicing Starlight and I have been doing for the rally. We've learned a lot, and I think we're ready to make a good showing tomorrow.

Stevie is in great shape, too. I was just thinking about what happened that day last week, when she and I decided that she should work with Prancer to practice for the rally, since Stevie needed to practice hard and Topside really didn't, and since Lisa didn't have time to give Prancer the extra effort she needed. It made perfect sense.

I'm not sure Max agreed with us at first. He stopped by to watch part of Stevie's first session with Prancer (I was helping them), and he seemed a little disturbed when we explained what we were doing.

"You know as well as I do," he told us, "that Lisa should be the one riding that horse. She needs as much ring time as possible before the rally, and instead she's getting less than usual."

So he had definitely noticed Lisa's crazed schedule. I tried to defend her, remembering how she had asked Stevie and me to cover for her as much as possible. "I know that, Max," I said, "and so does she. At least Prancer's getting ridden. That should help get her ready. And Lisa's really trying to get here as often as possible."

Max looked skeptical. "*Trying* to do something isn't always enough, especially when it comes to riding horses."

I knew he was right, but I wasn't sure what Stevie and I could do about it, other than keep trying to help Lisa fit everything in.

I think it was that same day that Mrs. Reg sat us down for her stable management talk. Actually what she was doing was telling us we had to fend for ourselves instead of getting one of the younger kids to act as our stable manager at the rally. There was some kind of birthday party planned for the same day, so there really wasn't anyone available except the six of us who were competing.

Stevie and I weren't too thrilled about that. At that point the rally seemed to be taking over our whole lives. Just when we thought we'd made progress in one area—getting Prancer ready to compete by having Stevie practice with her—Mrs. Reg had reminded us about another area that we'd been completely neglecting. We knew she was counting on us, The Saddle Club, to make things run smoothly at the rally. I mean, she had to know as well as we did that there was no way Veronica diAngelo was going to lift a finger to help out with stable management stuff. She usually doesn't even bother to tack up her own horse if she can help it. And Betsy and Polly are good teammates in most ways, but they're both a little lazy about stable chores. They tend to skimp on stuff like cleaning tack unless someone keeps after them about it.

We knew all that. But we still weren't feeling too good about the problem. "We're no good at this sort of thing, either," I told Stevie glumly.

"You mean *I'm* no good at it, right?" Stevie asked.

It's true that she's not exactly famous for her untamed enthusiasm for stable chores, but I shook my head. "No, I really do mean we," I said. "I love doing all that stuff on my own for Starlight, but I can never seem to get everyone else as excited as I am."

It looked like a real problem, but we didn't have much time to worry about it. There were too many other things to think about, like whether our best friend would give up riding for acting. Stevie was still fretting about that wacky dream she had where Lisa was a big-time movie star who didn't even remember our names. I wasn't sure things could ever get quite that bad, but I didn't want to take any chances.

So we kept on with our plan. We had Prancer tacked up and waiting whenever Lisa rushed in before or after rehearsal. Of course, that didn't help a bit last Saturday when Lisa and Prancer turned in a totally disastrous performance at our lesson. Max didn't say a whole lot, but it was clear that he was disappointed, and Lisa ended up rushing off in tears. The worst part was that Stevie and I didn't even get a chance to talk to her about it, since she had to race off to another rehearsal.

Meanwhile the rest of us had our hands full, trying to get organized for the rally without a team manager. It wasn't a pretty sight. We spent a long time arguing about it (Stevie, Betsy, Polly, and I did, anyway—Veronica took off right after class, as usual). Finally we just agreed to get our own stuff ready as much as possible and pray that we found somebody to step in to manage the team's equipment and everything when show time came. That didn't seem like much of a solution, but it was the best we could do.

After that was settled, Stevie and I decided to call Lisa to see how she was doing after her tough day. "I'll bet she's calmed down by now," I said. "Maybe she has time to meet us."

Stevie was doubtful about that, but we figured it couldn't hurt to call her and see. So we called her house. Mrs. Atwood answered.

"Is Lisa there?" Stevie asked politely.

"You mean she's not with you?" Mrs. Atwood asked.

"Us?" Stevie said. "No, she left Pine Hollow hours ago."

Mrs. Atwood sounded confused. "But I thought she must be with you because the director of the play has called three times looking for her."

"You mean she's not at rehearsal?" I demanded.

"No, she never showed up." Lisa's mom was starting to sound concerned. "Do you have any idea where she might have gone?"

Stevie and I looked at each other. I knew we were both thinking the same thing. "Don't worry, Mrs. Atwood," Stevie said into the phone. "We know where to find her."

Soon the two of us were heading out across the fields behind Pine Hollow. We hadn't bothered to put saddles on Starlight and Topside, just bridles. We entered the woods on our favorite trail, and before long we had reached our favorite spot by the creek. Lisa was there, sitting on that big rock that juts over the water, staring down at the rushing creek and muttering to herself. Her eyes were red and her skin looked blotchy, the way it does when she's been crying.

"Phew! I'm glad you're here," Stevie greeted her brightly as we dismounted and headed toward her. "We thought a Broadway director might have whisked you off for a starring role."

"Fat chance," Lisa replied bitterly. "At the rate I'm going, the only starring role I'm up for is Queen of the Failures. I'm a failure at Pony Club. A failure at *Annie*. A failure at school . . ."

That last part was pretty bogus, of course. For Lisa, failing at school means getting an A-minus instead of an A-plus, which I guess is what happened on some quiz or other she'd taken that week. Stevie and I were a lot more concerned about the other two items on her list. We launched into a pep talk, reminding her how hard she'd been working and how talented she was—at riding *and* acting.

"No one ever said acting was easy, you know," I told her, remembering how worried she was because she was the only first-time actor in the play. "But you walked in out of the blue and got the lead."

"Sometimes I wish I'd never auditioned." Lisa's voice was cracking a little. "This is such a familiar feeling—being a beginner. Everyone else seems to have been born riding or acting."

Stevie and I nodded sympathetically. Lisa's such a good rider now that both of us had practically forgotten that she hadn't been riding as long as either of us.

"At least I'm over the hump in riding," Lisa went on. "I don't have to ask what a martingale is or how to pick out a hoof anymore. I can't even remember not knowing. But being in *Annie* is like that time my French class went to Montreal. Everyone looks at you funny because you can hardly speak the language. At first it's fun. But pretty soon you want to go home to Willow Creek—or Pine Hollow."

"You mean you're not going to quit riding after all?" I asked.

"Quit riding?" Lisa repeated incredulously. "What ever gave you that idea?"

"We—We, ah—" I stammered, not quite sure how to explain.

Stevie jumped in to save me. "We thought you might be having so much fun acting that you'd decide you liked the stage better than horses and that you'd want to be in a lot more plays," she said. "And then you'd start hanging around with the theater crowd at school, and pretty soon you'd get a personal acting coach and join a mime troupe and run off to Hollywood to star in movies and forget our names when we asked you for autographs."

I gave Stevie a surprised glance at her mention of the mime troupe, wondering if maybe she'd had a dream that she hadn't told me about. But then I turned back to Lisa. "Or at least want to be in a lot more plays," I said with a shrug.

Lisa looked a little overwhelmed. "That does it," she said. "I'm going to give up the part."

"What?" Stevie and I cried in unison.

"I'm dropping out of the play," Lisa said.

"But what about all the people counting on you to play Annie?" I asked.

"They'll find someone else," Lisa replied eagerly. "I don't want to let you and Max and Mrs. Reg and Prancer down. Besides, my true loyalty is to The Saddle Club and riding, and dropping out will prove it."

"True loyalty? But this isn't a *life* choice," Stevie reminded her. "It's just to help you get through the next two weeks."

"Yeah, and what about all those lines you memorized?" I added. Now that I knew Lisa wasn't planning to ditch riding for a life on the stage, it suddenly seemed kind of, well, *wrong* for her to just give up on *Annie*.

"But I'd be able to memorize my dressage tests instead," Lisa said, though she didn't sound quite as eager this time.

"But this is your big chance!" Stevie cried.

"It's Prancer's big chance, too—to prove she can do dressage," Lisa said.

"She'll have other chances," I told her.

"And how do you know you'll get another lead role? Actors can wait years for this kind of thing!" Stevie exclaimed.

Lisa laughed, seeming surprised at our reaction. "Is this The Saddle Club talking?" she asked. "Because it sounds like the Willow Creek Community Theater."

Stevie waggled her finger in Lisa's face, looking stern. "You've got a part to play, missy, and don't you forget it."

"What happened to 'The show must go on' and all that?" I asked.

"All right! All right!" Lisa practically shouted. "You win! I'll play Annie!"

We all started talking excitedly about coming to see her in the play and stuff like that. I could tell that Lisa was kind of upset about not being able to take part in the dressage rally, but I suspected she was kind of relieved, too.

"I guess I can still help out with the rally behind the scenes," she commented at one point.

I nodded. Then I did a double take.

Stevie was obviously thinking the same thing I was. "Behind the scenes? *Behind the scenes?* How can we be such idiots?" she cried.

"You're telling me!" I agreed.

Lisa looked pretty confused, but we knew she had to get to her rehearsal. So we promised to fill her in later, after the rehearsal was over.

It was worth the wait, too. Lisa was thrilled when we explained how our team desperately needed a stable manager for the rally. She immediately agreed to take on the job.

"This really is the perfect solution," Lisa told us happily. "I have *some* time to devote to the rally—I just can't be responsible for getting Prancer ready."

"And even though you're not riding, you're still making a huge contribution to the team," I pointed out.

Lisa started making notes about equipment and schedules even before we finished that conversation. So now here we are, the night before the rally, and everything is beautifully organized, Lisa Atwood–style! Plus, now Lisa says she learned a valuable lesson from what she went through last week: When you try too hard to do *everything,* you end up not enjoying *anything!*

Oh, and I almost forgot—getting Lisa to be our manager wasn't the only change of plans we've had getting ready for the rally. In our lesson this Tuesday, Stevie and I were practicing together while Max was across the ring working with Polly. I watched Stevie run through all the transitions in her test, impressed as always by how clean and professional Topside was.

131

"Better and better," I commented appreciatively when they finished.

"Thanks," Stevie said, pulling Topside up beside Starlight. "But I'm not sure if we *are* better and better. Most of the time I feel like we're always the same."

"Okay, you're always the same, and that's always good," I agreed. "The judges will love him."

"Exactly," she said grimly. "They'll love *him*, and he deserves all the praise he gets."

"I didn't mean it like that. You look great, too," I added hastily.

"Sorry," Stevie said. "I really wasn't fishing for compliments. It's just that I can't stop thinking that no matter how great a score I get on Saturday, Topside will be the reason. We might get a blue ribbon; we might not. It hardly matters. If we do, it won't be a big deal anyway. Topside will have earned it, but he's gotten blue ribbons at international competitions. What would it mean to get one at a little Pony Club rally?"

"It would mean—" I started automatically. But then I paused, really thinking about what Stevie had said. I wasn't sure how to answer her. I'd never had her problem. I'd never gone into a show *expecting* to get a blue ribbon. And whenever Starlight and I did well, I knew it was because we had both worked hard.

"It's hard to answer, isn't it?" Stevie said. "The whole point of Pony Club is to learn. But I'm not learning anything. On Topside I'm just sitting back and enjoying the ride."

"Are you saying that you want more of a challenge?" I asked. That sounded like Stevie.

She nodded, a slow grin creeping across her face. "I've decided to ride Prancer at the rally if it's all right with Max."

I clapped my hands excitedly, knowing immediately that it was another perfect solution. "That's a great idea! It'll be wonderful for you *and* Prancer. Why didn't you just say so?"

Stevie tossed her head airily. "Oh, I wanted to build up the dramatic suspense."

"Humph," I muttered. "Maybe *you're* the one who ought to be onstage!"

Anyway, I guess Max thought the idea was just as perfect as we did. He actually gave Stevie a *hug* when she told him! Stevie was so shocked that she just stood there speechless while Max exclaimed, "Good for you! Good for you, Stevie Lake!" about ten times in a row. Finally he stepped back, looked her in the eye, and said, "We might make a horsewoman out of you yet."

Stevie was pretty thrilled about that. Coming from Max, that kind of compliment is about as rare and hard to earn as a Nobel Prize!

So I guess this means that Stevie doesn't have to worry about that crazy dream of hers anymore—*either* part. I mean, I'm no psychologist (despite what I wrote in here a while ago about becoming a horse psychologist, ha ha!), but her dream wasn't exactly hard to figure out. In the first part, she was obviously worried about holding up her end of her partnership with Topside in the rally. Now that's taken care of, since she'll probably be doing more to help Prancer tomorrow than the other way around.

I guess the second part of the dream was pretty obvious,

too. We were worried that Lisa would stop riding. And since riding has always been such an important part of our friendship, we were afraid that if we didn't have that in common anymore, we might stop being friends. As if that could ever happen! Still, I'll admit that I was just as worried about it as Stevie was. Pretty crazy, huh?

I guess it's only natural, though. Even though people live in the present, it seems like they're always thinking about the past and the future. For instance, the main reason that Stevie and I were so worried about Lisa's possible future (the one we thought she'd have if she gave up riding) was because our past together was so great. And haven't I been spending the past few months worrying about my future, trying to figure out what I'll be doing? It's important, too, since in that case the future really could have an effect on the present, and I could be preparing for that future right now, just like the rider in Cam's article did in her past. . . .

Well, I still can't go to sleep, even though I know I should. I'm too excited about tomorrow. And all this talk about the past is making me think about my old diary again. I sort of don't want to keep reading it, because I know what happens next. But for some reason I can't help wanting to read on. Maybe I'll just take a quick peek at the next entry before I turn in.

Dear Diary:

It's starting to look like spring outside. All those flower bulbs Mom planted are coming up, which doesn't seem quite fair somehow.

I thought I was starting to deal with things pretty well. Mom has been going in for regular treatments, and it's starting to feel almost normal. Well, not really—but at least a little closer to normal than the first month or two after her diagnosis.

Then her doctor put her on some new drug, I forget what it's called. It's brand new, and it was supposed to help her body handle the other treatments better or something like that. I think. It's hard to keep track of all the medical stuff sometimes.

Anyway, Mom started the new drug last Monday. On Tuesday night, she woke up at two A.M. with a fever. She was shaking so hard she could barely stand up. Dad didn't want to wake up a neighbor at that hour to come over and stay with me, so I went along with them to the hospital. It was awful. Even though the hospital's only a short drive away, it seemed to take forever to get there. I sort of thought it might all be another nightmare, like the ones I had all the time right after we found out about the cancer.

But it was real. And scary. The doctors say Mom's back on track now, and the new medication they put her on to replace that one is working so far, but I guess it was a pretty close call. They're not saying so to me, of course. But I can tell. There's just something about the way Dad looks at Mom sometimes now—like he's already missing her. That sounds horrible when I write it down like that, but it's what I think he's thinking. And that makes me think things I don't want to think. Like how maybe Mom won't be with us much longer.

I can't believe I just wrote that. It seems totally impossible. There's just no way I can imagine how Dad and I would go on without her. I can't imagine Mom not being there to see me ride my first horse of my very own (not that we've been talking about that whole topic much since this happened, naturally). Or not cheering me on at my high-school graduation. Or not watching me get married someday.

Not only that big stuff, though. It's almost harder thinking about all the littler stuff she might miss, like finally taking that family vacation we had to cancel this year. Or even having her own garden like she planned.

Okay, this is making me too sad. I think I'd better stop it and go over to Pine Hollow, even though my riding class isn't for almost two hours. That will take my mind off this if anything can.

(later)

I just got back from Pine Hollow and decided to add on to what I wrote earlier today. Someone at the stable said something that gave me an idea.

Actually, it was Stevie Lake. I've been spending more time with her since Dinah Slattery moved away to Vermont last month. Also, she's still one of the only kids in my riding class who doesn't get all weird whenever I mention Mom. Some days she asks how she's doing; some days she doesn't. It's like she trusts me to tell her what's going on if I want to. I like that feeling. It's so much better than Lauren saying, "Oh, Carole, everything will be all right," or Polly and Betsy giggling nervously and then looking guilty.

Anyway, today Stevie didn't ask about Mom at all. That's because she was really mad at Veronica. I guess Veronica said something snobby to her at school yesterday; she wasn't too clear on that. But she was out for revenge, and she had a plan. She'd overheard Max saying he was going to make a surprise stall inspection after our class. I guess he wanted to make sure we'd all taken care of our horses properly and not skimped on grooming or mucking out. So Stevie wanted to take a whole pile of manure from the manure pit and dump it into Princess's stall right after class so that Veronica couldn't possibly clean it all out in time (if she even bothered to check the stall, that is, instead of handing Princess off to Red O'Malley after class like she usually does). At first I wasn't sure why Stevie was telling me about her plan, but then I realized she was asking for my help. She wanted me to help her fill a couple of the stable's wheelbarrows with manure and hide them in an empty stall so they'd be ready for us to dump in Princess's stall right before Max's inspection.

I'm sure she normally would have asked Dinah to help her. But since Dinah isn't here anymore, she asked me. I was sort of flattered, actually. I mean, I haven't known her nearly as long as Betsy or Polly or Lauren or some of the others. But I guess Betsy and Polly are better friends with Veronica than they are with Stevie. And I sometimes get the impression that Stevie doesn't like Lauren that much.

I was a little nervous about what she wanted me to do, even though she swore there was no way we'd get caught. I finally agreed when she offered to do the second part by herself (dumping the stuff into Princess's stall) if I would just help her get the wheelbarrows ready.

I was totally nervous the whole time we were doing it. I kept looking over my shoulder every two seconds, expecting Max or

Mrs. Reg to catch us. (Especially since Mrs. Reg sometimes seems to have eyes in the back of her head. She knows everything that goes on around the stable!) But the only one who saw what we were doing was Lauren. She walked by when we were pushing the third wheelbarrow full of manure into the empty stall across the aisle from Princess's. "What are you doing?" she asked, wrinkling her nose the way she does when she's unhappy about something. "Never mind," Stevie snapped, glaring at her. "You didn't see a thing, okay?"

I didn't think that was very polite, so I smiled at Lauren apologetically. "Please don't say anything to Max, okay?" I begged her.

Lauren just shrugged, so I thought she was agreeing. And for a while Stevie's prank went perfectly. She rushed straight to Princess's stall after class, while I walked Comanche for her (mostly behind the building so that nobody would get suspicious). When Max started making the rounds a little while later, he came to Princess's stall and found Veronica staring in disbelief. Princess was still standing in the hall, since the manure in her stall was about six inches deep! It was actually sort of funny, though of course it shouldn't have been because if a horse had to stand in manure like that it would be really bad for its feet and everything. And it would have seemed like a really mean thing to do, except that Veronica is always so nasty herself. The horrified look on her face as she stared into that stall was priceless!

So Max bawled Veronica out for about half an hour, yelling at her about being more responsible and realizing that riding is a privilege and not a right, and all sorts of other things. Stevie and I hid in Delilah's stall, which is just a couple of doors down, and tried not to giggle too loudly.

Veronica was just stunned at first, I think, but soon enough she got suspicious. She interrupted Max's lecture to insist that the stall was almost clean before class (which it was) and that someone had done this as a prank. "It was probably that immature Stevie Lake," she added loudly. "She's always out to get me."

Stevie started giggling even harder at that. But then we heard another voice.

"She's right, Max," Lauren said. She was nearby, too, listening. "It was Stevie Lake. I saw her bringing in extra manure earlier."

Stevie's jaw dropped and her face turned bright red. I just froze, waiting for Lauren to mention me, too. I imagined how upset Mom and Dad would be when Max called to tell them why he was kicking me out of Pine Hollow for good. And I would have felt horrible about upsetting them right now, since the whole week has been upsetting enough.

But Lauren didn't say a word about me. She just told Max exactly what she'd seen. "See?" Veronica said angrily. "I told you."

Max was quiet for a moment, I guess thinking that over. Then he told Lauren to find Stevie and ask her to come see him.

Beside me, Stevie gulped. "I guess I'd better go out there," she said.

"I'll go with you," I offered. I knew it was the right thing to do, even though Lauren hadn't told on me.

But Stevie shook her head. "Don't," she said. "It was my idea—my plan. That Goody Two-shoes didn't say anything about you, and Max will totally believe I did this on my own. There's no reason both of us need to get in trouble."

I started to insist, but she was firm. Finally I gave in, mostly because I was still thinking about what Mom would say if she found out what I'd done.

So Stevie walked out to face the music herself. I peeked out over the stall door, still feeling guilty. Max yelled at her for a while and then made her apologize to Veronica, which was probably the hardest part for Stevie. After that, Veronica turned to Max and said, "Well? Don't I have another apology coming?"

Max gave her a stern look. "Perhaps if you were more reliable about doing your own chores, I wouldn't have believed the worst," he said. "Now, why don't you and Stevie get to work cleaning out this stall—together."

Veronica was so shocked that she just sputtered for a few minutes, and by the time she got hold of herself, Max had moved on. So she just made obnoxious comments to Stevie for the next ten minutes, working really slowly the whole time. Then, when Max disappeared around the corner to inspect the stalls in the next aisle, Veronica threw down her pitchfork and left. She just left Princess cross-tied in the aisle and took off for home, leaving Stevie with most of the work. As soon as she was gone I came out of hiding to help, and Stevie and I managed to get the stall clean and Princess comfortable in no time.

We talked a little while we worked, and that's when Stevie

said the thing I've been thinking about ever since. I was telling her how bad I felt that she'd gotten busted and stuff like that. But she was really pretty calm about it.

"It's okay," she said as she shoveled another forkful of straw and manure into the wheelbarrow. "At least I got my revenge."

I wasn't sure I'd heard her right. "But you got in just as much trouble as Veronica did!" I exclaimed. "Maybe more."

Stevie just shrugged. "I know. And I'm sure Max will call my parents, and I'll probably be grounded for a week or two. But I can survive that. I never could have lived with myself if I hadn't done what I needed to do."

I suspected she was a little more upset than she was letting on. But I was pretty sure she meant that part about needing to do what she'd done, and not being able to live with herself if she hadn't at least tried to get back at Veronica.

That's what's making me think so hard right now. Stevie is always doing stuff. Maybe it sometimes gets her in trouble or whatever, but at least no one can say she just sits around waiting for something to happen. She makes things happen herself.

Maybe that's what I need to do. Maybe instead of sitting around waiting for Mom to get better—or worse yet, worrying about horrible things that probably won't even happen (like Mom missing all those important moments in my life), I should try to help her more now. Make good things happen for her. Try to be sure she has fun even though she's sick.

After all, like Stevie said, doing something is a lot better than sitting around being unhappy and doing nothing.

141

ANNIE A SINGING SUCCESS!

The Willow Creek Community Theater has done it again! After the warm reception to last season's *My Fair Lady,* they have returned stronger than ever with their latest production, *Annie.* Held as usual in the high school auditorium, the musical drew a full house every night of its two-weekend run, and the audiences seemed to feel that they were getting their money's worth.

"I love all their shows," gushed local painter and theater fan Reginald Jarvis. "But this was one of the best."

This reviewer has to agree with Mr. Jarvis. The direction, by WCCT veteran Ellen Spitz, was brisk and well paced. New-comer Lisa Atwood, a student at Willow Creek Junior High, won the role as Little Orphan Annie. She displayed a strong, flexible singing voice and a natural command of the part, making the young heroine come to life for the audience. George Ryan's portrayal of Daddy Warbucks was also particularly strong, which will surprise no one who witnessed his fine performance in the lead role of *The King and I* several years back. Other standouts in the cast included Margaret French as Miss Hannigan and Hollie Bright as the head of the orphan chorus.

Congratulations to the whole cast and crew for a job well done!

LOOK OUT, BROADWAY—LISA ATWOOD SHINES IN STARRING ROLE!

By Stevie Lake

Those of us who attended the Willow Creek Community Theater's production of *Annie* last weekend were treated to a wonderful show. More importantly, we also witnessed the birth of a star—the most talented, most wonderful star ever to grace the stage in this town, or maybe anywhere! Miss Lisa Atwood, perhaps the finest actress ever to memorize a line, gave an earth-shatteringly brilliant performance in the lead role. Even though she had never acted onstage before (except for a few elementary-school pageants and stuff like that), Miss Atwood seemed born to bring Little Orphan Annie to life. Her voice was sweeter than the singing of angels, and her dancing was so graceful that it was hard to believe if you didn't know that she's also a terrific horseback rider, which helps your balance a lot. Anyway, watching her play Annie was truly amazing.

At the few moments when it was possible to tear my eyes away from Miss Atwood's spellbinding performance, this reviewer also noticed that Miss Hollie Bright was also very good as the head orphan. Most of the other actors were fine, too, which had the effect of making the play's wonderful star seem even better.

CAROLE HANSON'S RIDING JOURNAL:

I just stuck those two newspaper articles in here, even though they aren't about riding, because I wanted to make sure I didn't lose them. I meant to paste in that blurb they printed in the *Gazette* about how well our team did at the dressage rally, too, but I think Snowball must have eaten it or something because I can't find it anywhere. Oh well. Anyway, I definitely always want to remember how great Lisa was in her play, and I figured a couple of glowing reviews would help remind me—especially Stevie's. Actually, hers is really only a first draft of the review she wrote for her school paper. When she turned it in, for some strange reason, the editor insisted that she rewrite it so it focused just a *tad* less on Lisa. Ha ha! But I decided I liked her first draft better, so I asked her if I could keep it.

Speaking of Stevie, she's all excited about this new horse that's staying temporarily in Phil's family's stable. Stevie got to ride her when she went over there for dinner. The horse is a light bay mare, part Arabian and part Saddlebred. She has four white socks, an upside-down exclamation point on her face, and, according to Stevie, a real sense of humor. The horse actually started dancing in place when Stevie and Phil were about to kiss! The only problem is, the mare has allergies—she broke out in hives during Stevie's ride. Nobody seems to know what she's allergic to, though, not even Judy Barker. But Stevie wants to try to figure it out. The horse doesn't have a name as far as anyone knows (she's part of a bulk lot that Phil's riding instructor, Mr. Baker, just bought), so Stevie started calling her No-Name. Sounds like a typical Stevie idea!

By the way, Lisa's friend Hollie from the play came riding with us today. She seems really nice. She used to take riding lessons a few years ago, but she hadn't gone riding lately, and I think she had a good time. It's always great to see someone discover—or rediscover—how wonderful riding is!

FROM: Steviethegreat
TO: HorseGal
TO: LAtwood
SUBJECT: No-Name's allergies
MESSAGE:

I've been lying in bed for hours thinking about what could be causing those hives. I really, really, really want to figure it out. It's not fair that such a great, friendly, happy horse should have to deal with stupid old hives. Since I couldn't sleep anyway, I figured I'd drop you two a note in case you had any brilliant insights about it in the morning (or whenever you read this).

Okay, so here's what I've thought of to check so far:

food
fly spray
bedding (straw)
saddle soap
paint in stall
Phil (ha ha!)
???

Dear Diary:

I haven't written in here in a while because I've been so busy lately! I'm trying to stick to my plan to help Mom by doing everything I can to make her happy and keep her spirits up. I'm almost dizzy with everything we've been doing together lately. Last weekend we went on a picnic in the state park on Saturday, and on Sunday Dad took us out to that nice Italian restaurant Mom loves so much. The week before that, Mom was feeling pretty strong, so we drove into Washington and went to all our favorite museums—the National Air and Space Museum for Dad, the National Gallery of Art for Mom, and for me, of course, the Museum of Natural History. I could tell Mom was kind of tired by the end (she slept the whole way home in the car), but I think she had fun.

Dear Diary:

Still busy. I'm supposed to be downstairs right now making popcorn. Casablanca is on TV tonight, and since that's one of Mom's favorites (mine and Dad's, too), I thought it would be nice for the three of us to watch together. Anyway, I just had to write down what happened this afternoon. We went on a trail ride! That's right. I actually convinced Mom to climb in the saddle. She rode Patch, and I rode Delilah as usual. We didn't go very far, since Mom was afraid of getting tired, just to the edge of the woods and back. But I think that still may have been a little too much for her, because she was kind of shaky by the time we dismounted. I was pretty

146

worried, especially since it was Red's day off. I knew I had to take care of the horses, but I also knew I should stay with Mom until Dad got there to pick us up. Luckily Stevie happened by just then, on her way out after a trail ride or something. When I explained things to her, she joked about sitting with my mom while I scrubbed tack, but then she just took Patch's and Delilah's leads and headed off. I was really grateful—I was hoping she might help me with one of the horses, but instead she insisted on taking care of them both! It was really nice of her to help me out like that.

Dear Diary:

Casablanca ended a few minutes ago. Mom was tired afterward, so she went straight to bed. I'm sitting in my room now writing this and trying to be quiet so she can sleep.

Maybe watching that particular movie wasn't such a hot idea—the ending always makes us all cry, even Dad. And afterward, when I asked Mom if she'd like to come to Pine Hollow with me tomorrow after school, she just sort of smiled a little and rubbed my back. "Thanks for the offer, sweetie," she said. "But I think I'll stay here tomorrow and do a little weeding if the weather's nice."

"Okay," I said quickly. "I can stay and help." I was thinking that if we got all the weeding done, maybe we could do something fun afterward.

But Mom shook her head. "You don't have to do that," she said. "You can go riding just like you planned. I'm sure your friends at the stable will be glad to see you."

147

I started to insist that I like weeding just as much as riding, trying my best to sound like I meant it. But Mom can be stubborn when she wants to be, and she was being stubborn then. For some reason she really, really thinks I should go to Pine Hollow tomorrow without her. And finally Dad stepped in and agreed with her, giving me one of his famous no-nonsense looks to stop me from arguing. So I stopped, and Mom went to bed, and here I am, wondering if maybe my plan isn't working well enough. I thought Mom was having fun doing all the stuff we've been doing lately, like going to museums and on trail rides and all that. But maybe not.

So maybe I need to try a little harder. I keep thinking about that list I made before of all the important things Mom and I might not get to share: high school graduation, getting my own horse, getting married.

I know I was just being stupid and silly and worried for no reason. I mean, she keeps telling me that the doctors are really happy with her latest treatments. It's not as if she's really going to miss out on any of those things on my list. Still, I can tell Mom feels tired most of the time, and pretty sick sometimes, too. Maybe if something really important were happening, she'd think about that less and feel better. Something important like the stuff on that list. Obviously there's no way I can graduate from high school in the near future. (With all these extra movie nights and things, I'll be lucky to make it to junior high! Ha!) And, of course, the horse thing isn't too likely right now, either. And that's okay, really. Then there's the getting married thing—even less likely than the other two, since I'm only—

148

Wait a minute, though. I just had an idea. Maybe there's no way I'll be getting engaged anytime soon. But maybe I could at least find a boyfriend. Seeing my first love is something that would be sure to distract Mom a whole lot—I mean, Dad was just teasing her again tonight, when she was crying during the movie, about how she's so crazy about sappy love stories.

I think I may be onto something here! So here's my new vow: Starting tomorrow, I'm going to go out there and find myself a boyfriend!

Dear Diary:

I figured the best place to find a cool boyfriend was at Pine Hollow. So today I checked out all the possibilities. At first the most likely person seemed to be Adam Levine, this boy from my school who just joined our class last month. He's a pretty good rider (he took lessons at a different stable before), he's around my age, and I guess he's sort of cute.

Our regular lesson was today, so I figured that would give me a chance to get to know him better. I went over to Tecumseh's stall while Adam was tacking him up.

"Hi," I said. Brilliant, huh?

He looked at me. I'm not sure, but I think he was sort of surprised that I was talking to him. I guess that's not so strange, since I think it was the first time ever.

"Hi," he said back.

I wasn't sure what to say next. "Um, so how do you like Tecumseh?"

149

This time he gave me a really weird look. "I wouldn't marry him or anything," he said, kind of sarcastically. "Why? Do you want to ride him today or something?"

"Um, no," I said. Things weren't going the way I'd planned at all so far. But I wasn't willing to give up yet. "So what else do you like to do besides riding?"

"Pick my nose," Adam said, sticking his finger toward my face. "Want to see my collection?" He laughed so hard he started to snort.

I wrinkled my nose and backed away. That just made him laugh harder. He wriggled his finger at me and stepped closer.

I decided it was time to make my escape and move on. Besides, I was going to be late if I didn't tack up Delilah soon. I rushed around the corner of the aisle. Luckily, Adam couldn't follow me because of Tecumseh. Otherwise I'm sure he would have chased me all over the stable with his stupid nose-picking finger joke. Who knew he could be so immature?

My next choice was Joe Novick. He's kind of a goof-off, but a lot of the girls are always talking about how cute he is, so I figured Mom would like him.

He was out in front of the stable, waiting for his ride, with his friend Roger. I was happy about that, since Roger was next on my list. Actually, he was last on my list, too, since there are only three boys in our riding class right now.

But I didn't have much more luck with Joe and Roger than I did with Adam. When I found them, they were in the middle of some kind of martial arts battle. At least that's what they called it. To me, it looked more like they were just running around in circles, trying to kick each other in the knee.

"Hi, you guys!" I said brightly, raising my voice so they could hear me over their own yells.

They stopped in mid-kick and looked over at me. "What do you want?" Roger asked.

I shrugged. "Nothing. I just came over to say hi." I was starting to wish I'd paid a little more attention to the love scenes in all those old romantic movies Mom likes. What did the women in them say to get the men to like them? All I could remember was that they usually either gave the men compliments or insulted them. Both methods always seemed to make Cary Grant or Jimmy Stewart or whoever fall madly in love sooner or later. "Um, I like those shirts you guys are wearing," I said uncertainly. "But you look ridiculous kicking each other like that."

"Oh yeah?" Joe said, smirking at me. "Well, you look ridiculous all the time."

Gritting my teeth, I thought of Mom and how happy she would be if I brought home a cute boy like Joe. "That's not very nice," I told him. "I just gave you a compliment. Didn't you hear what I said about your shirt?"

"Carole and Joe, sittin' in a tree . . . ," Roger sang out.

Joe turned and punched him in the shoulder. "Shut up, jerkface. There's no way I like Carole. She smells like a horse."

"You do too like her, lamebrain," Roger said, punching him back. "You love her!"

151

"Do not," Joe insisted, punching him harder. "You love her, you weenie."

"Do not!" Roger tackled Joe, pinning him to the ground. "Take it back, and admit you're the one who wants to marry her."

I sighed and turned away as the two of them started to scuffle in the dirt. So much for my brilliant plan to find true love in my riding class. All the boys I know are way too immature to take me seriously. So I guess there's only one solution. I just have to figure out where to meet some older men!

I'm not giving up on this. I know that when Mom finds out I have a boyfriend, she'll be so happy that she'll have to get better.

Dear Diary:

I had another idea for a boyfriend today. I was talking to Stevie while we were cleaning tack after class, and she started complaining about something her younger brother, Michael, did. I think it had to do with putting his pet turtle in her shoe, but I wasn't paying that much attention to the details. I'd suddenly remembered hearing her complain about brothers before, and I was pretty sure she had a lot of them. So I asked her about them, and it turns out she has three. Michael is younger than us, Alex is Stevie's twin, and Chad is a couple of years older. I figured either Alex or Chad would be perfect. After all, Stevie is really nice, so her brothers are probably just as nice, right? And even though

Alex is our age, maybe he's not as immature and weird as those other guys.

I was kind of embarrassed about telling Stevie about my plan, though. She may be nice, but she also loves to tease people. So I was afraid to just come out and ask her if I could meet her brothers sometime. Luckily I remembered something she said to me once—namely, that there's always more than one way to get what you want if you're willing to be creative. She said it when she was trying to figure out a way to convince Max to let us play mounted games in class a couple of weeks ago instead of practicing bandaging. It didn't work that time, but it still makes sense.

So I decided to approach my problem creatively, just like she would. "Boy, I'm really hungry after that class," I remarked as I scrubbed Delilah's bridle. "Max worked us hard today."

"You're telling me," Stevie agreed.

I sighed as loudly as I could. "Too bad I'm stuck heating up a lousy frozen dinner again tonight." I made my voice as sad as I could.

"Really? How come?" Stevie asked. "I thought your dad was a great cook." She's only met Dad quickly a couple of times when he's come to pick me up, but I guess I'd talked about him some.

"He is," I said.

I felt kind of sad suddenly, since I wanted to tell her about how Mom was a fantastic cook, too, before she got sick. Now she hardly cooks at all anymore, since she doesn't even feel like eating a lot of the time because of her treatments. I forced all that out of my mind. After all, I was doing this for Mom, right? I had to make it work.

"He is," I said again. "But he has to take Mom to the doctor tonight, so I'm on my own."

"You get to stay home by yourself when your parents are out?" Stevie actually looked sort of jealous. "My parents always get a baby-sitter." She snorted. "Unless they're only going out for a little while, and then they put Chad the Chump in charge. That's even worse."

I didn't bother to tell her that Mom and Dad always get Emily Robinson from across the street to come and watch me when they're not home. It didn't seem important at the moment, especially since Mom and Dad weren't even going to the doctor that night at all. "Um, sure," I said. "But it's kind of lonely sometimes."

Stevie immediately looked concerned. "Really? Well, then why don't you come to my house for dinner tonight? I'm sure my folks won't mind."

Bingo! I felt like cheering. Being creative was easier than I thought! "Really?" I said, pretending to think about it. "Thanks, Stevie. I guess that would be fun. Are you sure it's okay?"

Stevie grinned. "I'll go call home right now and check, if you'll finish cleaning Comanche's girth for me," she offered.

"Deal," I said with a smile, taking the sweaty girth from her.

A few minutes later, it was all set. Stevie's parents said of course it was fine for me to come, and I called my parents and told them. They were fine with it, too. Dad actually sounded kind of relieved when I asked him.

"Have a nice time, sweetie," he told me. "That Stevie seems like a really nice girl."

"She is, Dad." I smiled secretly to myself. Maybe someday soon, he and Mom will be saying the same thing about one of Stevie's brothers! (Well, except for the "girl" part, of course!)

Anyway, I'm writing this in Delilah's stall while I'm waiting for Stevie to get ready to go. Max is making her clean out stalls for an extra hour after lessons for a whole month because of the prank she pulled on Veronica a few weeks ago. I would help her, of course, except Max always keeps a close eye on her to make sure she does the work herself.

I hope she finishes soon. I can't wait to get over to her house and meet the man of my dreams! Or maybe I should say men of my dreams—Alex and Chad. I wonder which one I'll like better? Carole and Alex. Carole and Chad. Hmmm. They both sound okay. So I guess I'll just have to wait until I meet them—and hope I can make up my mind!

Dear Diary:

I just got back from Stevie's house—or maybe I should start saying Chad's house now, if he's going to be my new boyfriend! Yes, that's right—I think my plan is actually working!

I was disappointed at first when I found out Alex was having dinner at a friend's house that night and wouldn't be around. But I figured maybe that was just as well. Chad is older, after all, and that's what I decided I wanted, right?

155

By the way, I also met Stevie's parents for the first time. They're both lawyers, and they're really nice. It's funny how much Stevie looks like her mom. She doesn't think she does—she gave me a funny look when I said something about it—but it's true. They both have the exact same shade of dark blond hair, and the same chin and eyes. They even laugh the same way! I wonder if Mom and I look that much alike to other people. I never really thought about it. Probably not, I guess. Mom's so beautiful, even now when she's so thin and is losing her hair from her treatments. I just hope I start to look like her someday.

But back to my dinner at the Lakes' house. When we first got there (Stevie lives within walking distance of Pine Hollow—lucky!), the only brother who was around was Michael. I thought he was adorable at first—he's about seven years old, with this round face and these big innocent-looking eyes—but then he brought out his insect collection to show me, and I changed my mind about him. Especially since his insects are all alive!

Finally, when it was almost time to sit down to dinner, Chad got home from baseball practice. He turned out to be kind of tall and gangly, but cute I guess. You can definitely tell he's older than those boys I was talking to (or trying to talk to!) at Pine Hollow. He's also sort of hyper—he never sits still for a single second, sort of like Stevie. I guess that's good. It means he has a lot of energy.

Anyway, Stevie introduced us. "Hey, dork," she said as Chad walked in. "This is Carole."

Chad nodded politely at me. Then he looked at Stevie.

"So you tricked another poor innocent person into being your friend, huh, Skeevie?"

"Chad!" Mrs. Lake said sternly. "No name calling."

"But she called me a dork," Chad protested.

Stevie smirked. "That's because that's your name, dork."

"Stevie," Mrs. Lake said warningly.

I just kept smiling through all that, trying to act normal. But I was pretty nervous. I mean, I really wanted to make a good impression on Chad. I didn't want him to think I was too immature to be his girlfriend.

We sat down to dinner soon, and for a while Mr. and Mrs. Lake asked me all kinds of questions about myself, like what it's like living on a military base and how I adjusted to moving so much. But finally the two of them started chatting about some lawyer-type topic, and Stevie started talking to me about Pine Hollow.

Normally I would have been perfectly happy to talk about horses all day long, but Chad didn't seem that interested in the topic, so I figured maybe I should try to change the subject. When Stevie paused to take a bite of her food, I turned to her older brother with my brightest smile.

"So, Chad," I said. "Do you like horseback riding, too?"

Chad paused with his fork halfway to his mouth and stared at me in shock. Michael started snickering.

Stevie rolled her eyes. "You can take that as a no," she told me. "My brothers don't like anything cool like riding. They're more interested in idiotic hobbies like capturing reptiles from the backyard or watching boring kung fu movies."

"Oh." I wasn't sure how to respond to that. It wasn't

too hard to guess that Michael was the reptile chaser, so I figured that meant Chad was the one interested in kung fu. I tried to think of something to say on that topic, but my mind drew a blank. "Um, my dad's in the Marines," I told him at last.

It was kind of a stupid comment, I guess—I mean, what does that have to do with kung fu? Besides, he should have figured it out already from what I was talking about with his parents. But I wasn't sure he'd been paying attention to that, and besides, it was the only thing I could think of right then that might impress a guy like Chad. It seemed to do the trick.

"Really?" he said, looking at me for the first time with real interest. "That's cool. Has he ever been in active duty in a war?"

"Um, I don't think so," I said. "But he has a collection of antique war medals."

"Cool!" Chad said again. "Which wars are they from?"

"The war of the dorks," Stevie muttered under her breath.

I ignored her. "I'm not really sure," I said. "Uh, but you could come over to my house and see them sometime. If you want."

Stevie turned and goggled at me. "Carole, no! You don't want a dork like him in your house. It's bad enough I have to have him in my house."

Mr. Lake interrupted his conversation long enough to turn and glare at his daughter. "Stevie!" he said sharply. "What have we told you about name calling?"

"Sorry, Dad," she said contritely. As soon as he turned back to Mrs. Lake, she stuck her tongue out at Chad. "Dork," she mouthed silently.

Chad just grinned at her. Then he turned to me. "Why, thank you so much, Carole," he said. "I'd love to come and take a look at your dad's collection. When would be convenient for you?"

"Never," Stevie snapped. "Say never, Carole!"

"Um, anytime, I guess," I said, desperately trying to remember my mother's treatment schedule. I wanted to make sure she met Chad on a day when she was likely to be feeling well. "How about the day after tomorrow?"

"Wonderful!" Chad smiled at me. "How's four-thirty? I can stop by right after baseball practice."

So that was that! I had a date! At first I couldn't wait to tell Mom. Then I thought about it and decided to surprise her instead. I just told her a friend was stopping by for a visit. She looked pretty happy about that. "Is it that lovely girl Stevie Lake?" she asked.

"Um, not exactly," I said, trying not to giggle.

Speaking of Stevie, she didn't seem too happy about the whole situation. She kept grumbling about how I would regret ever letting a dork like Chad in my house, and how I was just too nice and trusting for my own good. But I'm sure she'll get used to seeing me and Chad together before long.

And I know Mom will love him!

Dear Diary:

This day started out totally embarrassing, but it ended up okay. Chad was so late getting to my house that I was afraid he wasn't coming at all. But he finally rang the bell at ten minutes to five.

"Come on in," I told him, feeling kind of shy. "I want you to meet my mother."

He nodded agreeably. "Is your dad home yet?"

"Uh, not yet," I said.

Chad looked a little disappointed. "Too bad. I wanted to ask him some stuff about the Marines." He glanced at his watch. "Maybe I should stop by some other time when he's here."

"No!" I cried in a panic. "I mean, he might get home soon. Why don't you come meet Mom now?"

He shrugged. "Okay."

I led the way to the kitchen, where Mom was reading a magazine and sipping some tea. She looked tired, but otherwise nobody who didn't know better would guess that she had cancer. Her thinning hair was covered by a bright scarf, and she was dressed in jeans and a sweatshirt.

"Hey, Mom," I said. "I want to introduce, uh, a special friend of mine. Chad Lake."

Mom gave me a surprised look. But she smiled politely at Chad. "Hello," she said. "It's always nice to meet Carole's friends."

"Nice to meet you, too, Mrs., uh . . ." Chad looked helpless.

I suddenly realized that he didn't even know my last name! "Hanson," I supplied quickly, feeling my cheeks turn red. "Mrs. Hanson."

Chad just nodded, looking sheepish. He glanced around the kitchen. "Nice house." He looked a little uncomfortable. "Uh, so do you mind if we go take a look at those war medals now? I sort of need to get home soon."

"Oh, are you sure you have to go?" I said quickly. "Why don't you stay for dinner?"

Out of the corner of my eye I saw Mom giving me another surprised look. But that was nothing compared to the strange glance Chad gave me. "Is Stevie up to something?" he asked suddenly. "Come on, tell me. Is that what's going on? There actually are no old war medals, are there?"

"What?" I had no idea what he was talking about. But I had the unpleasant feeling that I was losing control of things. "Of course there are. They're in the den. This way."

I hurried out of the kitchen. Moments later, Chad was bent over Dad's collection. He seemed pretty impressed, and he kept talking about different battles and stuff. But I wasn't really listening. This date wasn't going anything like I'd planned, and I wasn't sure what to do about it.

When he finished looking over the medals, he stood up straight and glanced toward the front door. "Okay, well, thanks," he said. "I guess I'd better—"

At that moment I spotted Mom coming into the room. I knew I had to do something, and fast, if I was going to convince her that I had a boyfriend. So I did the only thing I

161

could think of. I grabbed Chad's hand and held it. "Okay," I said, smiling up at him. "Thanks for coming over, Chad."

He jerked his hand away, seeming startled. "What are you doing?" he said. "I'm telling you, when I get ahold of Stevie . . ." He shook his head and raced off, an angry and confused look on his face.

I slumped down onto the couch as the front door slammed. Mom had been standing in the doorway, watching the whole thing. Now she came forward. "Carole, sweetie," she said softly.

"Leave me alone," I muttered, burying my face in my hands. I felt ready to cry. How could I have been so stupid? Now I'd scared Chad away, and my plan was ruined. "I don't want to talk about it."

Mom sat down on the couch beside me. A second later I felt her warm hand stroking my hair. "Carole," she said gently. "You really don't have to do this."

"What do you mean?" I asked.

Mom grabbed my chin, tilting it up so that she could look into my face. "Oh, sweetie," she said, her voice sort of thick and sad. "Don't you think I've noticed how hard you've been trying these past few weeks? I mean, all the picnics, the museums . . ."

I gulped. "I'm sorry," I whispered. "I was just trying to help." I blinked back a few tears.

Mom pulled me to her and hugged me tight for a long moment. "Thank you, sweetie," she murmured into my ear. "Thank you for doing that, for wanting to make me feel better. For creating so many nice memories. But maybe it

162

would be better if we just looked for special moments as they come." She pulled back and smiled at me. "Like this one, for instance."

"What do you mean?"

"I mean sometimes we get so busy we start to miss the little things, like sitting in the den hugging each other," she said, brushing my hair out of my face. "If you're too busy doing anything, even something wonderful like trying to make someone else happy, you can end up not really enjoying your life. You know?"

I nodded. I was starting to see what she meant, a little. Still, I didn't like the idea of wasting time waiting for her to get better. I mean, who knows how long that could take?

As if reading my mind, sort of, Mom spoke again. "And honey, please remember: Nobody knows how long they're going to have together or what's going to happen next. The best thing to do is just to live for today, try to appreciate all the times you have, good and bad, large moments and small ones."

That idea was kind of scary, but it made sense, too. I nodded again as I thought about it. "Okay," I told her. "I'll try."

Mom hugged me again, smiling. "Me too, sweetie," she promised. "Me too."

CAROLE HANSON'S RIDING JOURNAL:

I can't believe I haven't written about the dressage exhibition at Cross County yet! It was over a week ago already. I

163

meant to make some notes in this journal while I was watching, but I was so distracted by other things that I forgot.

We first heard about the exhibition when Phil mentioned it to Stevie a couple of days after she first met No-Name. It turned out that he wanted her to come over and give him some pointers. Personally, I think he was probably just looking for an excuse to spend more time with her; but when I told her that, she just turned up her nose and sniffed. "Face it, Carole. You're not the only amateur riding instructor around here."

She was kidding, of course. I think she was just as thrilled about spending time at Phil's as he was at having her there. Maybe more, actually. She was already totally intrigued with No-Name.

So she went over there to watch Phil and Teddy practice their dressage test for the rally. Of course, as soon as she did, she saw that Phil didn't really need any pointers. He and Teddy are both good at dressage and were doing just fine by themselves.

That's when Stevie and Phil came up with their plan. They decided to do a dressage duet at the rally. Leave it to those two to think of something like that!

But there's more. We were sitting around the tack room a day or two after that, trying to explain to Lisa's friend Hollie why dressage is so important. (We'd just spent an unmounted Horse Wise meeting listening to a new speaker Max brought in. She's a dressage judge, and even though her topic was interesting, she had kind of a blah way of presenting it, so I guess Hollie hadn't thought it was very much fun.)

164

"Riding isn't so different from learning to act," Lisa told Hollie. "You have to master technique, study the greats, and tune your instrument."

"I didn't know you played an instrument," Stevie said, popping open a soda can and glancing at Hollie.

"An actor's body is her instrument," Lisa explained. "She has to keep it fit and well tuned."

"Same thing with dressage," Stevie said. "Horses are basically kind of stiff and bulky. Dressage makes them supple and graceful."

"It's a total body workout," Lisa added.

"And a total mind workout," I reminded her. "The heart of dressage is rider-horse communication. It has to be based on a set of shared signals, which can be anything from the pressure of a knee to a slight change in the balance of the rider."

I was getting ready to go on in more detail, but Stevie interrupted. "It's like dancing," she said suddenly. "That's what it's really like. When things are going right, you and the horse don't even have to communicate with each other— you just know."

That was pretty poetic stuff for Stevie, but it was accurate, too. Hollie seemed to catch on at last. "I know what you mean," she said, sitting up straight. "When you're performing, you have to forget about everything you've learned and dance the music. You have to dance it like you're hearing it for the first time, as if you don't know what note comes next."

"That's it!" This time Stevie jumped up from her seat on a

tack trunk, sloshing her soda all over her breeches. She looked really excited. "I was telling Phil that we needed to add something extra to the dressage exhibition, something with music." She looked at Hollie. "You could help us. You could be our choreographer!"

Hollie was a little skeptical at first, but Stevie can talk anyone into anything when she puts her mind to it. Before long, it was all settled. Hollie and Stevie started planning their masterpiece right away, and when Phil heard about it, he was just as excited as they were.

At that point the only thing that seemed like a possible problem was Hollie's cold. She'd been sneezing and stuffy off and on ever since she'd started coming to Pine Hollow with us. Stevie hoped that her cold wouldn't get in the way of her choreography.

Stevie and Phil started practicing as much as they could. They also got Lisa to agree to sing the song they'd decided to use, *Always*, for the rally. In the meantime, Stevie was still trying to figure out the cause of No-Name's allergies. She was trying to expose her to different possible allergens one at a time, but she couldn't seem to pinpoint the thing that was causing the hives.

Speaking of allergies—I don't remember exactly what day it was, but the four of us (me, Lisa, Stevie, and Hollie) were at TD's one day when we finally figured out the real story behind Hollie's "cold." See, while we were eating, Hollie's mother came by to pick her up. The way Hollie rushed her mom out of the restaurant, like she didn't want us to have a chance to talk to her, made us wonder. Finally, from a few things Hollie had said, we realized that she was allergic, just like No-Name. Only Hollie was allergic to *horses*! That's why she'd seemed to have a cold for so long. And why she always got all stuffed up when she was at Pine Hollow and sounded fine the rest of the time. My friends and I were pretty stunned when we figured it out. I, for one, couldn't imagine anything more horrible. Poor Hollie!

"I guess she doesn't want her mother to know she's allergic to horses," Stevie said.

"But we know," Lisa pointed out. "Do you think we should do something? Should we tell someone?"

I was still thinking about how awful it would be to wheeze and sneeze anytime I got near Starlight. "Hollie has a good time with us," I said. "I think she really enjoys hanging out with The Saddle Club and learning more about horses."

Lisa nodded. "I was worried about her being lonely after *Annie* finished."

"What's the big deal, anyway?" Stevie commented. "She coughs, she sniffles, she sneezes from time to time. That's nothing compared to not being able to ride."

So that settled it. "If Hollie wants to keep her allergy a secret, it's a secret," Lisa said firmly, speaking for all three of us. "That's what friends are for."

That took care of Hollie's allergies, at least for the moment. No-Name's were another story. By the day of the dressage exhibition, Stevie still had no idea what was causing them. Luckily, though, the mare was showing no signs of an outbreak that day, which meant that Stevie would be able to ride her in the exhibition.

We were all there to cheer her on, of course. Max had decided our whole class should go to watch the exhibition as a learning opportunity. Lisa, Hollie, and I found seats near the front of the bleachers by the main ring. Mr. Baker stood up and welcomed everyone to Cross County Stables, then explained the day's events.

"We'll start with a medley of dressage steps by members of Cross County," he said into the microphone. "And then we'll end with a duet by Phil Marsten and Stevie Lake, which incorporates these steps into a choreographed event."

Lisa and I exchanged looks when we heard that. "A choreographed event?" Lisa whispered. "That sounds a lot fancier than *horse dance!*"

I giggled, then turned to watch as the Cross County riders entered the ring. Their demonstration was really interesting. When it ended, Mr. Baker and the dressage judge he'd invited said a few words. Meanwhile, Lisa slipped away to get ready for her song.

Soon Mr. Baker introduced Phil and Stevie, and they entered the ring as Lisa sang the first few words. I was really impressed with Hollie's choreography. She'd worked it out so that the horses really did seem to be dancing with each other, sort of. And of course, the whole time they were actually demonstrating just how carefully Stevie and Phil had worked with them.

I was even more impressed with No-Name. Even though she'd come from a bulk lot and nobody knew much about her, it was obvious she'd had some dressage training, or there

168

was no way Stevie could have gotten her to perform so well in just a short time.

Anyway, the crowd loved the performance. And one of the best things that happened that day was that Stevie finally did figure out what was causing No-Name's hives. It turns out she's allergic to weeds! Stevie was pretty proud of herself for figuring that out. See, the day of the exhibition she tied No-Name in a different spot than she usually did. No hives. And when Stevie went back to look at the first spot, she saw that it was full of weeds.

To celebrate all of that, Stevie and Phil decided they were in the mood for more riding after the show—namely, a nice long trail ride. Mr. Baker was so happy that Stevie had figured out No-Name's problem that he offered to supply horses for me and Lisa and Hollie, too. So the five of us set out, along with Phil's friend A.J., who'd been in the demonstration.

We rode out of the stable area and across some flat land and through the woods for a while before coming to a clearing with a fierce-looking outcropping of rock. Phil stopped Teddy and gestured for the rest of us to gather around and listen.

"I know you're used to the country around Pine Hollow," he said, "so I have to warn you that under the grass there are rocks, and in the bushes there are ravines. Be sure to stay on the trail, because the footing here is full of surprises." He looked around to make sure we all understood.

"I've dot it," Hollie said. "I'll stay dight on the drail." Stevie, Lisa, and I knew that she was talking funny because

169

her allergies were acting up, though none of us said a word about it to Phil or A.J.—or Hollie herself, of course.

We rode on, enjoying the wild landscape and the nice late-autumn day. I'm not sure how long we'd been on the trail when Phil led us to a rise, from where we could see a sliver of water winding through the green fields far below. "That's the Silverado River," he told Hollie, who was next to him.

"It's fantastic," she said. But she didn't sound right. The words came out slowly and painfully, as if she had to force them.

"Are you okay?" Stevie asked her.

Hollie didn't respond at first. Instead she was taking shallow breaths that didn't seem to satisfy her.

"I'm dine!" she said at last, tossing her head carelessly. But I couldn't help noticing that she had turned pale, and there were faint bluish shadows under her eyes.

A.J., who had just met Hollie that day, looked concerned. "You look like you're going to faint," he told her.

"It's her horse allergy," Stevie explained. She reached across to feel Hollie's forehead. "You're allergic to horses, aren't you, Hollie? Tell us the truth."

Hollie didn't answer. Her eyes were glassy and vague, and her skin was getting still paler.

"Can you hear me?" Stevie shouted at her, looking worried. "Hello!"

Hollie turned her head toward her slightly. "Yes," she whispered. It came out as a horrible wheezing sound.

I was feeling really scared by then. Hollie looked awful.

"We've got to get her back," I said, my voice shaking a little. "She's got to get to the hospital."

We knew that carrying Hollie on horseback wasn't going to help any with her allergic reaction, but there wasn't any other option. "Help me put her on No-Name," Stevie told Phil. "We've got to move her fast."

Phil looked a little doubtful, and I guessed he was thinking the same thing I was. No-Name was an untested horse. Who knew how she'd react to a second rider? But Phil did as Stevie said, and soon Hollie was sitting on No-Name's back in front of Stevie.

They took off as fast as they could go on the rocky trail, veering off at the bottom of the rise into the dark hemlock forest to one side. The rest of us followed more slowly, not wanting to risk the other horses' safety—or our own—on the challenging trail.

We reached the stable shortly after Stevie. She had gotten Hollie onto the grass, where she was sort of slumped over, and was shouting for help. But the stable was deserted. Everyone had left for lunch or somewhere after the exhibition.

We were pretty panicky. Hollie didn't look good at all. I was afraid that if we didn't get her some medical help soon, she might not make it.

Luckily, Stevie had learned a lot about allergies that week because of No-Name. Of course, what she knew about was mostly horse allergies, but I guess she figured she had to try something. So while Lisa called an ambulance and then Max, so that he could track down Hollie's parents, Stevie

171

sent me for Cross County's first aid kit. When I brought it, she took out the EpiPen, which Judy Barker had taught her how to use to treat equine allergies. Stevie broke it open and gave Hollie a shot. And miracle of miracles, it worked! Hollie's eyelids fluttered, and she started to look a tiny bit better. By the time the ambulance arrived, she was sitting up and asking what had happened. Stevie showed the ambulance attendants the EpiPen as they checked Hollie's breathing.

"That was a good move," the attendant told Stevie. "I think you saved your friend's life."

They took her off to the hospital, and in the end she was fine. But Stevie, Lisa, and I realized it had been really stupid of us to keep the secret about Hollie's allergies. We've decided we're never going to do anything like that again. Because if it hadn't been for No-Name's incredible bravery—Stevie still can't stop talking about how the mare plowed through brambles and over rocks and down steep hills without the slightest protest—and the good luck of Stevie's knowing about the EpiPen, things might have turned out really horribly.

But our Saddle Club luck held this time. Not only is Hollie as good as new, but after the whole incident was over, Stevie's parents dropped a huge, wonderful bombshell on her. They'd bought No-Name from Mr. Baker. Isn't that great? See, they'd noticed how crazy Stevie was about the mare. And they knew how much Stevie had been wanting a horse of her own ever since the time last summer when she almost bought Stewball. Well, okay, even before that. And when they saw how brave and heroic No-Name was during Hollie's emergency, they knew she was the horse for Stevie.

Stevie's thrilled beyond belief, of course. She and No-Name are perfect for each other. The Marstens brought her over to Pine Hollow last week, and she's all settled in now in the stall next to Starlight's. Now all Stevie has to do is come up with a name for her. She's certainly taking her time about that. I named Starlight the day I got him!

Needless to say, Hollie hasn't been riding with us since all this happened. She told us her doctors may be able to work out some kind of special medication so that she can go horseback riding once in a while, but for now she has to stay away from the stable altogether. I guess it's a good thing she's so crazy about acting, instead of being horse-crazy like me and my friends. After getting to know her lately, I've really come to respect how strongly she feels about acting. I mean, she loves it so much that she already knows it's what she wants to do with her life. I only wish I were that certain about what I want to do. . . .

Actually, I've realized that one possibility I haven't spent much time considering yet is becoming an equine vet, like Judy Barker. After everything we've all learned about allergies lately (human and equine), I think I'm more impressed than ever with everything Judy has to know to be so good at her job.

Hmmm. My friends are always teasing me about being a walking horse encyclopedia. Maybe that's a sign that I should follow in Judy's bootprints. . . .

FROM:	CamNelson
TO:	HorseGal
SUBJECT:	Merry Christmas!
MESSAGE:	

Hi! I hope you're having a great holiday. Did you get any presents that have to do with horses? (Ha ha!) I did. I got a new turnout sheet for Duffy, a nice pair of all-weather riding gloves, and a bunch of horse books. One of the books is a guide to horse behavior, one's about combined training, and the other is a mystery about show jumping. (I think my mom gave me that last one because she wants to read it herself!)

Anyway, I hope you're doing well. Maybe we'll get to see each other during our school breaks. Say hi to Starlight for me, and your human friends, too.

CAROLE HANSON'S RIDING JOURNAL:

It's funny how things happen sometimes. Whenever Christmas approaches I always start feeling kind of bitter-sweet, even though it's still my favorite holiday. This year was no different. I was looking forward to a nice, quiet holiday with Dad and a school break full of riding and more riding. Then, right before vacation, my teacher assigned a family tree project, saying we should try to talk to our relatives over the break and study our families through oral history, which means getting relatives to talk.

Well, that sounded pretty interesting, and it didn't take me long to decide I wanted to concentrate on Mom's side of the family. I really don't know that much about them, and I thought it would be really interesting to find out. I was pretty excited about it when I told Dad, but at first he didn't seem interested in the project at all. I soon found out why. He was just hiding a surprise for me: We're going to Minnesota to stay with my relatives over the break! It's all arranged. We leave right after Christmas and we're staying for almost a week.

I can't wait. I already know I have two aunts on Mom's side. One is Aunt Elaine, who lives in North Carolina. The other is Mom's younger sister, Jessie, who lives in Minnesota with her brother, my uncle John, Uncle John's wife (Aunt Lily), my great-grandmother, Grand Alice, and my cousin Louise, who's just a couple of years younger than me. Actually, my grandparents also live on the farm part of the year, but they're down in Arizona for the winter.

I can't believe Dad arranged this trip for me. It's the greatest Christmas present ever! (Well, except for Starlight, of course.) I can't wait to see my relatives again after all this time and ask them about our ancestors for my project. At the same time, I have to admit I'm kind of sad to miss a whole school holiday of riding and hanging out with my friends at Pine Hollow. I'm going to miss the latest Saddle Club project, which is planning a birthday party for Prancer and Topside and the other Thoroughbreds at Pine Hollow. It was Lisa who thought of that. She remembered that every registered Thoroughbred officially turns one year older on January first.

But I'm still glad we're going. I'm really excited about getting to see Mom's relatives again, especially after reading parts of my old diary recently. I want to know more about her life, especially the parts before I was born. Who knows? Maybe learning more about Mom will tell me more about myself, too. And maybe that will help me figure out what I'm meant to do with my life.

Because that e-mail I got from Cam, where he talked about that combined training book he got, just reminded me how much time I've wasted already trying to make up my mind. I was planning to take care of this question way back in June. Here it is, December already, and I'm no closer to an answer!

So maybe this trip really is just the push I need. As soon as my family tree project is finished, no more excuses. I'm going to sit down and figure out which career is right for me.

FAMILY TREE NOTEBOOK:

Well, here I am in Nyberg, Minnesota! It seemed to take forever to get here—we had to take two planes to get to northeastern Minnesota, and then Uncle John and Louise, who picked us up at the airport, told us it was another two hours' drive in their four-wheel-drive vehicle. Plus it was so cold outside that I started to wish I'd packed my electric blanket. Actually, I kind of wished I was *wearing* it! The thermometer at the airport said it was negative five degrees. Yes, that's right—*negative* five! But when we finally arrived at the farm, which is just outside the tiny town of Nyberg, my relatives gave Dad and me a really warm welcome that made up for the cold weather. Well, most of them did, anyway.

I want to write down a few things that may be useful for my project. First, something kind of weird happened when we were chatting on the way here from the airport. I asked Uncle John to tell me about the family.

"Well," he said, giving me his wide, friendly smile in the rearview mirror. "You've met me, and now Louise. Your aunt Lily, my devoted wife, is more of the same. You'll like her. And your aunt Jessie is the baby sister—she's thirty-four."

"She's the greatest!" Louise interrupted. "She takes photographs and sells them to magazines all over the country. She's very talented, you know."

I was a little surprised at her enthusiasm. Louise had been kind of quiet before then—almost unfriendly, I couldn't help thinking, although maybe that's just because Uncle John is so friendly and talkative.

"I remember hearing Mom talk about Aunt Jessie," I said. "Didn't she used to live in New York?"

There was a long pause.

"Well—" Uncle John began at last.

But Louise jumped in. "Don't talk to Aunt Jessie about New York," she told me fiercely. "Carole, don't *ever* talk to Aunt Jessie about New York."

I was a little confused by that. I didn't say anything, though, and Uncle John started talking about Grand Alice and how she would be able to tell me a lot about the family.

He was right about that. . . . But I'll get to that in a minute.

When we arrived at the farm, everyone was there to greet us, including the family dog, a big, hairy, friendly mutt named Ginger. A little later we ate dinner, then Louise showed me around the farm, which is really more of a compound. There are several different buildings with living quarters for the whole family, most of them connected by covered walkways because it's so cold and snowy a lot of the time. My favorite building, of course, was the barn. There are four horses living there. Jiminy Cricket, a registered Morgan, is Louise's horse. Aunt Jessie has a beautiful Arabian mare named Kismet. And there's also a couple of big workhorses named Sugar and Spice.

"I know a horse named Spice," I told Louise, remembering the mare that had come to Pine Hollow to be bred with Max's stallion, Geronimo. "She's a Thoroughbred."

Louise laughed. "This Spice is no Thoroughbred. He and Sugar are plain old mixed-breed part-draft workhorses." She patted Spice on his shaggy back, which looked as thick and rough as a polar bear's. "We actually still use them for chores, especially in the wintertime. They start a lot more reliably than the tractor."

When Louise and I got back to the main house, we found that Louise's friend Christina Johnson, a neighbor from down the road, had stopped in to visit on her snowmobile. I liked her right away. She has a really open, welcoming way about her and a friendly smile. (Unlike my cousin. I know that's not very nice, but I can't help it. For some reason, Louise seems to be on her guard with me, even though we're related and everything.)

178

Anyway, pretty soon after that we all gathered in the living room to talk and toast marshmallows. That's when Grand Alice told a story about one of our ancestors. I'm writing it down because that's what I'm supposed to do for my project, even though I'm not sure it's something I want anyone outside our family to know about. It makes me feel weird to think about what Grand Alice told me about Jackson Foley—but never mind. I'm going to try to write it down just the way she told it.

My late husband's great-grandfather was born into slavery on a cotton plantation in the middle of Georgia. No one knows quite where it was—ol' Jackson never told what his master's name had been, and when he got away from there he didn't bother to read the road signs on his way out. So we don't know who owned him—owned, Carole, think on that—or where it was he was born. Master had given him the name Jackson Washington.

He had a wife. He had three little babies, born one after another, scarcely a year apart. Then one day he had a chance to escape. The Underground Railroad. A train, so to speak, had come for him.

I don't blame him for leaving. I don't blame him one bit. Think what it meant: freedom! The work he did would be his own; the money he earned, his own to spend. He could go where he pleased. He could name his own children, instead of having Master do it for him. And those children, growing up, could not be sold away from him. Freedom is a mighty and precious thing, but I don't think any of us, here in this room, can understand what it must have meant to a person who was born a slave. So I say, I don't blame ol' Jackson for leaving.

179

His babies were too young to go—too young to keep quiet during all those dark and dangerous nights of travel. His wife, they say, would not leave her children. But Jackson, he had to go. He promised her that he would come back for them, just as soon as he earned the money to buy their freedom.

Well, word came back to them by that same Underground Railroad. Jackson had made it safe to the North. They heard he was in Boston. They heard he had a job and was working hard. Then they heard nothing. A few years went by.

The Civil War began. It became impossible to send messages between the North and the South. Finally the war ended, and the slaves were freed. Jackson Washington's family didn't know what to do. They didn't know how to find him. They didn't know if he was dead or alive. They thought he was dead, for sure. The children—two boys and a girl—were now eight, nine, and ten years old. With their mother, they set off north to find their daddy.

They went to Boston and found that Jackson had been there but had moved on, so they moved on, too. There were freedmen's societies—blacks helping blacks find their families. Many families had been split apart by slavery. With the societies' help, that woman and those children tracked Jackson Washington from place to place. They looked for him for the better part of two years, working when they needed to, traveling when they could. They found him finally. I'm guessing that they wished they never did.

Jackson was working for a logging company in a tiny town in Minnesota, on the Great Northern Railway line near the Mississippi River. Name of the town was Foley. Jackson, never much liking the name Washington, had changed his name to Foley, too.

180

He'd given the name Foley to his wife. And to their four children.

When Grand Alice said that, I wasn't sure I'd understood her right. "But his wife and children were looking for him," I said.

"His first wife and children," Grand Alice corrected. "His second wife and children were with him in Foley." She sighed. "I don't blame him for leaving. I sure do blame him for never going back."

Aunt Jessie spoke up then. Her dark eyes were angry. "You see, Carole, slave marriages weren't legal. Legally, only Jackson Foley's second wife was actually married to him."

"But legally—What difference did *legally* make?" I was horrified. "While they waited and waited for him, and tried so hard to find him, he'd just given them up?"

"He'd just given up," Grand Alice confirmed sadly. "Apparently he'd decided that he'd never be able to afford to buy his first family's freedom, so he just started over. He didn't know the war would come, of course. He didn't know they'd all soon be free. But I say, he shouldn't have given up." She set her mouth in a firm line and folded and unfolded her hands.

"What happened next?" Christina asked.

"There was a ruckus that shook the streets of Foley. My husband's grandfather was the eldest of the second batch of children—he was five years old—and he could remember the women shouting back and forth and the children crying. Finally, Jackson's first wife and children renounced him and his lack of courage. They went back to Boston. His second wife stayed on, but I don't know if she forgave him. They'd had four children together already." Grand Alice chuckled. "They never had another after that. But that's where we come from, all of us Foleys."

"What happened to the Washington family?" I asked.

"No one knows, honey. No one knows."

So that was the story. It's really given me a lot to think about. Actually, my whole family has given me a lot to think about. While love and warmth seem to pour from Aunt Lily, Uncle John, and Grand Alice, Aunt Jessie seems to hold herself away from me, and Louise is so friendly to Jessie and Christina but not to me.

Worst of all, I can't seem to stop thinking about my great-great-great-great-grandfather, Jackson Washington/Foley, and the way he betrayed his own wife and children. I'd already known there was a runaway slave in my family history, but I had always figured he was a hero, a brave man—not a traitor. Were all my ancestors like him?

And if they were, what does that say about me?

FAMILY TREE NOTEBOOK:

Well, the new year starts in just a few hours, so I thought I should sit and write down what's been happening in the past few days here in Minnesota. Everyone else is resting or cooking or otherwise getting ready for the big neighborhood New Year's Eve party, which is at Christina's house this year. It should be fun.

Let's see, where did I leave off? Oh, right—Jackson Foley. Hmmm. Well, maybe it's time to write about some other stuff. Like how much fun I had exploring the area the other day with Christina on her snowmobile. Maybe I shouldn't write about that, since it doesn't really have anything to do with my family tree. As much as I like Christina, she's not a relative.

Okay. Then what else? I could write about how snotty Aunt Jessie can be—but that probably isn't something I want to include in my project, either. It's just that she makes me mad sometimes. Like the other day, after I came in from snowmobiling with Christina, I was telling Dad what Christina had told me about how up here in Minnesota, snowmobiles are real transportation, just like cars are where we live. Aunt Jessie happened to be at the sink, and she turned around with a smirk. "I'm sure to a delicate child like you, coming here from way down South is something of a novelty," she said in this sarcastic tone. "You don't even know what winter is, or what it means to be up here in the wilderness. Up here, the roads aren't always passable, and the phones don't always work. We have to take care of ourselves. You wouldn't know how to do that. You'd better let Louise take care of you when you go riding later."

I didn't say anything, but I felt really hurt by her words. I know I wasn't raised up here, and I'm not used to winter the way they know it in Minnesota. But I can take care of myself!

I couldn't help thinking that Jessie was a little bit like Jackson Foley. She didn't seem to care much about me, just

183

like Jackson didn't care about his family. Of course, I'm related to both of them, and I don't know what to think about that. . . .

Louise and I went riding after that, and that was fun, even though I had to put on more clothes to protect myself than I would wear in a whole week back home. It was great seeing the woods from Kismet's saddle—all that snow made things really peaceful and beautiful. Louise showed me all the sights, including this dramatic spot called Lover's Point. It's a spot over a lake where this huge pile of rocks juts into the sky. It's really wild and really special. Louise says they climb on the rocks sometimes during the summer, but it's way too dangerous now because of the snow.

"But Aunt Jessie is going to go out there at midnight during the next full moon," Louise added. "She's going to take a picture of the moon rising over the lake. She's not afraid."

I was surprised and kind of worried, especially when Louise said that Jessie planned to make the trip by horseback. But Louise didn't seem very concerned. I just hope she's mistaken about what she said.

But never mind about that now. I'm tired of thinking about Aunt Jessie and Louise. Besides, I still haven't written anything about my visit to Grand Alice's apartment. I was a little nervous when she invited me over there for a private talk and a cup of tea. I wasn't sure I was ready for any more family surprises, like the story about Jackson Foley.

But Grand Alice's apartment immediately helped me relax. It was sunny and colorful, with lots of plants and a bright quilt on the bed. Also, it turns out that Grand Alice is a

184

painter. There's a whole series of her watercolors decorating one wall. Another whole wall is lined with Jessie's photographs. I hadn't really looked at any of my aunt's photos up close before that, and I was impressed by them, especially by one that was an extreme close-up of a row of icicles.

That's winter, I thought when I saw it. *That's what winter feels like around here.*

"There's more than one way of looking at things," Grand Alice told me as I was looking at the photos. "Some angles are more interesting than others, but some are just more confusing. When Jessie takes photographs, she goes hunting for different angles. Problem is, she sometimes does the same thing in her life."

I wasn't sure what she meant by that, so I waited for her to explain. She poured me a cup of tea, then reached down and pulled a small wooden box out from under the table.

"I got this ready for you when I heard you were coming," she told me, handing me the box. "I can't be sure what I'm telling you is true, nobody can, but this is the story that's been passed down, generation to generation, on my side of the family. My mother told me. Her mother told her. Way back, to at least the late eighteenth century, one woman told another. The story is that the first woman in my family came over from Africa on the slave boats and brought this with her, around her neck."

I opened the box. It was lined with yellowed satin. Inside was a small, finely carved wooden amulet on a leather thong. I held it up and saw that it was the figure of a four-footed animal—a horse was the first thing I thought of, but it might be

185

a donkey or even a zebra. The wood was dark and smooth and the carving was really good. I held it up to the sunlight pouring through Grand Alice's large windows, amazed that something so delicate had survived first a trip in a slave boat and then over two hundred years, passed down from hand to hand . . . to my hand. The thought of the little amulet's history took my breath away.

I thanked Grand Alice, then flung my arms around her, feeling a little choked up. I never would have thought that anyone in my family would have such a treasure—let alone myself.

We drank our tea, then Grand Alice pulled out some photo albums to show me. She started with a big black album whose stiff cover crackled with age. "These are the old ones," she said. "There aren't too many of them—photographs were a rare luxury in those days. We start with Jackson Foley. Here he is."

I was surprised to see that Jackson Foley looked like an ordinary person, not like a villain. He was thin and slightly stooped, and he looked a little stiff in his formal clothes, but he was smiling and his eyes looked kind.

She showed me a lot more old pictures then. I'd forgotten to bring this notebook, so I jotted down the names and info on a piece of paper she gave me. I already put it in my suitcase so that I wouldn't lose it before I write my report.

After we looked through the old album, we moved on to more recent ones. She showed me a lot of pictures of my mother when she was young. Those were my favorites. I noticed that Mom even looked a little like me when she was my age! We looked at lots of pictures of her playing with John and Elaine, and some with her holding Jessie, who was quite a bit younger. There were also photos from a little later, after Mom met Dad. I giggled when I saw one of those. "I've never seen my father with that much hair," I said.

Grand Alice nodded and smiled. "First thing the Marines did was shave it all off."

There was also a picture I recognized, because we have a copy at home. It was Mom and Dad holding me when I was a baby. After we looked at that one, Grand Alice turned the page of the album again, then very quickly flipped it forward to the next page. But I had already seen the picture she'd tried to skip. It was Jessie, perhaps ten years younger than she is now. She was standing in front of the Statue of Liberty in New York, a huge smile on her face. A tall man stood with his arms around her, and Jessie was holding a young girl, two or three years old, with pigtails and a smile that matched Jessie's own.

"But who was—" I started to say.

"We don't talk about that."

"But I thought—"

"We don't talk about that," Grand Alice repeated firmly. And that was the end of that. But I can't help being curious. Who are that man and that child? Is this another family skeleton?

I still have no idea. And wondering about all the things that might be hiding in my family's past was making me kind of homesick. So I was thrilled when Lisa and Stevie called to say hi. They told me that my friend Karenna Richards was visiting Willow Creek. I'm sorry to be missing her, but it sounds like Stevie and Lisa are showing her a good time. They even arranged for her to ride Starlight on a trail ride, which is really nice.

After we hung up, I felt more homesick than ever. So when Aunt Jessie wandered by and started making snotty comments, I couldn't help defending myself. Somehow I ended up mentioning how I'd gone to watch the American Horse Show in New York. "Did you go to the American when you were in New York?" I asked Jessie.

She sort of flinched when I said the words *New York*. "No, I never went there." She looked confused for a second, then her face turned angry and hard. "I never was *in* New York," she went on. "That part of my life is dead. Gone. Over!" She ran out of the room.

"What did I say?" I asked Louise, who was the only other person in the room.

"I told you not to talk about New York in front of Aunt Jessie," Louise snapped, looking worried. She got up and ran after Jessie.

I felt bad. I hadn't meant to upset Aunt Jessie, but I couldn't imagine why the mere mention of the words *New York* was enough to set her off like that. Then I remembered the man and child with Jessie in the photo. Could they be Jessie's husband and daughter? Could Jessie have abandoned them in New York, just like Jackson Foley had abandoned his family all those generations ago?

I've got to stop thinking about it. It's been driving me crazy ever since. Anyway, I should probably sign off now and

188

go get changed for the party. It's taken me a while to write this, mostly because I keep stopping to look down at the necklace Grand Alice gave me. So far the little horse amulet seems to be the one thing about this trip that isn't confusing or mysterious or upsetting—just wonderful.

FROM:	Steviethegreat
TO:	HorseGal
CC:	LAtwood
SUBJECT:	WELCOME BACK!!!!!!!!!!!!!!!!!!!!!!!!!!
MESSAGE:	

I know you aren't due home until late tonight, and for some crazy reason my parents frown on my making phone calls after midnight. But I wanted to be the first one to welcome you home and tell you it's about time you got back here. We all missed you like crazy! (Especially Starlight, ha ha!)

So how was Minnesota? Let me guess—COLD! I looked up that town where you were in my dad's atlas, and it's so far north I thought it had to be, like, Canada or someplace. Oh well—at least you probably got to see some snow, right? I wish it snowed more around here.

But never mind that. Your first order of business now that you've returned (besides telling us all about your trip, that is) is giving me your opinion of my latest brilliant name ideas for

No-Name. (You too, Lisa—that's why I'm sending this to you, too, in case you didn't figure that out.) Here's the list:
    Dirham
    Tunisia
    Sandy (as in desert, get it?)
    Tripoli
    Shahrina
What do you think? Call first thing tomorrow. We've got a whole bunch of trail rides and Saddle Club meetings to fit into the next forty-eight hours before school starts again!!!

FROM:	LAtwood
TO:	HorseGal
CC:	Steviethegreat
SUBJECT:	WELCOME BACK!!!!!!!!!!!!!!!!!!!!!!!!! (2)
MESSAGE:	

Hi, Carole! Ditto for me on the welcome-home stuff in Stevie's e-mail. It seemed like you were gone forever! All we had in your place was your friend Karenna, and believe me, she was no substitute. (No offense to her—she's just definitely not *you*.) I'm sure you'll be at Pine Hollow first thing tomorrow checking on Starlight. So I'll see you then, okay? And I want to hear all about your trip.

As for your latest names, Stevie, I think you'd better go back to the drawing board. If your poor horse doesn't already have a complex from being called No-Name all these weeks, she'd *definitely* get one from being called Shahrina!

FROM: HorseGal
TO: Steviethegreat
TO: LAtwood
SUBJECT: WELCOME BACK!!!!!!!!!!!!!!!!!!!!! (3)
MESSAGE:

Hey, guys! Dad just turned on the computer to check for e-mails from work, so I figured I'd check for messages, too, even though it's almost two A.M. and I'm so tired I feel like a zombie! It was great to have your notes waiting for me—it really makes me feel like I'm home!

I can't wait to see you guys tomorrow. (Even though right now I feel like I might want to sleep right *through* tomorrow—and maybe the next day, too!) I have so much to tell you about my trip, including one story that is so amazing you might not believe it. I'm not sure I believe it myself, and I was there. Stevie, remember how you were kind of overwhelmed and scared and freaked after you and No-Name rescued Hollie last month? Well, let's just say that now I know how you feel. . . .

191

CAROLE HANSON'S RIDING JOURNAL:

It's great to be home!

That sort of makes it sound like I didn't enjoy my trip to Minnesota, doesn't it? Well, that's not what I meant. I wouldn't trade the trip for anything. But it's still nice to be back where I belong. Even if Minnesota did start to feel a little like home toward the end there . . .

By the way, I finished my family tree project yesterday after I got home from hanging out with my friends at Pine Hollow. It didn't take that long to do, since I already had so much information from the trip. I'm sure my teacher will like it. It's really detailed, thanks mostly to Grand Alice and her stories.

But even though I'm proud of the way the family tree project turned out, I can't help thinking that it doesn't even come close to telling the whole story of my family. There just didn't seem to be a way to work in all the extra stuff I learned, the stuff that didn't really have anything to do with who was married to whom or who had how many children or whatever.

I wasn't expecting anything very dramatic to happen when we all arrived at the New Year's Eve party. Christina's family lives about four miles away, and the night was really cold—even by Minnesota standards. The house was warm, though, and crowded with what had to be the entire population of Nyberg. Everyone was laughing and talking and eating and having a good time, and we dove right in.

Aunt Jessie got there a little later than the rest of us. She came over to me soon after she arrived. "Happy New Year, Carole," she said. "Are you having fun?"

I was surprised—she actually sounded friendly! "Sure," I said. "Everyone here has been super nice."

Aunt Jessie smiled, a small but not unfriendly smile. "Everyone's been nice to you except maybe me. I thought I should apologize. I know that I haven't been as friendly as I should have been. After all, you are my niece, and I do want to get to know you better. Sometimes I've got a real attitude. I'm sorry, okay?" She held out her hand.

"Okay." I shook her hand gladly. I still felt a bit strange toward Aunt Jessie—it seemed like every time I talked to her, she was angry about something—but I was happy to be on better terms with her.

Soon Christina came over to drag me onto the little dance floor in the family room, and I forgot about Aunt Jessie for a while. But when I stopped to catch my breath later, I saw her standing at the window and staring out at the night sky. I walked over to her.

"Hello," I said.

Aunt Jessie turned with an excited smile. "Oh, Carole, this is just the kind of night I need to ride Kismet over to Lover's Point to take my pictures."

I was sure she couldn't possibly mean that, but I was horrified that she would even talk about doing something so foolish. "You'd have to be crazy to take your horse out on a night like this," I said. "You'd endanger her life, riding up there! It would be a pretty bad decision to go out."

"I make my own decisions," Aunt Jessie snapped. Her dark

193

eyes were blazing. "I don't need you to tell me how or when to ride my horse. And I don't need you—or anyone else—to tell me what to do."

Suddenly I felt myself getting angry, too. Every rude word my aunt had said to me, everything I suspected about her, came back to me then. "I don't think you've been making very good decisions with your life so far," I spat out. "This one might be minor compared to some of the other colossal bloopers you've made, but it would be dangerous for Kismet as well as for you. It's stupid and reckless, and I think you should know better."

Aunt Jessie drew herself up tall. "And I think I don't care what you think!" she shouted. Then she stormed out of the room.

I was staring after her, wondering how someone so different from my mother could look so much like her, be related to her, be related to me, when Louise came rushing over. "What did you say to her?" she demanded. "Why did you get her so upset?"

"I'm sorry she left. I didn't mean to upset her," I said stiffly. "But I don't understand what the big deal is. She's always getting upset. She was saying what a great night it was to ride Kismet to Lover's Point, and I told her I thought that would be a really stupid thing to do."

Louise looked horrified. I was glad that she seemed to agree with me. But then she spoke. "You mean she's going to the lake without me?" she cried. "But she promised I could come!"

I told Louise that Aunt Jessie had run into the kitchen and

maybe she should go talk some sense into her. When she had hurried off, I went looking for a friendly face to talk to. I found Grand Alice sitting in an easy chair, tapping her feet to the party music.

"You look flushed, child," she said when she saw me. "Sit down. Tell me, what's going on?"

"I don't know what's going on," I said, still feeling upset. "Jessie said she was going to ride out to Lover's Point and I told her she shouldn't. I told her she might have screwed things up in her life before, but she shouldn't do it again— she shouldn't endanger Kismet like that. Jessie ran off and now Louise is mad and went off to be with her. I don't know what's wrong with either of them."

Grand Alice looked very grave. "Oh dear," she said slowly. "Oh dear, you shouldn't have said that." She looked very unhappy.

"Said what?" Suddenly I had the feeling that I'd done something very wrong, though I still had no idea what.

"Said that to Jessie. That very wrong thing to say." Grand Alice shook her head. "You didn't know. How could you? But, oh dear, you shouldn't have."

"What is it?" I asked. "What did I say?"

"Let's go find a quiet place to talk," she said grimly, getting up from her chair. "You'll need to hear the whole story now."

Again, I'm going to try to write down the whole story just as she told it to me that night.

Fifteen years ago, when Jessie was barely out of high school, she met a man named Lawrence Freeman. He was an artist. He liked her photographs. She liked his paintings. He was tall and funny and as much in love with her as she was in love with him. I never saw anyone love someone so much as Jessie loved Lawrence Freeman.

They got married and moved to New York City. He painted and taught art, and Jessie took photographs full-time. They did well. They had a few art exhibitions and started selling some of their work, and they really enjoyed living in the city. They were as happy as they could be—even more so when, after two years, Jessie had a baby girl. They named their daughter Joy.

One fall weekend, they decided to take a short vacation. They rented a car and drove up to western Massachusetts to look at the fall foliage. The hills in New England are beautiful that time of year. They were driving down Route 9 when something went wrong. To this day we're not sure exactly what happened. Maybe something was spilled on the highway. Maybe something was wrong with the car. Anyhow, it skidded without warning, flipped over the guardrail, and tumbled down the embankment. Jessie was hardly hurt at all.

Lawrence and Joy were killed.

Unfortunately, Jessie had been driving. No one blamed her for what happened—there were witnesses who saw the accident and said that the car went completely out of control—but Jessie blamed herself. She still can't forgive herself. Now it seems like the only time she's ever happy is when she's taking photographs. It's the only time she can completely forget about her family.

We never talk about Lawrence and Joy, or New York, because it's easier for Jessie not to remember them.

After that, of course, I understood a lot more about Aunt Jessie. A whole lot more. I still don't really understand why she doesn't want to remember her husband and baby daughter—I think she would feel better if she talked about them and tried to remember the good times she had with them. But Grand Alice says that everyone grieves in her own way, and I guess maybe that's true.

Anyway, I knew as soon as I heard the story that I should go and apologize to Aunt Jessie for what I'd said. I told Grand Alice that.

"I think that's a good idea," she said. "You're a compassionate person, Carole. Be kind to Jessie. Her life hasn't been easy."

"Miss Alice?" Dad knocked on the door of the room where we'd gone to talk. "I came to see if you would favor me with a dance." He looked at us. "Or am I interrupting?"

"Carole and I just came in here for a quiet chat," she said. "I think we're finished now."

"We were talking about Aunt Jessie," I told Dad. "Grand Alice told me about Lawrence and Joy."

Dad nodded slowly. "So now you know," he said. "Lawrence was a good man, Carole, and you would have liked him as an uncle. You and Joy might have been good friends." He sighed. "I didn't like not telling you about them, Carole, but Jessie keeps that part of her life so private. I thought you ought to hear it from this side of the family."

I nodded. After what Grand Alice had told me, I understood why Dad had kept the secret. I also understood how wrong I'd been to think that Jessie was like Jackson Foley just because they came from the same family. Jessie's anger and grief were nothing like Jackson's abandonment and betrayal. I was starting to think that maybe bloodlines aren't as important in people as they are in horses.

Dad and Grand Alice went off to dance, and I headed to the kitchen, looking for Aunt Jessie. She wasn't there, and neither was Louise. As I was wondering where to look next, the door opened and Christina hurried in, bringing a blast of arctic cold along with her.

"*Brrr!*" she said through the folds of her scarf, which was wrapped around her face. "It's *really* getting cold out there."

I helped her unwrap, then asked if she'd seen Louise.

"Sure," Christina said, shrugging off her coat. "That's where I've been. I just gave her a ride home on my snowmobile. She said she wasn't feeling well, but her parents are having fun and she didn't want to make them leave the party."

I had a sudden bad feeling. "What about Jessie? Have you seen her?"

"Uh-uh. I think she's gone, too, because her truck isn't in the driveway."

At that point I still didn't believe that Jessie would really ride out to Lover's Point, but I was afraid she'd gone home because of the things I'd said to her, and Louise had followed. I felt as if I'd spoiled the party for both of them. Of course, in the back of my mind even then I was also aware of how terrible it might be if they *had* gone to Lover's Point, but I didn't let myself really think about that.

"May I borrow your snowmobile?" I asked Christina. "I'd like to go home and check on Louise."

Christina was reluctant at first to let me go out alone, but finally I convinced her. She already knew I could handle the snowmobile because she'd let me drive it when she was showing me around a few days earlier. And the moon was bright to light my way through the snowy woods.

I don't really want to remember that trip. The woods may have been brightly lit, but they were still strange and scary, full of weird shadows and threatening noises. The air was so cold that it felt hard to breathe, and I was really worried about losing the trail left by Christina's tracks and getting lost.

Finally the lights of the compound came into sight. It was a lucky thing, too, because just a few hundred yards from home the snowmobile sputtered to a stop. It was out of gas. I struggled the rest of the way on foot through the knee-deep snow, noticing as I did that more snow was beginning to fall.

Inside, I found Ginger, the dog, but nobody else. Biting back my panic, I went back outside to check the barn and found that Kismet and Jiminy Cricket were both gone. That was when I realized my terrible fears had come true.

My heart sank like a stone. I noticed that Kismet's blanket was neatly folded and her stall door latched shut, while Jiminy's door hung open and his blanket was crumpled carelessly on the ground. From that, I figured that Jessie had gone out alone and Louise had followed her in a hurry to catch up. Automatically I picked up Jiminy's blanket. It was still warm, so I knew Louise hadn't been gone long.

I ran back to the house to call for help, dripping snow across the kitchen floor. But the phone was dead. I remembered Aunt Jessie's words: *"The roads aren't always passable, and the phones don't always work."*

I couldn't use the phone. I couldn't use the snowmobile. So I did the only thing I could: I saddled up Spice, the big workhorse, and went out after them. I tried to figure out what I might need in an emergency. I brought some rope, a few extra stirrup leathers, and a large flashlight I found in the tack trunk. By the time Spice and I headed out into the snow, which was falling faster now, my hands were trembling—with fear, not cold. I couldn't shake the feeling that something was very wrong, that my aunt and cousin were already somehow in trouble.

Ginger followed as Spice trudged through the snow. I did my best to light our way with the flashlight, holding both reins in one hand. I was more scared than I've ever been. I wasn't sure I could find the lake again. I wasn't sure what I was going to do even if I did find it. But at least Spice's large, warm, solid presence was comforting. I wondered if the horse could possibly know how totally my life depended on him. I hoped he wouldn't let me down.

A few minutes later, I noticed that Ginger wasn't with us anymore. I looked around and called to him, but there was no answering bark. I didn't have time to worry about the dog then. I figured he must have returned home.

I was so cold I could barely move. The cold made me tired, and I was afraid of falling asleep, slipping out of the saddle, and never waking up again.

It seemed to take forever, but eventually the landscape grew rockier, and I was pretty sure we were getting close to the lake. Suddenly a sound came from ahead. Moments later a large shape galloped into my flashlight's beam, moving awkwardly through the deep, drifting snow. It was Kismet, his saddle empty and his stirrups flying. I gulped and felt another stab of panic. Then another horse came into view ahead—Jiminy. This time there was a rider in the saddle.

"Louise!" I shouted.

She waved frantically. "Carole! Carole, hurry!" When I reached her, I saw her eyes were wide with fear. "It's Jessie. She's on the ice—stuck in rocks. Oh, Carole, I didn't know what to do!" She let out a sob.

"It'll be okay," I said as soothingly as I could. "Tell me what happened so we can go help her."

Louise nodded tearfully. "She was up on the rocks. She wanted to get a picture from a certain angle, and she couldn't quite get it. She kept asking Kismet to turn—and she wasn't paying attention to the footing. Kismet slipped on the ice and threw her. She's fallen into a crevice in the rocks, and she's hurt and she can't get out." Louise drew in a long, quivering breath. "I've got to get help—I've got to get home—but it's going to take too long and I don't know what to do."

I understood and agreed. It was way too cold for Jessie to lie unmoving. She would freeze to death before either Louise or I could return with help.

"We'll have to save her ourselves," I told Louise.

"But I don't know what to do!" she wailed.

I felt a moment's frustration. By getting so upset, Louise was only making things worse. I wished that Stevie and Lisa were there to help me.

Even thinking of them gave me courage. Somehow I got Louise to stop sobbing and lead me back to Jessie. As soon as I saw her, I knew the situation was bad. I rode Spice as close as I could to the crevice where she was stuck, leaving Louise back at the foot of the rocks, and dismounted.

I knelt in the snow. "Aunt Jessie!" I called.

Jessie didn't move or open her eyes. "Go 'way," she mumbled. I could barely hear the words above the wind.

"Where are you hurt?" I shouted. I was afraid to try to move her without finding out whether she'd hurt her back or her head.

Jessie just mumbled a few things that didn't make sense. I could tell she was too tired to understand what was going on. I was afraid that if I didn't do something, she would fall asleep, and then . . .

Suddenly I thought of Stevie. *What would she do in a situation like this?*

The answer came to me. I bent my face to Jessie's ear. "Knock knock!" I said loudly.

Her eyelids fluttered open. "What?"

"Knock knock," I repeated.

"Who's there?" she responded automatically.

"Banana."

"Banana who?"

"Knock knock."

"Who's there?"

"Banana."

"Banana who?" By now Jessie looked a little more alert.

"Knock knock."

202

"Who's there?" This time she actually looked irritated.

"Orange," I said.

Jessie smiled. "Orange who?"

"Orange you glad I didn't say banana?"

Jessie laughed. "No more bananas." She blinked. "Carole."

I was relieved. She recognized me, and that was a start. I asked her again where she was hurt, and this time she understood.

"My arm. My left arm below the elbow." She grimaced. "It's hurt so badly that I can't pull myself out."

I examined the way she was stuck. Her hips were caught in a gap in the rocks. Her left arm had come down hard on a rock, but her head and shoulders weren't trapped. I tried gently pulling her while she wriggled to free herself, but that didn't work.

Jessie had started to shiver uncontrollably. "It's more of an . . . in-and-out . . . than an up-and-down," she said through teeth clenched in pain.

I studied the problem again. *What would Lisa do?* I wondered. Then it came to me. I took the rope I'd brought and looped it under Jessie's arms and across her back. With one of the stirrup leathers I buckled her upper left arm tight against her side to keep it from moving.

Then I looped the other end of the rope over the horn on Spice's Western saddle. "Pull, Spice!" I urged him.

Spice began to strain against the rope. Jessie slowly slid free of the crevice, crying out in pain. We'd done it!

I maneuvered Jessie to Spice's side and held her against the horse's thick fur, hoping she could feel some of the warmth of his body. When I looked up at him, Spice seemed to have grown twice as tall since I'd started out. How was I ever going to get Jessie, or even myself, up onto his back?

I barely remember the next few minutes. I think I decided to try to help Jessie mount from the right side, thinking it was the only way because of her arm. I seem to recall the two of us getting knocked over by an especially strong wind gust. I think getting both of us on our feet again took kind of a long time. I may even have used Spice's leg to haul myself up.

But then something broke into my fuzzy, cold brain: the sound of excited barking—and better yet, the roar of a snowmobile! It was Dad and Uncle John. Ginger had led them to us!

I definitely don't remember much after that, except Dad hugging me and Uncle John saying, "Let's get home." That sounded like the best idea I'd ever heard.

A few other memories, fuzzy ones, came back to me the next morning after a really long, really deep sleep: seeing Spice safely into his stall and giving him an extra helping of oats; watching Uncle John bundle Jessie into the truck for their trip to the hospital; sitting at the kitchen table with Louise while Aunt Lily made hot chocolate.

Aunt Jessie came home from the hospital that morning. She had a large white cast from her fingertips to her elbow, and a few bruises, but otherwise she was fine. She didn't even end up with frostbite, which was practically a miracle.

Actually, she was better than fine. She and I talked for a long time after that, and I think I understand her a little better now. I think we may even end up being friends after all. Louise was a lot nicer after what happened, too. I started to see the nice, caring, interesting side of both of them in addition to the more suspicious, prickly one they'd shown me before.

I also spent a long time with Spice that morning, feeding him special treats and thanking him for the fine, brave thing he'd done the night before. I think all horses are special, of course, but I know now that he's *especially* special, despite his shaggy fur and plain looks.

"Your heart, Spice," I told him, "is pure champion Thoroughbred."

Suddenly I remembered that it was New Year's Day, the day Stevie and Lisa were planning that birthday party for Prancer. It gave me an idea.

"You've got a Thoroughbred's heart," I told Spice. "So I guess that means today's your birthday, too." I sang "Happy Birthday" to him as he polished off more of the apple and carrot pieces I'd brought. It felt right.

After that I gave the rest of the treats to the other three horses and sang to them, too. After all, Jiminy and Kismet had shared the ordeal, too, and I knew better than to blame Kismet for slipping on the ice or being frightened when Jessie fell. And I was sure that Sugar would have been just as willing to go out as Spice had been.

And do you know the most wonderful thing? When I got home, I found out that Stevie and Lisa had done the exact same thing. What had started out as a birthday party for Prancer and the other Thoroughbreds had quickly turned into a celebration for *all* the horses at Pine Hollow. They decided every one of them, from the tiniest pony to big old Nero, deserved a birthday party just as much as the Thoroughbreds, fancy bloodlines or not. So in a way, it was sort of like the whole Saddle Club was together, even though we were physically so far apart.

Anyway, ever since I got home I've been thinking about what Grand Alice said about seeing all the interesting angles. I think from now on I'll remember that people—situations, too—can be complicated, and I should try to see all their angles before I make up my mind about them.

Of course, there's another lesson that I didn't learn from Grand Alice or anyone else in Minnesota. That's that good friends are always with you. So is family, I guess, if not exactly in the way I used to think. I thought before that I would be able to understand myself better by looking at my bloodlines, just the way horse breeders do. But I know now it's not as simple as that. I remember that every time I think of Jackson Foley and Aunt Jessie, or when I look at the beautiful amulet necklace that Grand Alice gave me. The amulet always makes me think of her, and my mother, and that long-ago woman—my great-great-who-knows-how-many-times-great-grandmother who came over to America on the slave ship.

It doesn't tell me anything more about what I'm like, what I believe, or what I should be when I grow up. But it makes me feel like a part of something larger, like an important link in a strong, living chain. And I kind of like that feeling.

Dear Karenna,

Hi! I'm really sorry I missed you when you visited Willow Creek over winter break. I'm sure my friends told you I was up in Min-

206

nesota visiting relatives, and it turned out to be a really interesting trip. But I wish I could have seen you. It would have been fun to go riding together, the way we used to back in California. Do you still love jumping as much as you used to? I do. Do you still love shopping as much as you used to? I still don't! (Ha ha!) Remember how you dragged me to the mall that time because you said we were going to shop for riding gloves, but instead you tried on high-heeled shoes behind your mother's back? Well, I know I complained a lot at the time. But I still smile when I think about how your mom walked into the shoe store just as you were tottering toward the mirror on those three-inch heels. Not to mention how she chewed out the salesperson for letting an eight-year-old try on high heels in the first place!

Like I said, I really wish we could have gotten together when you were here. Next trip for sure, okay? Anyway, I'm glad at least you got to meet Starlight. Can you believe I really have my own horse now? It's just like we always dreamed about back then, only better, because it's real.

Write back sometime and let me know how you're doing. Stevie and Lisa didn't give me nearly enough details!

Your (shopaphobic) friend,

Carole

P.S.—Meg and Betsy say hello!

CAROLE HANSON'S RIDING JOURNAL:

It's funny how The Saddle Club works sometimes. The three of us are such good friends that it's always a little surprising when we don't agree on something. For instance, when I got back from Minnesota after New Year's, I wanted to know all about Karenna's visit to Willow Creek. I was expecting Stevie and Lisa to have hit it off with her, since I like her so much. But it turned out that they didn't get along that well after all. Karenna ended up spending more time with Meg Durham and Betsy Cavanaugh than she did with my friends.

I guess it shouldn't be that surprising when I really think about it, though. I think Karenna's great, but she's always been just as interested in things like shopping and gossiping as she is in riding. That doesn't bother me a bit, because I've known her so long. But I can see why Stevie and Lisa might not really understand her. They thought she would be like me because she's my friend, but she's really not that much like me at all. Just like Stevie's not that much like me, and Lisa's not that much like Stevie, and I'm not that much like Lisa. I guess sometimes differences work together, like with the three of us, or with me and Karenna, and sometimes they don't, like with Stevie and Lisa and Karenna. Actually, it sounds like the only time they really connected with Karenna was when they were all talking about *me!* Ha!

Anyway, not much happened back home while I was gone. Stevie's still trying to come up with the perfect name for No-Name. She still wants to do something that reflects the mare's bloodlines, though personally I'm not sure that's the right approach. Bloodlines can't always tell you everything about a horse—or a person. Of course, that doesn't mean you should totally ignore where you came from, either. . . .

Dear Diary:

Summer vacation started a couple of weeks ago, and I've been spending almost every day at the stable. Our riding class is a little smaller now, since Roger (ugh!) dropped out and Lauren moved away. It's funny, when I first came to Pine Hollow a little less than a year ago, I was sure that Lauren was going to end up being a really good friend. I thought we had so much in common—same interest in horses, same age, same school. But now that she's gone, I realize I don't even miss her that much. We didn't end up getting that close after all, especially once I started spending more time with Stevie. Stevie can be kind of crazy sometimes, and I don't always understand how her mind works, but I really like her. And she definitely helps take my mind off worrying about things at home.

Mom seems to get weaker every day. Her doctors say they're doing all they can, but I can't believe that, because the treatments seem to hurt her more than they help. Still, whenever she has the energy, Mom spends time in her little garden in the backyard. Dad dug it out for her, and she's been planting all kinds of vegetable and flower seeds there, even a few little shrubs. Actually, Dad and I have done most of the digging and planting. Mom sits in the shade and supervises, or sometimes she'll sprinkle seeds in a trench we've dug or pull a few small weeds from between the tiny plants.

I don't really understand why she cares so much about that stupid garden. It's getting harder and harder to ignore the fact that she isn't getting better, that the cancer isn't going away.

It's kind of hard to watch her keep on planting things. I mean, what's the point if she'll never get to see the flowers bloom? It hurts to watch the plants in the garden grow stronger as Mom gets weaker.

Dear Diary:

I just got home from Pine Hollow. Max was talking about some Fourth of July picnic, which is coming up next weekend. I guess they have it every year. Stevie says it's fun—all the riders and their friends and families get together to eat and talk about horses and have fun, and then everyone watches the town fireworks from a hillside behind the stable. I told Dad about it, and he says we can go for a little while if Mom is feeling okay that day. Actually, he says I should go and have fun no matter what, but I really hope we can all go as a family. I think it would be good for Mom to go out somewhere other than the hospital for once. I even told her about the small rosebushes that Mrs. Reg just planted by the driveway at Pine Hollow, hoping that would make her want to go. But all she'll say is "We'll see."

Dear Diary:

After what happened yesterday, I wasn't planning to go to the Pine Hollow picnic at all. Mom went to the doctor for her usual checkup, and I was hoping they'd tell her she was looking better, so she could go to the picnic. Instead they said her blood cells were in more trouble than ever, or something like that, and they put her on this new medicine that makes her so tired she can't even get out of bed. She has to ring a bell whenever she needs to go to the bathroom, and then Dad or Nurse Thompson has to help her in there and stay with her.

So like I said, I wasn't going to go today. I wasn't exactly in a celebrating mood, especially after I woke up in the middle of the night and heard Mom crying in her room. But then Stevie called this morning to see where I was. I sort of explained—I didn't go into much detail, but she already knew I was hoping my family could come—and she asked to talk to my dad. I thought that was kind of weird, but Dad came to the phone and said hello. He listened for a second, then said, "Yes, I think that's a very good idea. Thank you." He hung up, then said that Stevie's parents were coming by to pick me up and take me to the picnic.

I was surprised and a little annoyed. I wanted to stay and help Mom, and I said so. But Dad put his foot down. He said things were under control there, and there was no reason I shouldn't go and have a nice time with my friends.

I was still pouting when Stevie and her family picked me up. It didn't help much that Chad was in the car, too. I still feel a little embarrassed when I remember that whole finding-a-boyfriend fiasco from a few months ago. Luckily I guess Chad really thought that Stevie was behind it all, so I think he's forgotten it ever happened.

Anyway, I felt a little better when we got to Pine Hollow.

I sat with Stevie's family while we ate, and they did their best to make me feel comfortable. At least Stevie and her parents did. Her brothers mostly made fun of the stable and teased Stevie until she started pelting them with grapes and watermelon seeds whenever the adults weren't looking. But that was okay, too. It took my mind off Mom and the way she'd looked that morning, so pale and still, looking really small and thin and weak in her big bed at home.

Later, Stevie and I decided to go for a ride before it got dark. We tacked up Delilah and Comanche. We didn't want to miss the start of the fireworks, so we decided to just ride in the fields surrounding the stable instead of going into the woods. Most of the picnickers were around at the side, and there were some skittish yearlings in the big back pasture, so we chose the front pasture, the one that runs along the road.

We played a few games, like follow the leader and Simon says. Then we just rode along the fence line for a while at a walk, side by side, letting the horses cool down. We didn't talk much, but that was okay. Part of my mind was letting me have fun with Stevie, but a much larger part was still occupied with thoughts and worries about Mom.

We were coming around the corner of the fence by the driveway when I noticed the roses. Those little rosebushes that Mrs. Reg had planted a while back were getting bigger, in their sunny spot, and as we got closer, I saw a tiny pink bud on one of them.

I'm not sure quite what happened, but something inside me snapped. It was totally unfair. Everything else in the whole world seemed to be thriving and blooming and living, except for my mother. My mother wasn't thriving, she was weakening. She wasn't blooming, she was fading. And she wasn't living anymore. She was dying.

I didn't stop to think. I just acted. I kicked Delilah, startling her into a trot, then a canter. Wheeling her around, I built up some distance, then turned her back toward the fence. I know I wasn't quite myself right then, because normally I would never ask a horse to jump a fence that high. But Delilah sailed right over it as if it were nothing more than a fallen log. When we landed on the other side, I turned her toward those rosebushes. The pink bud looked like a little mouth laughing at me. I rode right toward it, letting Delilah trample it into the ground. I didn't stop until all the bushes were flattened. Then I burst into tears.

I guess Stevie didn't know what to do, so she went and got Mrs. Reg. "Carole!" Mrs. Reg cried, running down the driveway toward me. It was dusk by then, and at first I was crying so hard I didn't recognize her. "Carole! What have you done?"

I slid down out of the saddle, suddenly horrified. My first thought was for Delilah's legs. I checked them quickly, but luckily the roses were too small to have large thorns yet. Aside from a tiny scratch on her left fore, she seemed okay.

The roses were another story. Their stems were broken, the leaves trampled into the ground. Just about the only thing that wasn't totally destroyed was that one pink bud. It was lying on the ground at the end of its stem, which had been snapped off. I bent and picked it up, staring at it as what I'd done sank in.

213

I think Stevie stepped forward around then and took Delilah's bridle to lead her back to the stable. I'm not sure. Mrs. Reg put her arm around my shoulders. "Carole," she said gently, lowering herself to the grass at the edge of the driveway and pulling me down with her. "Do you want to talk about it?"

I didn't. At least I didn't think I did. But suddenly I found myself telling her everything—about Mom's last doctor's visit, the new medicine, her garden in the backyard, everything. Mrs. Reg didn't say much. She just nodded and listened.

When I finished, she pulled a tissue out of her pocket and gave it to me to wipe my face. "I understand why you did what you did," she said gently, gesturing at the broken roses. "But Carole, it doesn't solve anything. I know it's hard for you to realize it, but the world goes on no matter what. I learned that when I buried my dear husband, Max, your Max's father, a few years ago. Some lives end, others begin, most just go on in between." She shrugged and sighed. "I think your mother knows that already. I expect her little garden is her way of looking to the future, creating something special during a very uncertain time. Those plants she's helped bring to life will go on, perhaps even after she's not around to care for them anymore. They'll grow and thrive and make people happy—perhaps they'll remind people of her own life—and that makes her feel a little better about the future. Probably the same way she feels when she looks at you."

That made my tears start to flow again. "But it's not

fair," I mumbled, dabbing uselessly at my cheeks with the soggy tissue.

"I know, Carole," Mrs. Reg said. She looked up at the sky then, where the first stars were beginning to come into view, and blinked a few times. "It certainly isn't fair. But the only thing we can do is work with what we're given and try to make the best of it. Try to make ourselves and the people we care about happy for as long as we can, however we can. We really don't have another choice."

I was thinking about that when there was a sudden loud boom. I nearly jumped out of my skin, and I felt Mrs. Reg start beside me as well. Then another bang followed, and we both realized that the fireworks were starting. We couldn't see them from where we were sitting—they were hidden by the crest of the gentle slope leading up from the road to the hill behind the stable building.

I'm not sure why, but we both started to laugh then. I think it was because the fireworks had startled us so much, or maybe because we were sitting there in the dark on the grass. Anyway, we got up and brushed ourselves off.

"I'm really sorry about your roses, Mrs. Reg," I said. "I'll save my allowance until I can pay for new ones."

She patted me on the shoulder. "Don't worry about it," she said. "You save your allowance for something more important. Max didn't like having the roses here, anyway—he started fretting the moment I brought them home, saying it was only a matter of time before a horse got into them and scratched itself to pieces."

I had a feeling she was only being nice, but I accepted it,

because she'd just given me another idea. As we walked up the driveway toward the stable, following the sound of the crowd oohing and aahing at the fireworks exploding somewhere over the hill, I stared at the rosebud I was still holding. Now it seemed to be smiling at me, as if to say that it liked my new plan. I only hope Mom likes it. I can't wait until tomorrow comes and I can find out.

Dear Diary:

This morning as soon as I got up, I emptied my piggy bank and asked Dad for this week's allowance. He seemed a little surprised, but he was distracted because Nurse Thompson was just arriving, so he said yes.

I still wasn't sure I had enough, though, so I took the bus over to Pine Hollow. Stevie was there, and when I explained my plan, she gave me all the money she had in her pockets. Unfortunately that was only about fifty cents. But then she went and somehow managed to borrow money from Red, Betsy, Adam, Max—just about everyone who happened to be around. She told each of them a different story about why she needed it, from needing to make a long-distance call on the pay phone (Betsy) to wanting to buy a new package of gauze for the first aid kit (Max). She even got a dollar out of Veronica diAngelo by claiming she was collecting for a food drive at her family's church and that all the best families in town were making big contributions.

In the end, I still only had about ten dollars total. But I figured that would have to do. After thanking Stevie for her help, I walked over to the garden center near the shopping plaza and went straight to the rose section. There were so many different types that I wasn't sure what to do. Then I noticed the tag on one of the roses: Sparkling Scarlet. That reminded me of Scarlett O'Hara, the heroine of Gone with the Wind, which is one of Mom's favorite movies. There were only a few of those, though, and only the smallest, scraggliest one was less than ten dollars. I bought it and carried it home on the bus as carefully as I could.

I was planning to head upstairs and show it to Mom when I got home. But as I walked toward the house from the bus stop, I spotted her in the front yard, watching Nurse Thompson watering the petunias Dad and I had planted earlier that spring. Mom still looked weak, but she was smiling and sitting up on her own, which was a big improvement from that morning. It turns out her body finally adjusted to that new medicine—it just took a couple of days.

I was so happy to see her looking better that I almost forgot about the rose plant I was holding. But Mom saw it and asked about it.

"I bought it for you. Well, for us," I explained, setting it on her lap. "I thought we could plant it together."

Mom seemed to like that idea. "Let's do it now," she suggested. So we went around to the sunny side of the house, with Nurse Thompson having to help Mom only a little. We picked a spot halfway between my bedroom window and Mom and Dad's, right up against the wall. Mom said the rose I'd picked was a climbing rose, and that she would ask Dad to put up a trellis so that the plant could climb up it as

217

it grew. She said eventually it might cover the whole side of the house!

I'm not so sure about that. Like I said, the plant didn't seem all that strong, and even though Mom didn't say so, I don't think it's really the right time of year to plant roses anyway. But I guess that's not really the point. We went ahead and planted it, with me digging the hole the way Mom told me to, and then Mom kneeling beside me to help settle the little plant in the dirt.

I can see her now if I lean out my bedroom window. I've started thinking of the rose plant as Scarlett because of her name. She looks so small that I can't imagine she'll ever have a flower on her, let alone climb all over the house. But like I said, it doesn't really matter. I'm still glad I got her.

FROM: Steviethegreat
TO: HorseGal
TO: LAtwood
SUBJECT: We rule! (or at least we will)
MESSAGE:

Okay, guys, are you psyched to beat Cross County (and the other teams, natch) in the second Pony Club rally? Because you know I am. Phil and the others won't know what hit them. No-Name and I may have been a little off our game at today's rally, but next time we're going to be ready for anything!!!

FROM: HorseGal

TO: LAtwood

SUBJECT: Stevie and Phil

MESSAGE:

Hi, Lisa. You know I hate to go behind people's backs. But I just had to ask you if you're getting worried about Stevie like I am. You know she and Phil have had trouble in the past when they've gotten too competitive with each other. I thought they'd learned their lesson, but I'm afraid it may be happening again with this upcoming rally, especially since Cross County just beat us out for second place at the last one. Am I crazy? I hope so. Let me know what you think.

FROM: LAtwood

TO: HorseGal

SUBJECT: Stevie and Phil (2)

MESSAGE:

I don't think you're crazy at all to worry, but I think Stevie is just excited about these rallies because she's so happy with how well No-Name is working out. I'm definitely going to keep an eye on her, and you should, too, just in case things get out of hand. But otherwise I think we should just sit back and let her enjoy herself—and No-Name. We'll only say something to her if she starts worrying so much about winning that she doesn't seem to be having fun anymore, or if things start to get weird again between her and Phil.

Speaking of weird things, what did you think about that strange blond girl at the rally today, claiming that No-Name belongs to her? It's hard to believe anyone could mix up No-Name with any other horse. She's really one of a kind, from that crazy upside-down exclamation point on her face to her wacky, Stevie-like personality. But we all know that No-Name belongs to Stevie—heart, soul, and crazy personality. And we know her parents bought her from Mr. Baker fair and square. So I guess we shouldn't waste any time worrying about it. Stevie certainly doesn't seem to be.

Anyway, whatever's going on with that girl, it can't possibly be even half as weird as what we were talking about at lunch today. It's hard to imagine that Mr. diAngelo's bank could be in so much trouble that it could change Veronica's whole personality. Can you believe how nice she was acting at the rally? And then afterward at TD's, she sounded pretty serious when she said she might have to give up Garnet soon. If she's thinking of selling the valuable purebred Arabian she's always bragging about—and telling the three of us, of all people, about it—then she must be *really* worried about fitting in among us ordinary folk when she's poor.

Then again, who knows? Maybe she's just acting weird because it's a full moon and she's secretly a bizarre kind of werewolf who turns nice instead of shaggy! (I think that second possibility is actually a little easier to believe! Ha ha!)

220

CAROLE HANSON'S RIDING JOURNAL:

I still can't believe what happened today. It's so bizarre and awful that it has to be a dream—or a nightmare. But I haven't woken up from it yet, so maybe it's true.

I guess it started back on Saturday, when that crazy blond girl at the first Pony Club rally was yelling about how No-Name belonged to her. At least we thought she was crazy then. Now nobody's sure. Because today when Stevie got home from our extra rally practice session, her parents were waiting with some horrible news. That girl—her name's Chelsea Webber—still believes that No-Name belongs to her. Her father sent the Lakes a letter claiming that Chelsea's horse was stolen out of their barn a few months ago, and that No-Name is the same horse. And that her real name is Punctuation, for the mark on her face—Punk for short. Stevie called to tell Lisa and me the whole story right away, of course. She said that if Chelsea Webber can prove that Punk and No-Name are the same horse, she'll be able to take her away from Stevie!

At least Stevie's parents are lawyers. Maybe they can figure out what to do to keep No-Name where she belongs—with Stevie.

On the good news front, I got a letter from Kate, which I've pasted in.

Dear Saddle Club (c/o Carole),

Hi! I haven't heard from you guys in a while, so I thought I'd drop you a note to ask what's new. How are you doing? How's

Stevie's new horse adjusting to life at Pine Hollow? Does she have a name yet? Stewball seemed a little jealous when I told him about No-Name, but I'm sure he'll get used to it if we give him enough time. Ha ha!

Anyhow, I also thought you might be interested in hearing the latest from the Bar None—namely, that we weaned Felix a few weeks ago. He was pretty upset at first (aren't they always?) but he's adjusted like a little champ. Now he's back to being his usual lively, curious self again. I've started working with him on halter training, and he's catching on really fast. He's probably the smartest weanling west of the Mississippi!

Moonglow is fine, too, by the way. She missed her baby for a few days, but now that she's settling down, Walter and John and I are starting to think about training her. It will probably be harder for her than for Felix, since she grew up in the wild. But she's such a sweet horse that I'm sure we can get her to accept a rider. All we have to do is get her to really trust us—convince her we only want what's best for her. And all it will take to do that, as John likes to say, is about eight tons of patience and a little good luck.

Write back soon!

Love,

Kate

Dear Kate,

It was nice to hear the update about Felix and Moonglow. I haven't showed your letter to Stevie and Lisa yet, though. It's been kind of busy around here lately, and not in a good way, either.

It has to do with No-Name, or rather, Punk. No, that's not what

222

Stevie decided to name her. It's what her old owner calls her. See, it turns out that No-Name was stolen from her last owner, a girl named Chelsea Webber. We're still not sure how No-Name ended up in that bulk lot that Mr. Baker (Phil's riding instructor) bought, but neither he nor anyone else had any idea that she'd been stolen. Now it seems she was, and that means she still belongs to Chelsea. Legally, that is. Because morally or emotionally or however else you want to look at it, she's Stevie's horse. Period.

Still, there doesn't seem to be much any of us can do to help keep them together. Chelsea's parents even got a restraining order to keep Stevie from riding No-Name until this is all settled. Isn't that awful? She can still groom her and take care of her, but she can't ride her or remove her from Pine Hollow's grounds.

Stevie isn't taking any of this very well, as you can imagine. I've never seen her so upset. It's hard to know what to say to help her, so Lisa and I are just trying to be there to support her and listen to her and do whatever she needs.

It was so awful when Mr. Lake gave us the bad news yesterday. Chelsea had brought a vet to Pine Hollow to examine No-Name, and afterward their lawyer called the Lakes. After the preliminary examination, it looks as if No-Name and Punk are one and the same horse. Not only are the markings identical (I know Stevie sent you photos of her, so you know how unusual her markings are), but there's also the matter of the identical weed allergy. Stevie was so proud of herself for figuring that one out, and now . . . Well, anyway, there's also an old bone splint—perfectly harmless, as Judy Barker told Stevie when she bought No-Name. It turns out Punk had the same thing. So it looks as if No-Name Lake really is Punctuation Webber.

We've all been practicing for this Pony Club rally we're in tomorrow, but somehow it hasn't been that much fun since we found out about Chelsea. Stevie was riding Topside during our practice today, and it didn't go very well. He's one of the best-trained horses I've ever seen, but he just doesn't seem to like mounted games that well, at least not compared to No-Name (I still can't think of her as Punk, no matter how many times people call her that!). So on top of all the other horrible stuff that was going on, we were starting to think we were going to come in last place at the rally, too. It's not Topside's fault, of course. He just doesn't have the right kind of personality for those games.

But then Stevie came up with her new plan. Actually I think it was inspired by Veronica diAngelo's hair—she just had highlights put in it. Stevie noticed that Topside and No-Name are both bays, and she came up with one of her usual crazy ideas. "That's it!" she cried, staring at Veronica's highlights. "That's how I can ride No-Name in the rally tomorrow."

"There's no way," Veronica said. (She's been acting a lot nicer lately, by the way, because her family may be going broke—but I'll tell you about that some other time.) "There's no way you'll be able to ride No-Name tomorrow. Chelsea Webber and her sister are both in Pony Clubs—their whole family will be there."

Lisa and I had to agree. At least until Stevie told us her plan.

"Are you saying what I think you're saying?" Lisa asked in amazement. "You want to dye No-Name's hair?"

"You got it," Stevie confirmed. "If I dye her socks and stripe, she'll look like a solid bay, just like Topside. Nobody will recognize her."

"Chelsea will," Veronica pointed out. "After all, she'll be watching you closely."

Stevie shrugged. "Even if she does suspect, what can she do about it? It took a vet and an X-ray machine to prove No-Name's identity even *with* her markings. She'll never be able to prove a thing this way. And we'll get to beat Phil in the rally."

Somehow, when she said that, I suspected it was only part of what she was thinking. I think she really just wants to ride No-Name once more before Chelsea takes her away forever. With something like that at stake, I had to agree to give Stevie's plan a try. So did Lisa, and even Veronica wants to help.

So now I'm just crossing my fingers that we don't get caught before the rally tomorrow. Never mind how much trouble we'd get in if someone found out. I just couldn't stand it if Stevie didn't get to ride her horse—because that's what No-Name is, no matter what some stupid law says—one last time.

Your sad and worried friend,

Carole

CAROLE HANSON'S RIDING JOURNAL:

It's amazing how things turn out sometimes. Life is so full of surprises, good and bad, you know?

At that Pony Club rally a couple of weeks ago, we were all really worried about getting caught switching horses. But it turned out to be worth it in the end. For one thing, Stevie got to ride her horse in the rally, and our team even beat Phil's team, just like she was hoping. And nobody said a word about her mount's slightly blotchy bay legs, or the fact that Topside, a gelding, had suddenly turned into a mare. We (The Saddle Club and Veronica, that is) managed to distract anyone from taking too close a look at Stevie's horse. Max was an exception, of course. He didn't get a good look at Stevie's horse before we unloaded at Cross County, but during inspection, he finally noticed.

"What are you thinking?" he whispered at Stevie.

"I had to do it, Max," Stevie whispered back urgently. "This is my last chance to ride her. I just couldn't stand it if I missed it. I really couldn't."

"Don't you think people will find out?" he asked quietly.

"Not if you don't tell them," she countered.

Max was silent for a moment. "Tell them what?" he said at last. Then he moved on down the row.

Anyway, after that the rally went totally our way. Stevie and No-Name were brilliant in the games. Even Max said he'd never seen a horse and rider so perfectly matched. (He said it when nobody but us could hear, of course.)

In the end, Stevie had to take No-Name over to the Webbers' house and give her back to Chelsea. I wasn't there—Stevie thought it was something she needed to do on her own—but I was thinking about her the whole time, wondering if she'd be okay.

For a while she wasn't. She didn't even come to Pine Hollow for the rest of that week. Lisa and I were really worried about her. We'd never thought anything could ever overwhelm Stevie's naturally optimistic, happy nature. But losing No-Name . . . well, that seemed to do it. Her parents offered to start looking for a replacement for No-Name right away, but Stevie wasn't interested. She said she'd rather just go back to riding Topside for the time being.

On Saturday, Lisa and I finally convinced Stevie to come

to Horse Wise. She did, but she didn't look very happy to be there. People kept coming up and saying they were sorry about No-Name. And then something weird happened. Veronica came to add her condolences—only in addition to that, she tried to convince Stevie to buy *Garnet* from her as a replacement for No-Name! At first Stevie actually considered it, but after she realized that Garnet wasn't a good match for her, she started to wonder about Veronica's motives. That's when she remembered seeing something odd—namely, Veronica talking to Chelsea Webber at the last Pony Club rally. She'd even seen Chelsea hand Veronica a piece of paper, which Veronica had dropped into Garnet's grooming bucket. Stevie hadn't thought much of the incident at the time because she was so focused on her plot to ride No-Name for the last time. But now that she remembered, she couldn't help feeling curious—and, since Veronica was involved, a little suspicious.

"I wonder what that was all about?" Lisa said.

"I have no idea," I replied. "But if Veronica put a piece of paper in Garnet's grooming bucket, I'll bet you an ice-cream sundae it's still there."

We hurried to find the bucket. *"Voilà!"* Stevie cried triumphantly, grabbing a slip of paper from inside. "Here's the answer to the mystery."

Lisa and I peered over her shoulder. "It looks like a reward notice," Lisa said.

Suddenly a lot of things made sense. We realized that Veronica must have been the one who'd told the Webbers about No-Name's weed allergy, and maybe the bone splint, too. She wanted the thousand-dollar reward they were offering for information about their missing horse, and she'd sold Stevie out. That was the reason she'd been acting so nice to us.

Of course, knowing that didn't really make much difference. The Webbers would have found out about No-Name's allergy eventually anyway. Chelsea had already seen her at the rally, so it was just a matter of time. Nothing changed—except we're once again certain that Veronica is the sneakiest, most selfish, and least trustworthy person we know. (Plus we found out later that her father's bank problems turned out okay in the end, so the family isn't going broke after all and Veronica's free to go back to being her usual snobby self.)

As we were discussing ways to get back at Veronica for her latest rottenness, Mrs. Reg called Stevie to the office for a phone call. And we never, in a million years, would have guessed who it was.

It was Chelsea Webber. And she wanted Stevie to take No-Name back!

It turns out that Chelsea had been having second thoughts. She still loves No-Name (or Punk, as she called her) a lot, but while she was missing, her parents had leased a different horse for her. And Chelsea had realized that the new horse was a better match for her than Punk had ever been. The same things that made No-Name/Punk so perfect for Stevie—her spirit, her sense of humor, her strong will—made her kind of difficult for Chelsea to handle. Plus, Chelsea admitted she'd known it was Punk that Stevie was riding at that second rally. She wasn't fooled by the dye job.

Seeing the two of them together, she'd realized (eventually) that they were meant to be together.

I really respect her for coming to that decision. Not only did it make Stevie the happiest girl in the world, but I believe it's the best thing for Chelsea as well. And also for No-Name.

Oh, but I've got to get out of the habit of calling her No-Name, because Stevie finally found the perfect name for her! Back over the holiday, before I left for Minnesota, she was coming up with all kinds of crazy possible names, like Sarouk, Tabriz, and even Princess Jasmine (which reminds me of Princess, the horse Veronica had a couple of years ago, before she got Cobalt and then Garnet—not that I reminded Stevie about that, of course! She would strangle me if she thought I was accusing her of thinking like Veronica, especially after what she did!). Anyway, I guess she was trying to come up with a name that had something to do with the Arabian part of No-Name's bloodlines. (I think Sarouk and Tabriz have something to do with Arabian-type oriental rugs or something like that, and of course Princess Jasmine was the heroine in the movie *Aladdin*.) But eventually she realized that that wasn't going to work. It was something Lisa said, about how No-Name was half Saddlebred and that was a breed from the American South, that finally made Stevie think of the perfect name: Belle. As in Southern Belle, those spunky, independent women of film and legend, like Scarlett O'Hara in *Gone with the Wind*. I think it suits her perfectly!

And I'm really happy that Stevie got her dream horse back. It's the kind of perfect happy ending I always love in books and movies. I only wish *everything* in real life could turn out that well.

Dear Diary:

Another year, another first day of school . . . It still feels kind of weird to be back at the same school this fall instead of getting used to a new place and new people. Of course, going back to school in the fall always feels a little strange. I already miss being able to hang out at Pine Hollow for hours every day. I wish Stevie and I went to the same school—at least then I'd have someone to talk to about horses! But at least I do have friends here at school now. More than I realized, actually. A lot of kids I didn't see all summer came up to say hi in the halls today. That made me feel like I really do belong here, and that's a pretty good feeling. I think it would be even harder to deal with Mom's condition if I were starting all over again.

Dear Diary:

A weird day today. Now that the first week is behind me, I was starting to think maybe I should get more involved with things at school. I mean, I never used to bother to join many extra-curricular activities or anything because I always knew I'd be moving away sooner or later, and usually sooner. Riding was always enough of an activity.

But now that I'm feeling more permanent, I thought joining something would be a good way to meet more people, make more real friends. Plus I'd seen a sign-up sheet for an after-school dance group, and I figured that kind of exercise would be good for my riding.

So I went to the introductory meeting after school today. It was fun. I liked most of the people I met there, including the club secretary, this girl I've seen around who's a grade ahead of me. Her name is Lisa Applewood or Atglen or something like that. She seemed nice, if a little serious, while she was taking down my name and everything. And the club president, Gretchen Something-or-other, was really interested when I told her how long I've been riding. She doesn't ride herself, but she knows it uses some of the same skills as dancing.

So I was feeling pretty good when I headed home after the meeting. All that changed when I got here. Dad was just pulling into the driveway. He didn't usually get home that early, so I knew something was wrong.

I ran over to find out what was going on. "Don't worry, Carole," Dad said as he climbed out of the car. "Everything's under control. We just had a little scare, that's all. Your mother's back in the hospital—they want to keep her tonight for observation."

Yeah, right. This time everything's under control. But what about next time? What if something really major happens and they don't even bother to let me know until it's too late?

Well, I'm not taking any chances. When Dad went upstairs, I picked up the phone. Pulling out the members' phone list Gretchen gave me at the meeting, I dialed

Gretchen's number, but it was busy. I didn't want to put this off, so I tried Lisa, the secretary.

"Hi," I said when she answered. "This is Carole Hanson. Remember? The new girl from the meeting today?"

"Oh, sure!" she said. "How are you? Did you have fun today?"

"Sure." I twisted the phone cord around my finger. "Um, but I have to drop out of the club."

"What? But you just joined!"

"I know," I said. "I'm sorry. It's just—Well, I can't do it. Sorry."

"Okay." Lisa sounded confused and maybe a little annoyed. "I'll take you off the list, if you're sure."

"I'm sure. Thanks."

I hung up, feeling kind of bad. It would have been fun to be in the dance club. It would have been nice to become friends with people like Gretchen and Lisa and the others, instead of making them think I was some weirdo who drops out of things the same day she signs up.

But it doesn't matter. The only thing that matters right now is being there for Mom. She's my top priority now. My only priority. Other people will just have to deal with that.

CAROLE HANSON'S RIDING JOURNAL:

Okay, this is getting ridiculous. Every time I open this book I end up writing stuff that doesn't have anything to do with riding. So this time I'm going to concentrate on what

232

this journal is supposed to be about—starting with some news Max gave us on Saturday after our Horse Wise meeting.

"I've always wanted to open up Pine Hollow to the local riding community and hold a schooling show here," he told us. "So I've decided that two weekends from now is the perfect time for the First Annual Pine Hollow Invitational Schooling Show."

Isn't that great? I mean, a schooling show is like the best of both worlds. You get to compete for real, with real judges and real horse show classes, but you don't have to go through all the efforts of getting ready for real. You don't have to bathe, braid, polish tack, and all the rest of it. And with the show being at Pine Hollow, we won't even have to get up early to trailer over!

Max went on to explain that he planned to invite a few other Pony Clubs to send riders, though all the competition will be individual. "The show will consist entirely of jumping classes in three divisions," he said. "Can anyone explain the difference?"

I raised my hand. "In jumper classes, they judge how fast and clean you jump. In hunter classes, they judge the horse's form. And in equitation, they judge the rider's form."

"Precisely," Max said. He raised his eyebrows. "Now, can anyone guess which classes I want all of you to ride in?"

"Hmmm . . . Equitation?" Lisa said, pretending she had to think hard about it. We all know that Max is more of a stickler for good equitation than any other aspect of riding.

She was right, of course. We'll all be going in Junior Equitation Over Fences. Max also asked us to write down our goals, like he does before every show.

I thought about it for a few minutes, and this is what I came up with: *My goal is for Starlight and me to enjoy ourselves, and for Starlight to get more exposure to competition, and for me to be able to keep him quiet in the ring and not let him speed up at the end of the course.*

As I finished, I heard Lisa asking Veronica if she was going to write anything down. It seems that Veronica had simply shoved her sheet in her pocket.

"No," Veronica retorted, "I'm not, as a matter of fact. I'm going to give Max a blank piece of paper, if you must know. Because I'm going to *blank out* all the other riders. Get it? I'm going to win, no matter what it takes." Then she strode off.

That's typical Veronica bluster, I guess. She and Garnet had had some trouble in class that day—which was almost totally Veronica's fault, of course. She's a pretty good rider when she tries to be, but she's so lazy that she makes a lot more mistakes than she should, and she relies on poor Garnet to pick up the slack. She won't be able to get away with that in the equitation classes, though!

But apparently she's doing her best to live up to her boast. Today, as we were getting changed in the locker room for our usual Tuesday lesson, Lisa asked Stevie and me if we'd heard the news about this Saturday's Horse Wise meeting.

"What news?" I asked. "As far as I know it's going to be a regular meeting."

"Not exactly," Lisa said. "It turns out that the judges for the schooling show are going to be there watching."

"You're kidding. Isn't that illegal or something?" Stevie asked.

Lisa shrugged. "Normally it would be kind of questionable, but since it's only a schooling show, it doesn't matter. They can even give us advice and help us out with problems. And it gives them a chance to get to know the lay of the land at Pine Hollow."

I was excited at the news, especially since Starlight had done so well on Saturday. "I think that's great," I said. "We'll have two chances to ride well for them, instead of one."

"How did you find out the judges were coming?" Stevie asked Lisa.

Lisa explained that she'd gone to Pine Hollow early Sunday morning to put in some extra jumping practice with Prancer, and she'd run into Max. Stevie and I were a little surprised at that. Not the running-into-Max part, of course. The part about Lisa practicing on Sunday. She hadn't mentioned it until then.

"I wasn't trying to be secretive about it," she explained. "But I did like the idea of working on my own for a while."

"I understand," I told her. "Sometimes it's better to work with just your horse, with no one else around. I love schooling Starlight by myself."

"That was my plan, anyway," Lisa went on. "It turned out to be mostly a waste of time, because about fifteen minutes after I got here, who shows up but Veronica."

That was really a surprise. At first we could hardly believe it—Veronica diAngelo, putting in extra practice time?—but when Lisa started telling us how much Veronica had been

235

showing off in front of her, being totally condescending and annoying, we knew it was true.

"Basically," Lisa said, "she told me that if I worked hard for about a hundred years I might be good enough to kiss her feet."

I had to laugh at that. Stevie laughed, too. But as we kept talking about Veronica, it became all too clear that Stevie was more annoyed than amused by Veronica's attitude. She really wants to beat her. Veronica has always been able to rub Stevie the wrong way (even more than the rest of us, I mean), and it seemed to be happening again.

And class today didn't help that situation one bit. Stevie and Veronica sniped at each other a couple of times when Max wasn't listening. And then after class, Stevie sort of grimly suggested we get together tomorrow afternoon for an extra practice. "If Veronica shows up," she added, "we can scare her off with our great equitation over fences. Okay?"

Wait a minute. This entry started off talking about riding. How did it end up talking about Stevie's endless feud with Veronica???

CAROLE HANSON'S RIDING JOURNAL:

What a weird day! I'm so worried about both of my friends, and I'm not really sure how to help either of them.

I guess Lisa's problem is a little easier, since at least I have some idea what the problem is there. But Stevie . . . I'm still feeling confused about that, especially after what just happened at TD's.

Today's Horse Wise meeting started out well. Everybody worked hard to groom their horses (and themselves) for the judges, and everybody looked great. Stevie, especially, looked fantastic. She'd arrived early to get Belle ready, and it showed.

First, Max asked us to line up with our horses so that the judges could walk around and meet all of us and familiarize themselves with the horses. The judges seemed very nice, and I was proud of Starlight for behaving so well.

Then, after that was over, we gathered at one end of the ring and waited to get started. All except Veronica, that is. She remained right in the middle of the ring, deep in an especially animated conversation with one of the judges.

"Look at her!" Stevie whispered fiercely. "She's trying to get on that judge's good side. Not that it's a surprise, considering it's Veronica, but she could at least be a little less obvious about it!"

Then Max happened by and mentioned that Veronica and the judge, Mrs. Gorham, know each other. Mrs. Gorham belongs to Mrs. diAngelo's bridge club.

It was right after that that it happened. The judges gave the order for us all to mount. Everyone quieted down, except for Veronica, who was still talking with Mrs. Gorham.

Finally she started to mount, too. Veronica put her foot in Garnet's stirrup, grabbed the pommel, and started to hoist herself up. But a second or two after her right foot left the ground and she started to swing it up over Garnet's rump, Veronica let out a wild, terrified shriek and tumbled hard to the ground. Then she started to cry hysterically. There was a huge rip all the way up one side of her breeches, and her chin was bleeding.

We all turned to watch, stunned. Mrs. Reg rushed over to help Veronica while Max rounded up Garnet, who had panicked and taken off. By the time he got back to her, Veronica was sitting up, holding her bloody chin.

"What happened?" Mrs. Reg asked her.

"I c-cut my chin when I fell," Veronica wailed. "I think I b-banged it on the stirrup iron."

"Her stirrup leather just broke in two!" Mrs. Gorham said in a shocked voice.

Max raised his eyebrows at that. Stirrup leathers generally don't just snap in two—*if* you take care of your tack, which Veronica rarely does. I was sure Max was embarrassed to have the visiting judges see that one of his riders was so careless about routine safety.

"Imagine not noticing a worn-out stirrup leather," one of the other judges commented.

"It is odd," another said, "especially in a group of horses that are so well turned out."

I was still watching Max, feeling bad for him. But Stevie was focused on Veronica. "She would never notice what shape her tack is in," she whispered to Lisa and me. "She hardly ever even puts on her own saddle. Today she even asked me to tighten her girth for her!"

Eventually Mrs. Reg got Veronica calmed down. Her cut didn't seem to be too serious, but it was still bleeding. Mrs. Reg decided to send her off to the hospital, just in case. First, though, Max reminded Veronica that the stable policy is that no matter why somebody falls off a horse, they have to get back on if they are physically able.

"You don't have to ride very far," he assured her. "Just a few steps."

"I'll t-try," she blubbered. "B-but how am I s-supposed to get on without a s-stirrup leather?"

"Oh, please!" Stevie muttered. "Anybody should be able to get on without a stirrup. What if you were out in the woods and something broke? What would you do then, hang around waiting for your groom to show up and hoist you on?"

Despite what had happened, I couldn't help giggling at the image of Veronica hopping around in the woods, screaming for Red to give her a leg up. Lisa giggled, too, and so did Stevie.

But we noticed a few of the other riders shooting us dirty looks, so we did our best to quiet down. I guess people didn't think it was appropriate to laugh at a time like that, which is probably true.

Max told Veronica he would give her a leg up. First, though, he wanted to remove the broken leather so that it wouldn't be in the way. He lifted the skirt of the saddle and pulled it out. Then he peered at the leather carefully.

I edged Starlight closer and peeked over his shoulder. I could see why he was taking a closer look. The leather didn't look worn at all. In fact, it seemed practically brand new.

Max held up the leather, looking angry. I gasped as I realized what had happened. The leather hadn't just ripped. It had been deliberately cut!

"Of all the dirty tricks to pull!" Max exclaimed. His next

words were hard and icy. "I would like to know who, in my stable, could have done a thing like this."

At his words, everyone turned—and looked straight at Stevie. Her rivalry with Veronica isn't exactly a secret.

Meanwhile, Veronica started shrieking more loudly than ever. "This is the worst thing that's ever happened to me!" she screeched. "Who could have done this to me? Why me? Why me?"

Finally Mrs. Reg dragged her off to the emergency room. I guess she and Max decided that making Veronica ride when she was so hysterical wasn't worth it. Max sent Polly and Simon to put Garnet away. As Veronica left, our classmates called out how sorry they were and stuff like that. Most of them also shot dirty looks at Stevie.

I felt awkward. I glanced at Lisa, who looked equally uncomfortable. But somehow, I didn't feel like saying anything to anyone just then, not even her. And certainly not to Stevie. She was sitting in Belle's saddle, staring straight ahead and ignoring everyone. Her expression was defiant.

As soon as Veronica was gone, Max started the class. It didn't go particularly well—most of us were a little sluggish and distracted. I know I was. Starlight got over the course well enough, but he didn't seem to enjoy it like he usually does.

Lisa had even more trouble than the rest of us. Prancer refused the first fence—twice. And when she finally made it over on the third try, the rest of the course was messy, with lots of mistakes.

I could tell Lisa was angry with herself afterward. But she

rushed off, not seeming to want to talk it over, so I left her alone.

After the meeting was over, as I was grooming Starlight, I debated with myself. I wondered if I should come right out and say, "Listen, Lisa, it's obvious you're having problems with Prancer, but I *know* you can fix them by next weekend." And what about Stevie? So far she hadn't said anything about the fact that everyone thought she was the one who'd sabotaged Veronica. Should I bring it up?

I decided the answer to the Lisa question was to keep quiet, at least for now. If she wanted my help, she knew she could ask for it.

Then I turned my attention back to Stevie's problem. It sort of annoyed me how quickly everyone had assumed that Stevie was guilty. Of course, Stevie's rivalry with Veronica had been escalating all week. Everyone had probably overheard at least one of the insulting remarks Stevie's made about her lately.

But I *know* Stevie. I know she wouldn't pull such a dangerous prank, no matter what. But then who had done it?

I decided it was time for a Saddle Club meeting. Maybe if we put our heads together, the three of us could get to the bottom of it. I found Lisa and Stevie and we headed outside.

Bad timing. As we reached the driveway, we saw the Pine Hollow station wagon returning from the hospital. Veronica emerged, wearing a bulky bandage on her chin.

She was immediately surrounded. Mrs. Gorham and a bunch of people from class flocked around her asking how she was feeling.

Veronica shakily explained that she wasn't sure she'd be able to jump next weekend, but she wanted to get back on a horse today. Everyone seemed terribly impressed with her bravery. I couldn't help thinking that she probably loved being the center of attention. But I felt bad for her, too. Missing the schooling show would be tough for anyone, even Veronica.

When I looked over at Lisa, her face was sympathetic, too. But Stevie's face was hard. "What are you guys looking at?" she demanded, noticing that Lisa and I were glancing at her. "Do you honestly think I care whether she rides next weekend?"

"Stevie," I said timidly, "aren't you at all sorry for her?"

"Hardly." Stevie's face was flushed. "How can I be? Veronica's blaming me for cutting her stirrup leather. I had nothing to do with it. So why should I pretend to care who did?"

I didn't have an answer to that. A few minutes later, we continued on to TD's. Some of the other riders from Pine Hollow were there, too, and they kept staring at Stevie. She did her best to ignore them, but even I couldn't help feeling a little like a criminal under their accusing stares. I knew I hadn't done anything wrong, and I was sure Stevie hadn't, either.

When Stevie got up to go to the ladies' room, Lisa and I held a quick consultation. Just like me, she really wants to believe that Stevie is innocent.

"We have to look at the evidence, though," she reminded me. "Stevie *is* the world's biggest practical joker."

"But isn't slashing someone's stirrup leathers a bit more than a practical joke?" I pointed out.

"Maybe she figured Veronica would see it right away," Lisa reasoned. "Or that the judges would find it and criticize Veronica during her inspection. Then Veronica would either have had to admit that she didn't clean her own tack, or she'd have had to take the blame for missing such an obvious problem."

I hated to admit it, but she had a point. "It was just a fluke that the judges didn't inspect us more carefully," I admitted. "If they had, we all would have thought it served Veronica right."

We continued to discuss it. I felt terrible—as if we were putting our friend on trial without her even knowing it. Lisa and I couldn't even touch our ice cream when the waitress brought it.

When Stevie returned, she grabbed her spoon. "Let's dig in!" she said enthusiastically.

Then she caught our eyes. I guess we're not too good at hiding our feelings, because she set her spoon down again with a clatter, suddenly looking very upset.

"Listen, you guys," she began, her voice quavering.

Just then, Veronica entered the restaurant. She stood in the doorway, scanning the crowded tables. The look on her face made my stomach flip nervously. It was obvious that she hadn't come in because of a hot-fudge craving. She had come to make Stevie pay.

She marched over to our table and took a deep breath. I cringed, waiting for her to erupt.

But before she could say a word, Stevie sprang up. She looked Veronica straight in the eye. When she spoke, her voice was perfectly calm. "You are going to be very sorry if you make any kind of accusation about anything at all," she said loudly enough for the whole restaurant to hear. "In case you've forgotten, my mother and father are lawyers. If you start telling stories about me, I'll slap a lawsuit on you so fast you'll wish you lived in Abu Dhabi!"

Veronica glared at her, but she backed down. A moment later, she had swept out of TD's again.

Stevie sat down. "Well, that might have kept her from talking, but it sure didn't make her change her mind about me. I know she still thinks I did it." Then she saw Lisa and me staring at her silently. I guess our questions about the whole incident must have showed in our eyes, because her face immediately lost its angry look. Tears gathered in her eyes, and she stood up again quickly. "I can take anything from Veronica," she said in a choked voice, "but I can't stand my two best friends in the world doubting me!"

She rushed out, leaving us with our melting sundaes and not much to say to each other. And she's right, too. I can't help doubting her—at least a little.

Does that make me a terrible friend?

Dear Diary:

This might have been my strangest birthday ever. This year I knew better than to ask for a horse of my own, or even to think about it. But that didn't stop Stevie. After lessons on the day before my birthday, she presented me with her gift—an "invisible horse kit." It's a halter that she some-

how got to stay stiff, I think with some kind of varnish or something, so it has the shape it would have if a horse were wearing it. There's a lead rope attached to it, too, also stiff and curving down from the halter. When I hold the end of the lead rope in my hand, the halter stands up beside me so that it really does, kind of, look like I'm leading an invisible horse! Everyone laughed when they saw it, even Max. Just about the only one who didn't think it was funny was Veronica diAngelo. She just sort of sniffed when she saw us goofing around with it and said, "Well, I guess that's the closest some people will ever come to having their own horse." I don't think she meant me, though—she was looking straight at Stevie when she said it. To quote my mother, those two get along about as well as oil and water!

Anyway, my celebration at home was nice, too, in a strange sort of way. Dad baked me a cake shaped like a barn (he said that he couldn't quite manage a horsehead shape—that's what Mom usually makes for me), and we ate it up in Mom's bedroom, since she'd just come home from the hospital the day before and couldn't really make it downstairs too well. She didn't say much—I think singing "Happy Birthday" with Dad kind of wore her out—but she smiled more than I've seen her smile lately. And she seemed really interested in hearing all about the little party at Pine Hollow and seeing the invisible horse kit. I went and got it and pretended to lead my "horse" around their bedroom, which made us all laugh, especially when Dad pretended the horse had taken a bite of his cake.

I was glad that Mom had fun. These days she seems to

spend more time sleeping—or trying to—than anything else. It's been like that for a long time, actually. I've sort of stopped hoping for her to start getting better, and just try to be happy that she doesn't seem to be getting any worse.

It's weird, but sometimes I even forget to think about it one way or another. It almost feels like our life has always been this way and always will be—Mom sick, spending a couple of days or a week in the hospital, and the rest of our lives going on in between.

Dear Diary:

Why is it that time always seems to slow to a crawl when you're waiting and worried? I'm sitting in the hallway outside the school office, waiting for Dad to get here. The ambulance took Mom this time, so he's coming to pick me up on his way to the hospital. It shouldn't take him long. . . .

It's hard to believe that less than ten minutes ago I was sitting in class, doodling horse pictures in my notebook and not really thinking about anything except whether Delilah is too high strung to make a good broodmare, since Max mentioned he'd like to breed her someday.

Then the teacher called my name. I looked up quickly, afraid that she'd noticed I wasn't paying attention. Then I saw that another student had come in with a note.

"Carole," Ms. Wagner said, "could you gather your things, please? Your father is on the phone for you in the office."

My heart started pounding, like it always does when this

246

happens. I knew what it meant—they'd taken Mom to the hospital again. That's the only reason Dad ever calls me out of class. It's happened twice already this year, plus I don't know how many times last year, so you'd think I'd be used to it by now.

But I'm not. I could barely form complete words or sentences when I spoke to Dad just now, and my heart still feels like it's pounding twice as fast as usual.

Last week (or was it the week before? I can't seem to remember anything right now except my own name, and I'm not even positive about that) when Aunt Elaine came for Thanksgiving, she said one of the things she was thankful for is that we never know what's going to happen next. I thought it was kind of a weird thing to say, though she probably just meant she still hoped Mom would get better. Right now I wish I knew what was going to happen next. Or at least I think I do.

Actually, I don't know what I think. After all, this kind of situation is pretty normal for us these days, so I probably shouldn't feel this scared. But it's one thing to know that and another to believe it.

CAROLE HANSON'S RIDING JOURNAL:

Wow! Things around here never slow down, do they? I haven't had a chance to write down any of the things I've been working on with Starlight, and now the schooling show is over already. It sure was a busy week!

As far as I can remember, it started with a phone call from

247

Lisa the day after the stirrup-leather-cutting incident. She'd been at Pine Hollow and overheard Max talking to Mrs. diAngelo on the phone. It was pretty clear to her, even from hearing only one side of the conversation, that Veronica's mother wanted Max to punish Stevie for what she'd done—namely, by banning her from the schooling show.

But that wasn't all. Lisa had also run into Veronica herself. It seemed her chin was feeling *much* better, so she was there working with Garnet. Lisa made some totally innocent comment, like "It's great that you're recovering so fast," and Veronica blew up at her. I guess she thought Lisa was being sarcastic, because she started saying how *she* was the one who should be suing, and how Stevie had gone way too far this time, and stuff like that.

Lisa kept her mouth shut. Unfortunately, she also got stuck practicing with her again, and once again Veronica criticized everything she did. And the more she criticized, the worse Lisa ended up riding.

But none of that was the main reason she was calling me. The main thing was that she'd realized, all of a sudden, why Stevie couldn't have done it. No matter how much she wanted to get back at Veronica, or how irrational she could be about some things, this simple fact remained: she never would have done something that might have ended up hurting a horse. If that stirrup had broken while Garnet was going over a jump, she could have been unbalanced and ended up with a broken leg or worse. It was so obvious when Lisa put it that way that I couldn't believe I hadn't seen it myself earlier.

Knowing that Stevie was innocent—instead of just sort of hoping she was—made us feel better. Apologizing to Stevie for doubting her made us feel better, too. We did that right away.

But none of that really solved the problem. As Stevie put it, "I sure look guilty, don't I?"

Lisa, naturally, was looking at things logically. "There's only one solution," she said. "We have to find the real perpetrator and expose him or her to Max."

We agreed to meet at Pine Hollow that afternoon to get started. We didn't have much time if we wanted to clear Stevie's name before the schooling show, which was less than a week away.

That afternoon, the first thing we did was put in some practice for the show. Lisa was having some trouble, and Stevie and I were doing our best to help her, but it didn't seem to be doing any good. Lisa and Prancer just did worse and worse each time they went over the jumps.

"I can't seem to get into any kind of a rhythm," Lisa complained, sounding frustrated. "I'm either ahead or behind."

"That's because you're too worried about it," Stevie told her. "You've got to relax."

That was easier said than done in Lisa's case. "I'm really beginning to think I'm cursed," she said, sounding as though she were only half kidding. "There's got to be some kind of witch jinxing my jumping."

We decided enough was enough. Sometimes the best thing to do in a situation like that is take a break. Stevie suggested that we go for a trail ride to relax, and we all agreed.

But a simple trail ride wasn't all Stevie had up her sleeve. When Lisa went to tell Max where we were going, she filled me in. She wanted us to trick Lisa into jumping something—anything—so that she would forget about her form and Veronica's criticisms and the schooling show and all the rest of it and just *do* it. She thought that might give Lisa her confidence back, and I agreed it was worth a try.

It worked perfectly. We waited until we were a short distance from that old stone wall at the edge of Pine Hollow's property, near the woods. Then Stevie slipped away (she was riding third in line) and rode off as quietly as she could. When she was safely on the other side of the wall, she started shouting for help.

Lisa reacted just as we'd hoped. She whirled Prancer around and urged her into a canter, then a gallop. She aimed her straight at that wall and, without a second's hesitation from either one of them, they sailed right over—with perfect form!

That was all it took. Once Lisa understood what we'd done—and it didn't take her long once she'd landed on the far side of the wall and gotten a good look at Stevie's huge grin—she realized what she'd done. And she remembered that jumping was easy. And fun. Suddenly she couldn't wait to do it again.

Somehow, once that problem was solved, the answer to the other one came to us, too. We were sitting by the stream after Lisa's surprise jumping lesson, talking about the way she'd psyched herself out. She'd been so worried about doing well at the schooling show that she'd let her self-doubts take over and cripple her.

Or at least that's what Lisa and I thought. Stevie was more inclined to blame Veronica and her snotty "advice" that was really more like plain old criticism.

Lisa thought that might have had a little to do with it, though she wasn't convinced that Veronica had really plotted it out as carefully as Stevie made it sound. "I don't know what Veronica thinks she has to fear from me. If she wanted to psych someone out, I'm sure she'd go after one of you."

That was pretty much all it took. Suddenly the answer clicked for all of us. Veronica had done it! She'd cut her own stirrup leather, knowing that everyone would think Stevie had done it because of all the things she'd said about wanting to beat Veronica at the show. Plus, by making herself look like an innocent victim, she'd probably hoped the judges would give her higher marks out of pity.

It was Lisa who remembered the clue that cinched it. Veronica had been wearing an old pair of breeches when she fell—the pair that had been ruined in the incident. "She would never, ever have appeared in anything but her best in front of the judges that day," Lisa pointed out. "Not unless she had a good reason—like she knew they'd get ripped."

So we had the answers we needed. All we had to do was figure out how to prove it to Max. Once again, Lisa came through. She remembered that Veronica had dropped something in the locker room the day of the incident and kicked it out of sight under the lockers before Lisa could see what it was. She figured out that it had to be the knife she'd used to cut the stirrup leather. And by confronting her in a locker room full of riders and subtly threatening to spill the secret, she not only convinced Veronica to confess to Max, but also to withdraw from the schooling show in front of everyone! It was a pretty amazing scene.

The schooling show was amazing, too. Starlight and I took top honors in Junior Equitation Over Fences. He stayed slow and in control as I'd hoped, and we soared over every fence on the course with no trouble at all. My friends did really well, too. Lisa still dropped her hands too early once or twice and looked down instead of up a few times, but I could tell her confidence was up all the way around. Even better, it was obvious that Prancer really enjoyed jumping, and we all think that with a little more work she'll be really good at it. I've already got some ideas to suggest to Lisa for their training.

Speaking of training, I'm starting to wonder again if that's the career for me. It's so satisfying to see a wonderful horse like Starlight or Prancer or Belle improve and learn. It's even more satisfying to know that you had something to do with that improvement.

I want to think about that some more. Maybe I can find some extra time to focus on it during spring break. I know it's still almost a month away, but I'm already looking forward to spending the whole week at Pine Hollow. After the schooling show—after I've seen his strengths and weaknesses, and mine, too—I've got a lot better idea of where to go next with Starlight.

So the break will be a great time to work with him more intensively. And, I might add, a good time to write *a lot* more about that training in this journal, instead of all the other stuff that keeps sneaking in.

FROM:	Steviethegreat
TO:	HorseGal
TO:	LAtwood
SUBJECT:	URGENT!
MESSAGE:	

Okay, I just *had* to complain about my idiot brothers right away, but Mom is tying up the phone. The weirdest thing is that she's not having one of her boring lawyerly conference calls, or even gossiping with my aunt in Maryland. She's talking to Colonel Hanson. Yes, you read that right, Carole— your dear old dad. Do you have any idea what they're so busy chatting about? Because Dad (mine, that is) won't let me near the kitchen to listen. Weird . . .

But not half as weird as my psychotic brothers. Do you want to hear what they did this time? See, Michael has this new lizard he brought home from school the other day, and my riding boots were lying in the hall for the perfectly good reason that I'd forgotten to put them away, and—

Yikes! I just remembered one reason the Colonel might be calling. I think I might have mentioned the grade I got on my last history test in front of him the other day at your house, Carole. And I haven't quite gotten around to mentioning it to my parents yet. He wouldn't do that to me, would he? *Would he?*

I hope not. Or I'll probably be grounded straight through spring break!

CAROLE HANSON'S RIDING JOURNAL:

I can't believe it! Here I was, looking forward to spring break in an ordinary way. A nice way, but totally predictable. Riding at Pine Hollow. Hanging out at TD's. The usual.

Instead, we're going back to the Bar None! And when I say "we're going," I don't just mean Stevie and Lisa and me. Our whole families are going! (Well, okay, not Stevie's brothers; they all have other plans. And not Lisa's brother, of course, since he's off in Europe or Africa or Antarctica for all I know, as usual. But all the adults are going, and the three of us, and that's what matters.) Our parents have been planning it for weeks as a big surprise. And boy, were we surprised!

We leave in a week. I can't wait to see Kate again, and her parents, and Christine, and John and Walter, and Berry and Stewball and Chocolate and Moonglow and little Felix and, oh, everybody! I can't wait to show the Bar None to Dad so that he can finally see all the stuff I've been raving about all this time. It'll be really neat to share an experience like that with him.

Dear Diary:

First I spent what felt like a million years sitting in the school hallway, waiting for Dad to pick me up. Now I've spent at least six million sitting here in the waiting room at the hospital. I'm really starting to understand why they call it that—a waiting room. Because today it seems like all I've

been doing is waiting. Waiting for Dad. Waiting to get here.
And now, waiting for someone to tell me what's going on.

I've only seen Mom once since I got here, for about two
seconds. She looked pretty bad, just like the last time some-
thing like this happened, and the time before, and the time
before that.

But this time feels different somehow. I'm not sure how
to describe it, but nobody is talking much about Mom's con-
dition. The nurses just keep smiling at me and saying, "Try
to be patient, dear," whenever I ask what's happening.

But it's hard to be patient when you're worried. And
waiting.

But waiting is all I can do.

I hate waiting!!!!

CAROLE HANSON'S RIDING JOURNAL:

It's weird the way things never turn out the way you expect them to, isn't it?

I mean, a week ago I thought that coming here to the Bar
None with Dad would be the greatest thing in the world.
And I still think it *should* be really great. So why doesn't it
feel that way most of the time?

At first everything seemed just as wonderful as expected.
All the parents, Dad included, loved the Bar None. We all
decided to go on a trail ride together soon after we arrived
two days ago. That started out pretty well, too, except for a
few minor things, like Mrs. Atwood mounting her horse

255

from the right side instead of the left. It's amazing how some people don't know the simplest things about riding!

Probably the only thing really bugging me at that point was Dad's hat. It's this huge, black, ten-gallon monstrosity that makes him look like the dude of the century. But every time I say something about it, he just laughs and starts teasing me, saying that I'm jealous. As if I would ever wear such a thing even on a bet!

Anyway, as we got ready to head out, I guess the three of us must have been fussing over the adults a lot, telling them what to do, how to hold the reins, stuff like that, because Mr. Lake spoke up. "You know, you don't need to pamper us, girls," he said. "We haven't watched all those shows and lessons at Pine Hollow without picking up a thing or two."

"We're not as run-down as you think we are," Dad added with a wink at me.

Mrs. Atwood nodded. "You're treating us like a bunch of old bags!"

"That's right," Stevie's mom chimed in. "And if we're bags, we must really be *saddle*bags!"

Everybody laughed.

"Our very own nickname!" Mrs. Atwood exclaimed. "Maybe we should start our own club!"

The adults laughed again at that. My friends and I groaned and rolled our eyes. Then we set off. The ride itself wasn't bad. I couldn't help noticing about a thousand things the Saddlebags—Dad included—were doing wrong, but I tried to keep them to myself. After all, I reminded myself, the Bar None's horses were used to carrying all sorts of dudes, some of them probably even more clueless about riding than our parents. If that's possible!

My friends and I talked it over that night in our bunkhouse. "I think my mom ended up enjoying the trail ride," Lisa said. "She had a rough patch when she practically kicked a hole in Spot's sides, but she finally started getting the hang of it."

"It's fun to see my parents having such a good time," Stevie said. "I just wish my dad wouldn't try to show off. Did you see when he whacked Melody on the rump? She almost flew right up to the weather vane on the barn roof!"

I rolled my eyes. "Did you notice my dad, with his feet sticking way out in front of him? He was rocking from side to side so much, I thought Yellowbird might get dizzy! And when I said something about it, he just laughed it off, like it was some big joke."

"I know what you mean." Lisa nodded. "My mom certainly doesn't like me telling her what to do, either."

"I wish they would take the whole thing more seriously," I mused. "Just because *we're* the ones giving them suggestions on how to be better riders doesn't mean they shouldn't listen."

"They're acting like kids," Lisa said.

"Right!" I agreed.

Things got worse, sort of, yesterday morning. We found out that our parents had gone off on a trail ride by themselves, without even bothering to wake us. Walter told us he'd put them on their horses at seven-thirty that morning.

"What?" Stevie blanched. "All five of them?"

"All five," Walter confirmed. "Carole, your dad said they'd have no problem. Said he's a volunteer at your Pony Club. Seems he knows the ropes."

"*Seems* is right!" I exclaimed. Dad is a Horse Wise parent volunteer, all right, but that doesn't mean he knows very much about riding. "He doesn't have a clue."

"Neither do any of the others!" Stevie practically shouted.

Walter gazed at us, looking amused. "I've watched your folks ride. I'm sure they'll be okay."

Lisa shook her head. "You don't know our parents," she told Walter. "They don't understand that riding is serious business—not just fun."

"We'd better go find them," I said.

Walter shrugged. "If that's what you want to do." He told us where they'd gone—on the trail he calls the little loop. We saddled up quickly and set off, starting from the opposite end of the loop to try to head them off.

"I hope they're okay," Lisa said as we trotted along the dusty trail.

Stevie looked grim. "They've been gone over two hours on a ride that should take less than one."

"Could they have gotten lost?" Lisa wondered.

"What if one of them fell and got badly hurt?" I bit my lip, trying not to panic.

We rode in silence for a few minutes. Then Stevie spoke up. "Are there rattlers during this time of year?" she asked Kate, gazing around at the desert brush.

"There are always rattlers," Kate replied.

The first sign we saw of our parents was Dad's black ten-gallon hat. Then the rest of them came into view over a slight rise. The parents were riding out of a patch of woods and heading toward us. Stevie's father was serenading the others with his rendition of "Red River Valley," which he'd been singing off and on since we'd arrived.

"I can't believe it." Stevie stared. "They get us really worried and here they are, moseying along and singing. Couldn't you just scream?"

I was so relieved to see them all safe and sound that I couldn't answer. We trotted up to them. "Where have you been?" I demanded. "We were so worried!"

The Saddlebags chuckled. They seemed really amused by that, but we weren't feeling too amused. "Did you stick to the trail Walter mapped out?" Stevie asked them.

"What's the matter, don't you trust us?" Mr. Lake replied. "Of course we stuck to the trail."

"And what if we didn't?" Mrs. Atwood put in.

Lisa shook her head. "Mom, have you ever heard of rattlers?"

But they just didn't get it. So today at lunch, when Kate's father announced that there will be a cattle drive tomorrow, I was half excited and half worried. My friends and I love cattle drives, and we think they're fun, but we're afraid they're not the kind of fun our parents are expecting. We tried to explain that to them, but once again they wouldn't listen. They just dismissed our concerns and called us party poopers.

After lunch, while the Saddlebags were taking a siesta, we held a Saddle Club meeting to discuss it. Stevie, Lisa, and I complained a little more about how weird our parents were acting. But then Kate spoke up.

"Look, guys," she said. "Tons of the guests who come here are rank beginners. A lot of them know even less than your parents do—and they manage just fine. The only ones who really give us trouble are the people who think they can do more than they actually can. That can be dangerous."

"That's just it," I said, realizing she'd put her finger on the problem without meaning to. "I think—I *know*—my dad thinks he's much more capable than he really is." It felt strange to be saying that. Most of the time I think Dad is capable of just about anything. But not now. Definitely not now.

"Same with my parents," Stevie said.

Lisa nodded. "Mine too."

Kate tried to reassure us. "Dad made the cattle drive sound farther than it is," she said. "It'll take us only a few hours to ride to the pasture where the herd is. Then we'll sleep out. Next morning we'll bring the herd to the back pasture near the ranch. It's an easy ride, and the herd's not that big this time."

"So it's really a one-day drive that Walter and John could handle without any help from any of us dudes, young *or* old," Stevie said.

"Well, that's how we run the ranch," Kate agreed. "Guests come on a simple drive and get the feel and the thrill of riding the herd, sleeping under the stars, cooking out. You know. This same drive has been done by guests with less experience than the Saddlebags. What could possibly go wrong?"

We couldn't really argue with that. But I won't say I'm not

still worried. I just hope the Saddlebags don't forget that there's real work involved in riding well.

Speaking of which, earlier we got the chance to watch John work with his new horse, Tex. John's hoping to train Tex to be a really good reining horse, and as far as I can tell, he's most of the way there already. They're both really good—especially John.

Because of the way I've been trying (unsuccessfully, so far) to figure out my own career plans, I couldn't help wondering if John had thought about turning his skills into a career. I'm sure he could make a real name for himself on the rodeo circuit if he wanted to. Or he'd be a totally valuable addition to any working ranch or to a dude ranch like the Bar None. He could probably work himself up to head wrangler, like his dad, in no time at all.

So after dinner tonight, while the two of us were helping to clear the tables, I decided to ask him. "Hey, John," I said. "What are you going to do when you grow up?"

He looked a little surprised at the question. "I'm still trying to decide between rock star and international revolutionary," he joked. "Why do you ask?"

"No, really," I insisted. "Haven't you thought about it?"

He shrugged. "Sure, I think about it from time to time. But I really haven't made up my mind yet. What's the hurry?"

Then he changed the subject, so I didn't have to answer. But I've been thinking about it ever since. I mean, John is a couple of years older than me. Shouldn't he have at least some idea of what he wants to do with his life?

Dear Diary:

They moved Mom to a hospice today. I didn't even know what a hospice was until the day before yesterday when they started talking about it. She'd already been in the hospital for a week before that, and I was starting to wonder when they were going to let her come home. But instead they've put her in this place—it's really just another part of the hospital, sort of. I mean, it's on the grounds but in a separate building. It doesn't look much like the rest of the hospital, though. Instead of sterile white walls and bare floors, it's painted different colors and there are bright rugs on the floors. The furniture is a lot nicer, too. There are still hospital beds, but they're made up with pretty sheets and fluffy pillows. And there are plants on the windowsills and pictures on the walls. The picture across from Mom's bed is of a bouquet of flowers. If I stare at it long enough, I almost stop noticing the big respirator right underneath it.

Dad says they've moved her here so that she can feel more comfortable, more at home, but still be cared for round the clock by medical staff. I don't really understand the point, though. This place is pretty nice, I guess—at least nicer than the hospital. But she couldn't possibly feel more at home here than she does in her real home. And Nurse Thompson comes there every day to take care of her.

But every time I say that, Dad just pats me on the shoulder and doesn't answer. He seems really tired—he stays with Mom almost all the time now. I heard him tell Aunt Elaine (she drove up from North Carolina a couple of days ago)

262

that he's taken a leave of absence from work. Also, he let me skip school today to help move Mom in here.

So I guess maybe this really isn't part of our "normal" new life anymore. Things are getting weird, and I'm not sure what to do. I know the situation must be really serious. Just looking at Mom tells me that. She looks worse than ever, like each breath she takes is an effort. But she still smiles when she sees me, and she asks if I've been watering the rosebush or if I've gone riding that day.

But for once I don't even feel much like riding anymore. At least not right now. The only thing I want to do—the only thing that makes me a little less scared—is being with Mom. Watching her breathe.

Dear Diary:

I'm really scared. Mom has been in this hospice place for almost a week now, and I don't think it's working, because she's getting worse instead of better. I stayed here all weekend, along with Dad and Aunt Elaine. And when Monday came, neither of them said a word about me going back to school. I think Aunt Elaine called my principal; I heard her mention it to one of the nurses. I also heard her say something about Uncle John and Aunt Lily from Minnesota; I think maybe they're flying in soon.

But I'm not really sure about that. I can't seem to focus on much of anything except for Mom. I'm afraid to think too hard about what's happening to her. But I know one thing— I'm so worried I almost can't stand it. I thought I knew all

263

along that something like this might happen. But maybe I didn't know it as much as I thought I did.

That doesn't make sense, does it? I don't even know what I'm saying. I don't know what I'm thinking. All I can do is worry.

I wish I could talk to Mom about it. She's always been the one who could help me figure out what I'm thinking and feeling when I start getting all mixed up about things. But she's been pretty out of it for a couple of days now—a "semiconscious state," that's what I heard someone call it. Sometimes she still looks right at me and smiles when I come into the room or when she wakes up from sleeping. Sometimes she talks to me—mostly about things that happened when I was a baby. Or she asks me questions, and I try to answer them. That's hard. But not as hard as the times when she doesn't seem to see me at all.

So even though I want to, I'm afraid to talk to her about what's happening to her right now. Or how confused and terrified and angry I feel about it all at the same time. I'm afraid to talk to her about much of anything, really. Because I'm really scared that she won't talk back. And I'm not sure I could stand that.

I think maybe Dad feels the same way, because he doesn't talk much lately, either. We both just sit in Mom's room, watching the nurses work and trying not to think too much.

CAROLE HANSON'S RIDING JOURNAL:

The cattle drive is over. But I will never, as long as I live, forget it.

It started out well enough. Our parents were still being their Saddlebag selves, making a mess of their bedrolls and generally acting clueless about what we were really setting off to do for the next two days. Lisa's mother actually tried to pack an electric blow dryer in her bedroll!

But our parents were pretty well behaved once we hit the trail. They seemed impressed with the wild, beautiful landscape we were riding through, and they followed John's and Walter's instructions without a peep.

That was the first day. This morning, after a night sleeping under the stars, their mood seemed a little less chipper. Lisa's dad kept grumbling about having only beef jerky and coffee for breakfast. And the others, including Dad, kept cracking jokes about everything. I was afraid they might have hurt John's and Walter's feelings—after all, this was real work to them, not just a lark—but they didn't seem to notice.

Everybody felt a little better once we were back in the saddle. Well, okay, I'm not sure about the "everybody" part. But I know *I* felt better.

The rest of the morning was actually a lot of fun. The Saddlebags really seemed to be getting into the spirit of things, and by the time we stopped for lunch, each of them had managed to help out and make themselves useful at least once.

Well, make that each of them except for Dad. As far as I could tell, he hadn't done much of anything during the ride. "He spent the whole morning chitchatting at the back of the herd," I told my friends ruefully. "I almost wish something would come up that would teach him a lesson or two. About real riding and what goes into it."

Just then Walter called for us to mount up to continue the ride. I got up to obey, trying to forget about Dad and just enjoy myself.

By early afternoon, we'd reached an arroyo that I remembered from the day before. It hadn't been hard to cross it then. But today, with a herd of cattle, it looked like a much tougher job. I quickly realized that the safest place for the cattle to go down the steep side was very narrow. Walter and John started herding them down, but they had to funnel them practically one at a time into the narrow spot to take a drink. That would have been fine, except that a lot of the animals were too impatient to wait their turn. They tried to make their own way down the hillside, slipping and sliding and doing their best to break their own necks.

It was definitely a job for Stewball. And for The Saddle Club. We swung into action, with Stevie and Kate working the front of the line of cattle, herding them across the stream to John and Walter, while Lisa and I stood back and guided the cattle at the back of the line.

It was a slow process, and we all stayed intensely focused on what we were doing. Meanwhile, the Saddlebags were hanging back, watching and getting restless.

"These ornery beasts are sure taking their time," Dad said at one point.

I overheard him and couldn't help feeling irritated. The cattle weren't being ornery. They were just thirsty. That was why it took so long to get them across the stream.

Eventually the adults decided to take a ride upstream while they were waiting. They cleared it with Walter.

"Just don't go too far," he told them. "Fifteen minutes up and fifteen back ought to bring you back by the time we've got all these critters on the other side."

The Saddlebags agreed and rode off, and the rest of us continued with our work.

It took a long time, but finally we did it. The whole herd had made it across the arroyo safe and sound. We paused for a few seconds' rest and a drink from our canteens.

"Sure took a while, didn't it?" Lisa commented.

"Yeah," Kate agreed. "It's getting dark already."

Stevie checked her watch. "It's only three-thirty."

"That's weird," I said.

We all looked up at the sky. Above us was a low ceiling of sinister-looking clouds.

"Wow," I gasped. "I didn't see *those* coming."

"Uh-oh, I feel a drop," Stevie said.

We all grabbed our ponchos just in time. The drops started coming faster, and a moment later the heavens opened up in sheets. It felt like we were standing under a pounding waterfall. The land, which had been dry and parched, instantly developed puddles and lakes. The tiny winding creek where we had just watered the cattle was rapidly swelling upward in the arroyo.

"It's a good thing we got the cattle out of there before the storm hit," I called to my friends, having to raise my voice over the pounding of the rain.

"I hope the Saddlebags get to see this!" Stevie shouted back.

"Where are our parents, anyway?" I cried, looking around. It had been nearly an hour since they'd ridden off.

Suddenly I saw something that made my stomach turn over. The current below had torn a small tree out of the bank by its roots and sent it floating downstream. Behind it, rushing toward us, was a big black ten-gallon cowboy hat. Dad's hat.

"Oh no!" Stevie cried. "Our parents are in trouble!"

We shouted for Walter and John. Walter was already out of earshot, but John rode back to see what we wanted. As soon as he heard, he nodded grimly. "Let's go."

We rode upstream, looking for any sign of our missing parents. Nothing met our eyes except the rushing water and rain. My heart was pounding a mile a minute. What if something happened to Dad? I couldn't stand that. I tried not to think about it as I scanned the arroyo and the land around it.

After what felt like forever, we rounded a bend in the stream, which now looked more like a river. That's when we saw them. They were standing on a tiny patch of land in the middle of the arroyo, surrounded on all sides by rushing, tumbling water. All five of them were huddled together on their five very nervous horses, looking terrified. And the water was rising by the minute.

As soon as they spotted us, they started waving frantically and yelling for help. We swung into action, led by John. He pulled his lariat out from under his poncho and Kate tied it around a boulder on the bank farther upstream. Then he threw the other end of the rope, and it landed around one of the scraggly trees on the island with the Saddlebags. Stevie's dad tied that end around the trunk of the tree.

I'm still not sure how we did what we did next, but we knew our parents' lives were on the line. John and Tex made their way through the swirling current to the little island. He coaxed each of the horses out into the water, and then they began to swim across the river. Mrs. Atwood was terrified and we were all afraid that she might fall in, but John kept her calm and they finally reached the other side. Then she grabbed the rope John and Kate had strung up earlier, and we helped her pull herself to safety. And so it went until all the Saddlebags were safe. By the time the last of them had made it across, the little island where they'd been standing had totally disappeared below the raging water.

I've never felt the kind of relief I felt when Dad was back on the bank—when they were all there, safe and sound, but especially Dad.

As we rode away, I glanced back one last time at the flooded arroyo. I felt tears sting my eyes as I remembered Dad's silly cowboy hat floating downstream. It was almost too much to bear. I looked over at him, and I almost sobbed out loud. What if I'd lost him?

But I didn't. That's the important thing. Thanks to The Saddle Club, and to John and Tex, I didn't.

Dear Diary:

Mom died today.

I can't believe I just wrote that. Even more, I can't believe it's true.

I'm sitting here in an empty stall at Pine Hollow writing this. It feels weird to be here. Everything seems just the same—the horses look the same, the shuffling of their hooves sounds the same, the hay smells just as sweet as ever. It doesn't seem right. That everything can just go on like that, like nothing's changed. It seems so not right that I can hardly stand it.

It feels strange, stranger than I ever thought anything could feel. But it's still better here at the stable. If I couldn't be here right now, I think I might not be able to go on existing at all.

CAROLE HANSON'S RIDING JOURNAL:

It feels kind of weird to be home again after everything that happened at the Bar None. I mean, we left expecting a nice, fun, relaxing trip with our parents. Instead we ended up saving their lives. It just goes to show that nobody really knows what's going to happen next.

Which makes me think that maybe I've been trying a little too hard in the past few months to figure out the rest of my life. I mean, I should know by now that things are always going to change, no matter how carefully you plan. A horse can always throw a shoe five minutes before he's supposed to step into the ring. So I guess it's a little silly to spend so much energy worrying about my career when I could be doing other things, like enjoying all the different kinds of riding I love. And I'll just have to cross the career decision bridge when I come to it. John Brightstar is right—there's plenty of time for that.

In fact, I'm starting to think maybe I should call Cam and mention this to him. It's fine if he really wants to be a three-day eventer, and if he wants to spend extra time preparing for that. But I'd hate to think of him giving up any opportunities to do other stuff. So I think I will go call him—right now.

(later)

Well, what do you know? All this time I've been so worried because of what Cam said last summer, and it turns out he doesn't even remember! He was completely confused when I started babbling about his three-day event plans. That's because these days he's convinced that he's going to become the world's greatest polo player when he grows up!

So that's that. My brilliant future career can wait. I have other things to think about, like next weekend's Horse Wise meeting, and that book report I'm supposed to be writing before spring break ends in two days, and what to get Lisa for her birthday next month.

And also what I just read in my diary. Remembering that horrible day when we lost Mom was even harder, somehow, because of how close I came to losing Dad on the trip to the Bar None.

But I'm still glad I read it, because it also makes me think about the time we *did* have together before she died. That makes me miss her more than ever, of course. But it also reminds me of what she told me about looking for the special moments in life as they come. I guess I've had a lot of special moments recently. Stuff like seeing Deborah propose to Max. Or helping Stevie celebrate getting her own horse at long last. Or cheering Lisa on in her stage debut as Annie. Or touching that amulet for the first time as Grand Alice told me its story.

Those are all things I wish Mom could have shared. And somehow, I guess she did share them. Because just like I realized on New Year's Eve in Minnesota, friends are always with you—and the same is true of family. Mom will always be a part of me. So in that way she'll always be there to share the important moments, from the day I got Starlight to the day I get married. Not to mention all the smaller, but still special, moments in between.

But knowing that doesn't seem like quite enough somehow. I still wish I'd been able to say more during those last days in the hospice, when I wanted to talk to her so much but was afraid to. Plus I keep thinking about what my old instructor always said about how writing things down helps you focus. So I think I'm going to try something, an idea I just had. Here goes . . .

Dear Mom,

I've been thinking about you a lot lately. I wanted to let you know that Dad and I are getting along fine. Willow Creek really has become a true home to us, just like we hoped when we first moved here. That seems like such a long time ago now—I guess it's because so much has happened in the meantime. So many things have changed. I'm just starting to realize that that's the way of the world—everything is always changing one way or another, for better or for worse. We can't stop it, so there's no sense in trying.

Speaking of things changing, do you remember that rosebush we planted together? Well, it's grown from a scraggly little twig into a huge vine that covers most of the wall beneath my bedroom window. Buds are just starting to emerge as another spring begins. Each year when I smell the blossoms for the first time, it reminds me of you and makes me happy.

A lot of stuff has been making me happy lately, actually. Dad and I just got back from a nice vacation together out West. There were a few difficult moments (and some scary ones, too), but in the end the trip made me appreciate him even more. He's a great dad—but I guess you know that already, right?

Then there was our schooling show a little while before that. And of course the Pony Club rallies. And my trip to visit my— oops, I mean our—relatives in Minnesota. At first I wasn't too sure about some of the stuff I found out up there. But now I'm really happy I went.

Let's see... Before that there was Lisa's play. At first her role made me and Stevie unhappy because we thought she might be less interested in riding, and maybe in us, too. But we were incredibly happy to find out that that wasn't the case in the least, and that made us positively thrilled to cheer her on in her big debut.

Getting to know Marie Dana made me happy, too. Well, not at first, maybe. But it all turned out okay in the end. Her stay with Dad and me was one of those weird times where something that

273

seemed terrible at first turned out to be wonderful. Riding camp getting canceled was the same way—my friends and I were horribly disappointed at first, but it worked out great because it meant we got to go out to the Bar None and be in the Wild West show.

Oh, and how could I forget? It makes me *really* happy that Max and Deborah are getting married soon. And happier still to know that The Saddle Club was there to see them fall in love.

Wow! Remembering some of the stuff that's been happening in the last year or so just made me realize something. I've been thinking a lot about our family after rereading my diary. And I always sort of assumed that "family" just meant you, me, and Dad. But now I'm thinking that my real family is much larger than that. It also includes my two best friends, and Starlight, and our relatives in Minnesota, and Max and Deborah and the other people and horses at Pine Hollow, and Cam, and the whole gang at the Bar None, and old friends like Karenna and Margery Tarr, and newer friends like Marie Dana and Hollie Bright and Christina Johnson.…

So even though you can't be around to look after me, Mom, you don't have to worry too much about your daughter. I'll always miss you. But I've got plenty of family left to take care of me until we can be together again!

Your loving daughter forever,
Carole

ABOUT THE AUTHOR

BONNIE BRYANT is the author of more than a hundred books about horses, including The Saddle Club series, Saddle Club Super Editions, the Pony Tails series, and Pine Hollow, which follows the Saddle Club girls into their teens. She has also written novels and movie novelizations under her married name, B. B. Hiller.

Ms. Bryant began writing The Saddle Club in 1986. Although she had done some riding before that, she intensified her studies then and found herself learning right along with her characters Stevie, Carole, and Lisa. She claims that they are all much better riders than she is.

Ms. Bryant was born and raised in New York City. She still lives there, in Greenwich Village, with her two sons.

Don't miss the next exciting
Saddle Club adventure . . .

DRIVING TEAM
SADDLE CLUB #90

The Saddle Club is gearing up to learn all about driving—not cars, horses. Carole Hanson and Lisa Atwood have to do a report on the use of driving teams throughout history. The only problem is that they have too much information! Somehow they have to rein in their enthusiasm, or their ten-minute talk could take a lifetime. Meanwhile, Stevie Lake is facing her worst nightmare. Their riding instructor has assigned Stevie and Veronica diAngelo a special driving-team project: teaching their horses to work as a team. It's a great idea, but how are the horses going to work together if their owners can't? It's going to take more than teamwork to get through this project. It's going to take a miracle!

PINE HOLLOW

by Bonnie Bryant

*B*est friends Stevie, Carole, and Lisa have always stuck together. But everything has changed now that they're in high school. They've got boyfriends, jobs, and serious questions that they must grapple with on their own.

More and more they're discovering that sometimes even the best of friends can't solve your most serious problems.

Does this change in their lives mark the end of everything, or a brand-new beginning?

BFYR 240

Bantam